THE HOUSE ACROSS THE STREET

BOOKS BY JILL CHILDS

Gracie's Secret

Jessica's Promise

Invisible Girl

The First Wife

The Mistress

I Let Him In

Long Lost Girl

The Mother at Number 5

THE HOUSE ACROSS THE STREET

JILL CHILDS

bookouture

Published by Bookouture in 2024

An imprint of Storyfire Ltd.
Carmelite House
50 Victoria Embankment
London EC4Y 0DZ

www.bookouture.com

ISBN: 978-1-83525-579-7
eBook ISBN: 978-1-83525-578-0

This book is a work of fiction. Names, characters, businesses, organizations, places and events other than those clearly in the public domain, are either the product of the author's imagination or are used fictitiously. Any resemblance to actual persons, living or dead, events or locales is entirely coincidental.

For Janet

PROLOGUE

It was late. She shouldn't even have been there, not at that hour.

She drew her coat more closely around her body and shivered. The cold was piercing and mercilessly sharp, slicing through her flesh. Her ears whined and burned. When she sighed, she blew out a rapidly dispersing trail of white.

She'd meant to leave by ten but every time she'd tried to make a move, her elderly mother had looked so disappointed, she hadn't had the heart to leave her. Her mother was lonely, of course. Life wasn't easy, at her age.

A car drew slowly out of the darkness. She heard it before she saw it, caught the low throb of the engine in the buzzing stillness. It nosed its way round the bend, feeling carefully for ice. The lowered headlights cut the dark as it slid past, hard and bright as steel. Afterwards, the sound became muffled at once and the blackness settled and clotted behind the tail lights, as if it had never been.

She tutted to herself and checked the time again on her phone. The five to eleven bus was late. The last one. It should've come by now. Fifteen minutes she'd been standing here, stuck at the bus stop. She ached to be home, to catch up with her family, make sure they'd all eaten properly, hear how their day had gone. If the bus hadn't come by eleven twenty, she'd text and ask him to come out for her. He wouldn't mind and she couldn't stand here much longer – she'd freeze to death.

She hadn't been much warmer in her mother's living room. Her house was so cold, even with the electric fire. Her mother's hands, gnarled now and veined, had been like ice this evening and, however much she'd remonstrated with her, her mother had seemed determined not to put the central heating on. It wasn't healthy, not at her age. She frowned to herself, thinking about it. There must be some way she could persuade her mother to let her help out with bills, if that was the issue. She'd be more than happy to chip in.

A dog started barking, somewhere off across the fields. Sound carried for miles on nights like this. The earthy scents of soil and leaf mulch were dulled by the freezing air. She stamped her feet in her boots, trying to get feeling back into numb toes. The pavement glittered with frost.

She distracted herself by imagining the bus, the throaty drone of its engine as it approached the bend, the bright lights of the interior shining as it eased to a halt in front of her, then the swish of the opening doors and the flood of warmth as she climbed inside. She'd be home in fifteen minutes. Hardly any traffic at this time. She pulled her phone out again. Eleven sixteen. *For pity's sake.* If it wasn't here soon—

An engine roared. Sudden and angry. Not the bus, though. A car, growing from nowhere, too fast, a blast of sound on the icy road.

She pulled up her eyes from her phone to look as it swung round the corner. The headlights blazed, catching her full in the face. Her mouth opened, soundless. Blinded, she was paralysed, too shocked to move, sensing in that final moment that the car had swerved and was coming right at her.

It mounted the kerb, then struck her with force, full on, in a sickening crunch of bone and sinew. It careered onwards, crushing her as it veered across the pavement, then crashed into the dry-stone wall on the far side.

Her phone, knocked clean from her hand, spun on its back. Its screen emitted a soft blue glow in the night before it finally went dark.

1

NOW

Anna

'Love what you've done to the place! It looks amazing!'

'Thanks!' Anna, in the process of squeezing her way through the press of bodies back into the garden, turned and smiled. He was vaguely familiar. One of Tim's school friends from way back, when they were all still teenagers. Quite a few of Tim's old crowd had turned out to welcome him home. Most of them hadn't seen him for ten years.

But what was his name exactly? Sanjay, wasn't it? Or Sanjeev? He looked as if he'd done well for himself, handsome in a crisp white shirt and chinos. As he leaned into her, making himself heard through the wall of music and chatter, his warm breath smelled of white wine. She wondered how well the stock of champagne was holding up, whether three cases would be enough.

'Your dad would be so proud.' His eyes were kind. No need to explain to him everything they'd been through. It was left unspoken. The whole community knew.

'He'd have loved tonight, wouldn't he?' Anna nodded,

wistful as she moved past. Her father would hardly recognise the old house now. She'd spent a fortune bringing it bang up to date since he had died. If he'd been here tonight, he'd have been fretting about the expense. She could almost hear him: *Are you sure you can afford it, love? Really? Your mother never shelled out for caterers. Just put crisps and nuts out, that's all people want. They never eat much at parties, anyway.* She smiled to herself, imagining.

He'd have been impressed by the jazz quartet though. They were starting up again for the second half of their set, flooding the garden with the opening strains of 'The Lady Is a Tramp'. She recognised it from the first notes. She and Tim had grown up with their father's woefully old-fashioned music.

Faces turned to her as she stepped out into the garden. She shook herself back to the present and smiled brightly, kissing cheeks and accepting compliments on her dress, on the party, on the strings of softly glowing, multi-coloured lights which had transformed the garden and, most importantly of all, on having Tim home again after all these years. That was the real reason for the party. Sanjay was right: their father would be proud.

One of the young waitresses was working the crowd, passing round platters of smoked salmon blinis. Another, just beyond the patio doors, was topping up glasses. Cassie, chasing a school friend, surfaced on the far side of the garden, twisted through the crush and disappeared again. She was dizzy with excitement about being allowed to stay up so late.

'So, is it true, Anna? Are you really opening another shop?' Mrs MacKay, four doors down and pushing seventy now, always spoke her mind. 'How many have you got now? Four?'

Anna smiled. 'It'll be three if it goes through. I'm still nego-tiating the lease.'

'You get it from your mum,' Mrs MacKay said. 'She was always smart with money. Your dad was more cautious.'

Anna nodded. 'He certainly was.'

'Let's hope Cassie's got it too.' Mrs MacKay moved the conversation swiftly on to her grandsons and how profligate they were with her middle-aged daughter's hard-earned cash.

Anna let the older woman's chat wash over her, buoyed up by a sudden feeling of wellbeing. She'd known the MacKays all her life. Mrs MacKay's sister, a cheerful woman with ruddy cheeks and stout legs, had cleaned for her father for a few years. She would wear a polyester overall to clean and often kept a handful of flavoured toffees in the pocket. Anna used to hang around her, hoping to be offered one. Odd flavours, like banana and raspberry, but still a treat. Mrs MacKay had babysat for them too, once in a while, on the rare occasions her father went out.

Anna had been a newborn when Tim and their parents had moved to Riverside Road, to this house. She could have afforded something bigger now, if she'd wanted to move. One of the converted farmhouses up on the Chevin, the dark crags dominating the wooded hillside which overlooked the old market town of Otley. Some of them had stunning, picture-window views over the Wharfe valley.

But she'd never leave, no matter how much money she made. She loved the fact that so many people in the road knew each other. As children, she and Tim had been in and out of these houses, playing with the other kids, absorbed into their mealtimes without fuss. All their parents were friends.

It touched her that so many of them remembered her father, and the older ones, like Mrs MacKay, remembered her mother too. They reminded her, sometimes, of little things about them which she'd almost forgotten, or they explained to her, now she was approaching thirty, details that she'd been too young, at the age of seven, to understand when her mother had died. These things were far more precious than a great view. She wanted the same for Cassie.

'OK?' Tim touched her shoulder as he passed, heading back into the house.

She grinned at him. 'Very OK. You?' He'd already gone.

Mrs MacKay, seeing Anna look after him, interrupted her own flow to lean in and say, 'He's looking so well, isn't he? I saw him walking down the street the other day and I thought I'd seen a ghost. He's the image of your father.' She paused, then added meaningfully, 'Do you think he'll stick around, now he's come back? It's been a long time.'

Anna shrugged. 'I don't know. I'm just enjoying having him home.'

'I'm sure.' Mrs MacKay's eyes sharpened. 'Not easy being a single parent. And working too. I don't know how you do it.' She looked around. 'And George? Is he alright with it, you know, seeing Tim back here again, right across the road?'

Anna sensed herself flush. Trust Mrs MacKay to go straight to the one topic she knew many people here were thinking about but no one else was quite blunt enough to mention.

'George is here somewhere.' She looked round vaguely. 'And Lily, of course.'

'Well, you and Lily were always thick as thieves,' Mrs MacKay said. 'I can still see the two of you skipping off to school together when you were ever so little, plaits flying, cute as buttons. There was no separating you two.'

'I don't know what I'd do without her.' Anna seized her moment. 'Anyway, do excuse me, I'd better see if they need any help inside, in the kitchen.'

She put her head in at the kitchen door, just for long enough to see the caterers pulling out trays of mini quiches and sliding them artfully onto platters. One of the waitresses bustled past her to switch an empty platter for the fresh one. Here, inside the house, the sounds of the jazz quartet were suddenly distant and subdued. Anna felt the tension in her shoulders ease. She poured herself a glass of water and withdrew, headed down the hall to the front of the house for a moment's calm and slipped out of the front door.

Riverside Road was silent and still. Cool night air blew down from the moors, a reminder that already, now the year had tipped into September, the warmth was under threat. Anna leaned back against the brickwork and inhaled deeply. A rich scent of damp earth and foliage, of grass and a fading hint of flowers.

She sipped the water and felt her breathing slow. She'd head back inside shortly – she was enjoying the party – but she was grateful for this stolen, peaceful moment to herself. In the distance, a dog barked, a sudden volley of yapping which ebbed away to silence. From the corner, a car turned into the road and glided past, lazy and unhurried. Stillness settled again.

She peered over the fence to the left. The couple next door, Janice and Ricardo, had come to the party. They'd left their lounge curtains drawn back, the windows dark, empty sockets. She turned to look across to the neighbours on the other side, the Li family, recent arrivals to the street, lawyers with three young children and a practice in Leeds. A thin line of light fringed their closed curtains. She'd invited them, of course, but they'd looked embarrassed, made an excuse. A shame. She hoped the noise wasn't bothering them. She'd go round with Cassie and apologise tomorrow, maybe even take them some flowers. She didn't want to sour relations.

Riverside Road had always been desirable, with three- and four-bedroom family homes and patches of garden, close to the park by the river and walking distance from the ancient, cobbled market square at the heart of the town. Now, it was a mixture of the old families, like the MacKays, who'd lived here for two or three generations, and relative newcomers like the Li family, working in Leeds but drawn to the town community with its traditional pubs and the rolling countryside surrounding it, still dominated by farms and fields and stables, and some decent schools.

Gradually, the prices in the road were rising and the gardens shrinking to accommodate larger conservatories, patios and pizza ovens. Mrs MacKay had said the house next to hers had sold in the spring for more than £600,000. Anna's parents had paid a fraction of that in the nineties, but she knew it had still seemed a lot to them. Her father's job in the bank had been steady but he'd never earned a fortune there. In many ways, after her mother died, he'd struggled to bring up two young children on his own, but he'd always been careful with money, and he'd managed to leave the house, mortgage-free, to Anna and Tim, along with some modest savings. It had been this inheritance which had made it possible for her to rent her own shop in the first place and get her business off the ground, selling watches and jewellery.

Gradually, she felt herself relax, her skin pleasantly chilled by the light breeze rising from the river. She lifted the glass and ran the smooth, cold surface along her forehead. She ought to get Cassie off to bed. The jazz quartet would finish in another half an hour and it was getting late for a ten-year-old, however sophisticated she fancied herself nowadays. Cassie had recently discovered YouTube shorts and was spending far too much time cooing over cat videos and fashion makeovers. At other times, she'd regress and curl up in her pyjamas on the sofa with her stuffed toys to watch cartoons. It was a funny age.

The distant strains of 'Ev'ry Time We Say Goodbye' drifted through the night air from the garden. Anna smiled to herself and hoped that, wherever he was, their father was listening.

She thought about Mrs MacKay's question, about whether Tim would stick around. Anna wasn't certain but she really hoped he would. He and Cassie had barely had any contact with each other over the years but they'd really seemed to hit it off. He was a much cooler uncle than she was a mum. She might be glad of that when Cassie hit the dreaded teenage years.

He'd already hinted that, after ten years in London, forging a career for himself in the City, he wanted to come home. It wasn't about money. He'd clearly commanded an impressive salary in the south. It was about the insistent pull of their community, of family, of their town, of their road. A sense of belonging that was absent in London. She understood that.

But if Tim did choose to stay, it might not be easy. Mrs MacKay was right to mention George. He hadn't spoken much to Tim since he'd returned, but Anna had seen the strain in George's face this evening. It had taken a lot to persuade George to come at all. He was hard to read but Anna sensed that, for him, there was little chance of forgiving and forgetting.

She straightened up, composed again now and ready to head back into the fray. She'd find Cassie first and give her a ten-minute warning that it was nearly time for bed.

As she started to turn back towards the front door, an eerie flicker of light in a house across the road caught her eye. She stopped, trying to make it out, frowning. *What was that?*

It was the Taylors' house, there, on the other side of the road and just a couple of doors down. She peered through the gloom. Nothing. Darkness. She must have been mistaken. A reflection from the street, maybe, or a trick of the light.

She smiled to herself. Dr Taylor had popped across with a bottle of champagne at the start of the party. She'd tried to make him stay longer but he'd made his excuses after an hour and headed home. He'd been out on the golf course all day, he'd said, and needed an early night. Anna suspected he'd also been keen to escape the cluster of patients who'd gathered round him. Many of them were women of a certain age, admirers who seemed eager to share details of their ailments and ask his advice. He might have retired but, as far as many in Otley were concerned, he was still their kind, charming family doctor, however much he protested that they should make an appointment with one of the newer GPs at the local surgery.

She started to relax, ready to move. Then it came again. A faint glimmer. A low beam was bobbing upstairs, just visible through the dark windows. Unease chilled her stomach. That was odd. It didn't look right. It wasn't the steady gleam of a normal landing or bedroom light. It was more like a wavering torch. She looked away, back over her shoulder, thinking of Lily and George, wondering whether to go inside and find one of them, tell them what she'd seen.

But what had she really seen? She hesitated. What would she say? *I think I saw a weird light flicker upstairs in your dad's house. But I might have been mistaken.* She'd feel a fool. She'd be frightening them for nothing. No, there was no need to spoil their fun. And Dr Taylor hated a fuss. No, she'd just pop across herself and have a closer look.

She set the half-empty glass of water on the ground by the wall and set off down the path to the empty road. Her shallow breathing and the pounding of blood in her head buzzed in her ears.

She was making a fuss about nothing. They'd laugh about it, afterwards. She'd make a story of it, the drama of her clandestine, dead-of-night mission across Riverside Road which only ended in – in what? In finding Dr Taylor carrying a storm lamp round the house because he'd needed the bathroom in the dark and the landing light bulb had fused? It was bound to be something like that. Nothing to worry about.

The Taylors' gate was unlatched. It swung open with a shudder and she padded down to the front door. She only glanced as she passed it. It was always kept locked and usually bolted too. Their house had a path running down the side to the back garden. As a child – in and out of the Taylors' house as much as her own with her best friend, Lily – Anna had quickly learned that everyone used the back door. The front was reserved for visitors.

She followed the paving stones round towards the shadowy garden. A streak flashed across the lawn as she approached and made her jump. It disappeared into the untidy bushes. A fox, probably, or a neighbourhood cat, out hunting.

Anna steadied her nerves and carried on to the back door. It was locked, as she'd expected. Dr Taylor was diligent when it came to security. Lily liked to tease him about it.

Anna considered. She could go back to the front and ring the doorbell but he mightn't hear, and even if he did, it might alarm him. She looked back towards the road, towards her own house, feeling increasingly foolish. No one was there. The fringe of her back garden, just visible from here, shimmered with coloured light, that was all. They were all too intent on enjoying the party to notice what was happening in the street.

She reached under the plant pot for the back door key and let herself in.

The kitchen was ghostly. Thin tendrils of light reached in from the street, yellowed with sodium. Just enough to highlight the metal trim of the stove and the dull circle of the wall clock. A green dot pulsed on the fridge.

Anna stood stock still and listened. She felt a sudden chill. If Dr Taylor opened the door and found her in his kitchen, she'd give him the fright of his life. Maybe she should just retreat and pull the door closed after her.

A creak sounded upstairs. A floorboard overhead yielded to someone's weight. It could only be Dr Taylor. They'd lost his wife, Lily and George's mother, years ago, when Anna had been pregnant with Cassie.

She was here now – she'd call out to him, let him know she was here. She'd explain that she was just checking on him, making sure he was OK. She made it to the kitchen door and opened it.

It was unmistakable now, at close quarters. A weak play of light across the landing, spilling in a confusion of ebbing shadow onto the staircase wall. A torch.

She called into the silence. 'Dr Taylor? It's Anna. You alright?'

Her voice sounded tremulous in the echoey house. She thought of him fondly, imagining him fumbling around in the darkness. He was increasingly hard of hearing now, although he didn't like to admit it. She'd have to be careful not to startle him.

She stole across the hall and made her way to the foot of the stairs. The only sound was the steady tick of the grandmother clock in the corner. The swinging pendulum gleamed in the half-light.

She peered up the stairs. The landing windows were bare, and fragments of outside light seeped in. No sign now of the torch. She leaned a shoulder against the wall and eased herself upwards, putting her feet with care on the very edge of each stair, where the treads were most stable. Halfway up, she stopped and called again. 'Dr Taylor?' Nothing.

She carried on until she could see across the landing. The door to Dr Taylor's bedroom stood open.

She stared, transfixed. She'd known that room since she was a little girl. The wardrobe where she and Lily used to hide when they were children. Nearby, the best secret hidey-hole in the house, a long, narrow hollow behind a removable section of skirting board, unknown even to the boys, where she and Lily had once stashed sweets. The double bed where she and Lily used to bounce, pretending they were gymnasts. Later, when they hadn't been much older than Cassie was now, they'd danced and sung in front of that full-length mirror, the only one in the house.

What the mirror reflected to her now was a glimpse of hell. Barely visible in the darkness, she could make out the outline of a figure, head and shoulders raised but slumped sideways into a mound of pillows. Glassy, staring eyes glistened.

She couldn't breathe. Somehow, she found herself moving, almost losing her footing as her toes caught the top stair, then stumbling across the landing and into the bedroom, twisting round the open door to see for herself.

She couldn't scream. The sound stuck in her throat. All she heard in the silence was her own strangled, breathy wheeze. Her body started to shake. She put out a hand and found the chest of drawers, steadied herself against it. The smell hit her, the cold, metallic stench of spilled blood. Her stomach heaved and she tasted bile. She struggled to breathe, to stop her stomach roiling.

Dr Taylor's face was twisted, a frozen portrait of shock and fear. His cotton pyjama top, the bedding and the clawed hand on top of it were densely spattered with blood, centred on a dense, black hole in his chest.

2

'Are you OK?'

Tim's voice was full of concern, his face strained. He sat close beside Anna on the sofa. His broad thigh was warm against hers, comforting.

Anna was still getting used to having Tim around after all these years, to the sight of his face, to the fact that, after being absent for so long, her brother suddenly seemed so eager to take care of her.

Am I OK?

The early morning was brutal with sharp light. She felt a wreck, mentally and physically. She'd spent the night at the police station, answering questions, explaining what she'd seen. Now, finally back home, her head ached. Her eyeballs were scratchy with sleeplessness. Her hands, balled into fists, were clammy in her lap.

Dr Taylor. The man who'd been so central to Riverside Road, to the whole town. The doctor who'd treated and cared for them all, for as long as she could remember. And, more than that, the kind neighbour who, with his wife, had opened his doors to Anna and Tim after the death of their mother and then, more recently, of their father, and treated them as warmly as if they'd been his own children.

'I'm not great, to be honest.' She took a breath. 'Still can't believe it.'

Tim nodded. 'I know.' He too looked shell-shocked. 'Him, of all people, right? I mean, why would anyone…?'

They sat in silence, too distressed to speak.

Finally, Anna asked, 'Is Cassie OK?' She needed to go upstairs, to see her daughter, but at the moment her body wouldn't move.

'Still asleep.' His voice was hoarse. 'I put her to bed around eleven, just after you left with the police. I just said you were busy with the party. She didn't seem to cotton on. I think she was too tired.'

'Thank you.' Anna tried to steel herself. She had to face the prospect of telling her daughter about Dr Taylor's death. It made her suddenly nauseous. He'd been such a kindly fixture in Cassie's life. It was going to be a terrible shock for her. 'Let's hope she sleeps in a bit.'

'Can I get you anything? Cup of tea?'

'No, thanks. I've been drinking bad tea all night.'

'Something stronger?'

'Definitely not.' Alcohol was the last thing she needed. She blew out her cheeks. All the time she'd been at the police station in Leeds, she'd longed to be at home. She'd wanted to shower, to crawl into bed, to sleep. Now, she was afraid to close her eyes. She knew she'd see Dr Taylor there, waiting to ambush her, his face contorted with horror. She knew she'd smell again the metallic tang of blood. She shivered. She wasn't sure she'd ever sleep soundly again.

'What time is it?'

Tim checked his watch. 'Half past six.' He considered. 'Why don't you go to bed? I can see to Cassie when she wakes up. You look done in.'

I can see to Cassie. He didn't know how much she appreciated that. The relief of having someone else to help with Cassie was one of the most wonderful parts of Tim's sudden return. Cassie hadn't even been born when he'd left. Even though Anna could afford childcare nowadays, it still wasn't easy being a single mum, keeping all those plates spinning. She didn't have the energy for it right now. Plates were crashing to the ground all around her.

For so many years, Lily had been the only one around to help, really. Cassie called her Auntie Lily but she'd been more like a second mum when Cassie was tiny, stepping in when she sensed that Anna was teetering close to the edge and keeping her afloat.

Lily. Anna's flesh tightened. She couldn't imagine what her friend must be going through. Anna had only seen her briefly last night, after she'd gone screaming back to the house, barely coherent as she'd tried to tell them what she'd seen.

She hadn't been aware of Lily at first. Anna had berated herself afterwards for the clumsy way she'd handled it. She'd just been too much in shock herself to think about protecting her friend.

She'd suddenly spotted Lily, there, at the back of the hall, half-hidden by the gathering crowd. Lily's eyes had been wide with horror as she'd started to grasp what Anna was saying. Her own father, dear Dr Taylor, had been stabbed to death in his bed. Anna had seen Lily sway then reach blindly for the wall to steady herself. The colour had leached from her face. Anna had pushed her way through at once to wrap her arms around her friend and felt Lily collapse against her. It was unthinkable. Poor Dr Taylor. Poor Lily and George. George, white with shock, had set off at a run towards their home, but Anna had held Lily back, shielding her from a sight which, Anna knew, would haunt her friend for the rest of her life.

Now, Anna wondered if George would be the one to do the

formal identification. Maybe she should suggest it. Lily adored her father. She mustn't see him for the last time like that.

Tim, watching her, said, 'Do you want to talk about it?'

Anna's body, so desperate for sleep, was also rigid with tension. She wasn't sure she could go to bed just yet. The long hours in the police station, sitting around, waiting for so long to speak to one detective and then another, then, finally, to give a formal statement, had put her out of sync with the rest of the world. She felt dull, out of sorts, jet-lagged. But talk about it? She wasn't sure she could.

Outside, a gate clanged. One of the neighbours must be taking their dog out early. Freshly showered, no doubt, and ready for the day. It seemed impossibly normal, out of kilter.

'Tell me what happened. If you like. You went outside to get some air. And you saw something...'

'A light. Flickering. Inside their house. I wasn't sure at first. I think now it must have been a torch.'

He looked incredulous. 'You should have told me. I'd have gone instead.'

'I know. I just...' She tried to remember. 'I just thought it was something and nothing, just a problem with the fuse box. I didn't want to make a fuss.'

She remembered the look on the detective's face when she'd described entering the Taylors' house. The slightly raised eyebrow suggested surprise that she'd barged into a crime scene on her own, unarmed, late at night. But he didn't understand. She hadn't thought of it as a crime scene. Not then. She'd thought of it as the Taylors' house, practically her second home, where lovely Dr Taylor would be pottering around on his own upstairs, getting ready for bed.

'Sounds like you had a narrow escape,' the detective had said mildly. 'It could have been a lot worse.'

She'd known what that implied. She could be dead now too, a cold body on a slab alongside Dr Taylor.

Now, Anna said, 'The police say they've found signs of forced entry. A smashed kitchen window or something. I don't know. It was dark.'

'And you searched the house, on your own, in the dark?'

It sounded so foolhardy when he put it like that. 'I just wanted to check he was OK.' She paused, remembering. 'I heard someone, moving about upstairs. I thought it must be him. I called out but... Anyway, I went upstairs to see and—' She broke off, trembling as she remembered the horror of it.

'God, Anna. You could have been killed.'

She shrugged. In her lap, her hands shook. It wasn't something she was ready to think about.

'I'm sorry.' Tim took a deep breath. 'So you went upstairs. What did you find?'

'Him. Dr Taylor. In bed. In their bedroom, you know, at the front.'

Tim nodded. They'd both done a lot of their growing up in that house. 'And he was already' – he struggled to say the word, lowering his voice as if they were sharing a secret – 'dead?'

She gave a quick nod. She hadn't gone too close to the body, hadn't touched it. She'd been sure, just looking at him. The wound in his chest was recent, the blood still sluggishly flowing, but he'd gone.

'That's awful.' Tim's large, warm hand enveloped hers and squeezed her knuckles. 'I'm so sorry.' He looked stricken for her and it made her feel guilty. She wasn't the victim here. He should save his sympathy for Dr Taylor. Or for Lily and George.

'I heard footsteps. Someone running down the side of the house. I ran to the window on the landing and saw a man run out of the gate. He turned right, towards the river, going fast.' She'd been through all this with the police, back and forth, in detail. Already, the words were becoming stale.

'He was thick-set. I think maybe young, by the way he

moved, but I can't be sure. But broad-shouldered. He was wearing a dark hoodie. The hood up. That's all I could see.' She faltered. 'They kept asking.'

She hung her head, embarrassed. She'd disappointed the mild-mannered detective. She'd sensed it in his face as he'd pressed her, chasing her sketchy memory round and round her tired mind with his questions: *What can you tell us about his face? Even from the side, a glimpse, a glance at his profile? A beard, a moustache? And his clothes, what more can you tell us? Anything distinctive? Anything at all?*

She'd been useless. She'd let Dr Taylor down. She'd let everyone down.

'It was dark,' she'd kept telling them, pathetically. 'And it all happened so quickly.'

Tim tightened his hand on hers. 'It's OK,' he said. 'It's over now.'

They sat in silence for a while. Cassie would be awake soon. She knew she ought to stir herself, to shower, to haul herself off to bed and get a few hours' sleep, but she couldn't. It wasn't only that she didn't have the energy. She didn't want to be on her own.

She said, remembering, 'The police want a list of everyone at the party.'

Tim frowned. 'Why?'

She shrugged. 'I don't know. I suppose they want to talk to them. Check if they saw anything.'

Tim reached for his phone. 'OK. I can do that.'

Anna looked round vaguely at the lounge. Tim and the caterers had worked hard. The furniture was back in place and the carpet looked freshly vacuumed. Bulging recycling bags and cases of empty champagne bottles were stacked neatly by the front door. Apart from the strings of lights, still draped round the garden, it was hard to tell there had been a party here a matter of hours ago.

'Go on.' Tim gave her a nudge. 'Go up and get some rest. You must be shattered.'

Shattered. She thought of a glass, crashing onto a stone floor from a great height and splintering into shards.

She hesitated. She was frightened of being alone, of closing her eyes. Dr Taylor's deathly face hung there, waiting for her.

She shook herself. 'You're right. Wake me, will you, if anything happens?'

Tim grunted. He was already hunching forward over his phone, starting work on the guest list for the police.

She heaved herself to her feet and stumbled out into the hall. As she turned towards the bottom of the stairs, her eye was caught by the white rectangle on the mat. That hadn't been there when she'd come home. It didn't look like a printed flyer. It was a sheet of paper, neatly folded in half. The top flap stirred as she crossed to the front door and stooped to pick it up.

Thoughts flitted through her tired mind. An early thank you for the party, perhaps. Or, if news of Dr Taylor's murder had already spread, a condolence note. Everyone in Riverside Road knew how close her family was to the Taylors, just across the street, and to kindly Dr Taylor in particular.

So it was all the more of a shock when she opened the fold to see crude block letters in black ink spelling out a coarse threat:

KEEP YOUR MOUTH SHUT. OR YOU'RE NEXT.

3

'Mum?'

'Cassie?' Anna, deep in a pit of sleep, struggled to rouse herself. 'What time is it?'

She was lost, drifting, her limbs heavy. Then the stark events of the previous night burst back into her mind. Dr Taylor. The police. The threatening note, shoved to the back of the drawer in her bedside table.

'Like, eight something?' Cassie tugged at the duvet. 'What's going on?'

Anna ran a hand across her face and forced her eyes open against the burning daylight. Cassie's cheeks were pale, her eyes sharp with worry.

'What do you mean?' Anna stalled, playing for time.

'Outside. In the road. There's loads of people.'

Anna plucked back the edge of the duvet and opened her arms wide. Cassie bent down and submitted half-heartedly to a long, tight hug.

Anna felt her daughter's slight bones, bird-like, against the bulk of her own body. She buried her face in Cassie's hair and breathed in the faded scent of strawberry shampoo, of her daughter's young skin. All the times crowded in. The days Cassie was an infant and cuddled into Anna's lap, safe and secure, her cheek against Anna's breastbone. Now, older, Cassie squirmed and pulled away, impatient.

'Mum.' She tilted her face to her mother's. 'What's happened?'

Anna sat up in bed. 'I'm afraid I've got some bad news.'

'What?'

Anna swallowed hard. Cassie had known Dr Taylor all her life. He'd been as special as a grandpa to her in recent years, always making such a fuss of her and buying her little treats. They seemed to have forged a special bond, especially since Lily and George had moved out to rent their own small flats, leaving Dr Taylor to live alone. Cassie had never known Anna's mother, who'd died long before Cassie had been born, and she'd only been three when Anna's father had died suddenly, of a heart attack. She could barely remember him.

Anna said carefully, 'It's about Dr Taylor.'

Cassie frowned. 'Is he in hospital?'

'It's worse than that. I'm sorry.' Anna reached for the words. 'He's passed away.'

Cassie's jaw slackened. Her eyes slid away to gaze towards the window. A pigeon landed heavily on the outside sill. Anna watched it hop along, peck at the paintwork, then take off again in a flurry of feathers. She waited, letting her daughter absorb the news.

Cassie opened her mouth, then closed it again and frowned to herself. Her mind seemed to be whirring. Finally, she said, 'How old was he?'

'Well, not very old. Only sixty-eight.' Anna considered what Cassie might be thinking. Cassie woke crying sometimes after nightmares in which Anna had died. 'But he was a lot older than me. And Uncle Tim.'

Cassie nodded. She seemed to be making a calculation. 'And older than Grandpa was when he died?'

'And Grandma. She was only in her forties. But that's very unusual, for someone to die that young.' *Unusual and unlucky,* she thought.

Cassie pressed closer into Anna's side. 'Was it his heart?'

Anna thought of the dark wound in Dr Taylor's chest and the blood, so much blood.

'Not exactly.' She paused. She hadn't envisaged telling Cassie so much, not all at once. But maybe she had to. She'd have to find out eventually. 'Someone hurt him.'

Cassie's eyes widened and swung back to her mother. 'What? Do you mean he was' – she baulked at the next word, lowered her voice to a stage whisper – 'murdered?'

'Yes.'

'Oh!' Cassie stared, horrified. 'But why? Who did it?'

Anna sighed. 'The police are still trying to work out who did it, sweetheart. I'm sure they'll catch him soon. It's nothing to worry about.'

Cassie seemed to sink into herself, piecing the facts together. 'It was in his house, wasn't it? That's why all the police are there. Outside.'

'Are they?' Anna nodded to herself. 'Yes, of course.' She stroked her daughter's hair. 'I'm sorry. I know it's upsetting. It's unbelievable. For all of us.'

Anna soon realised, as she washed and hastily dressed, that Cassie was right about the scale of the commotion outside.

Riverside Road, their quiet, close-knit street, had broken out into a bustling crime scene. The calm and security they'd always prized had been fractured.

Across the road, the police had sealed off the Taylors' house. The front garden, the path down the side and, presumably, the area at the back of the house, had been swallowed up by voluminous folds of tenting. Gates clanged, paths and pavements thudded with boots and shoes, and loud voices shouted instructions. The pavements were clogged with police vans and cars. An hour later, media vans and TV reporters appeared, adding to the din.

The houses, which had always been so open to each other, so welcoming, closed their doors and curtains as neighbours retreated, huddling inside.

Anna felt under siege. Somehow, the reporters seemed to know that she'd been the one who'd found the body, that she'd spent her life darting in and out of the Taylors' home. When they'd been children, they'd all been so close, they'd felt like family. *We were family,* she thought, *in every way it mattered.*

In the midst of the commotion, the past seemed a still, steady anchor. She and Lily, Tim and George had grown up together. They'd drawn and painted side by side at the Taylors' scrubbed kitchen table while Mrs Taylor flitted in and out, folding laundry or preparing snacks. They'd shared birthday parties and summer barbecues in the Taylors' back garden and, as often as not, gathered round the Taylors' polished dining table to celebrate Christmas.

Now, Anna, lost in memories, jumped each time the doorbell sounded, long and shrill. Tim opened the door twice, telling the journalists in no uncertain terms to go away and leave them in peace, they had nothing to say. When his pleas had little impact, they simply closed the curtains, hunkered down and let the doorbell ring.

One woman, brassy, pushed open the letterbox and shouted into the hall, telling them she'd only be a minute, she just wanted a word. Others trampled through the front garden and pressed their faces against the lounge windows, trying to see through gaps in the closed curtains. One pressed a note to the pane offering money for their story.

In the midst of it all, several neighbours bravely fought their way to the front door through the chaotic mob, eventually managing to pass in bunches of flowers and notes thanking Anna for the party. Many said how sorry they were about the sad news. If there was anything they could do, anything at all...

Anna watched from an upstairs window as Janice from the house next door battled her way back down the path after handing a bunch of flowers to Tim on the doorstep. She was shielding her face from the onslaught with cupped hands as reporters pushed microphones towards her and fired questions. Anna thought about the crude note, warning her to keep her mouth shut. She didn't understand. Where had it come from? It couldn't be anyone she knew, she was sure. No one in the road would write something so vicious.

You're next. She shuddered. She'd hidden it at the back of a drawer in her bedroom, too frightened to tell the police, to tell anyone.

In the end, suffocated by all the intrusion, she, Tim and Cassie withdrew to the kitchen. Anna let Cassie play games endlessly on her iPad while she and Tim sat beside her in silence, drinking tea. Anna couldn't find words. She just wanted these strangers to leave them all alone.

She worried about Lily, trying to imagine her grief. She wanted to reach out to her best friend but didn't know what to do, what to say. When she finally reached for her mobile, wondering if she could compose a message at least, it started to ring. She answered the call from a number she didn't recognise only to hear a pushy male reporter start to fire questions at her. She didn't know how the journalists had got hold of her number.

She switched her phone off at once and sent it skimming across the kitchen table as if it were too hot to touch. Later, when she finally checked, a fleet of missed calls and messages from unknown numbers bounced into view. She deleted the lot without bothering to listen back.

Later, in the afternoon, Anna tried to numb herself by burying herself in routine. She batch-cooked for the week, put a wash on and folded laundry.

When she trudged upstairs with a pile of clean clothes, Cassie called out to her.

'Mum! Come and look!'

Cassie was kneeling on the end of her bed, watching events in the street from her bedroom window. Anna padded in to stand behind her and peer out.

There, on the kerb close to the Taylors' house, a mound of flowers had accumulated. A multi-coloured bunch of gerberas poked out of grey paper. Beneath them lay a bright yellow and pink seasonal bouquet, wrapped in cellophane. From the super-market, probably. Alongside, a cheerful bunch of pink carna-tions. There must have been a dozen bunches already. Handwritten condolence cards, taped to the wrapping, fluttered in the breeze.

Anna's eyes filled. Dr Taylor would have been so touched. She wondered if he'd really understood how much he'd meant to their community, to the road. How loved he'd been, by so many.

She wiped her eyes with the back of her hand before Cassie saw. 'Did you see who left them?'

Cassie bit her lip. 'Mrs MacKay put the pink ones there. That family with the black poodle put those fancy ones down. I don't know who left the big daisies. Should we leave some?'

Anna said quietly, 'Yes, sweetheart, let's do that.' She thought about it. 'I guess people have heard.'

Of course, they had. News travelled quickly along the street and so many of them had been gathered together right here, at the party, when she'd come stumbling back to raise the alarm. She imagined Mrs MacKay would have had a hand in spreading the word further afield at church that morning.

Everyone would be horrified. It was enough of a shock that someone had been murdered, here, in the middle of their close, sleepy community. But it wasn't just anyone. It was Dr Taylor. A man known and respected by everyone in the street. Over the years, he'd attended half the local population, treating several generations, in the early days in the draughty old surgery where he and a colleague had seen patients in the front room, and then, once it opened, in the new, purpose-built building on Leeds Road.

Anna blinked. The reporters had all moved out of the street now and were standing at its entrance by their vans, drinking from plastic cups and chatting to each other. They were separated from the street by a fluttering police tape, blue and white, which secured the entrance. A police officer stood beside it, watching them.

'What's happening?' Tim appeared in Cassie's doorway, behind them.

'They've put a cordon up, look.' Anna pointed. 'It won't affect us, will it? I mean, residents can still come and go?'

'I'm sure we'll be fine.' Tim craned round the curtain to see. 'Good that it's keeping the reporters at bay. That's something.'

Cassie said suddenly, 'Does Auntie Lily know yet?'

Anna put a hand on her daughter's shoulder. 'Yes, my love, she does. We need to be extra kind to her for a while. And Uncle George. Remember, they've just lost their dad.'

Tim said, 'Have you called her?'

Anna didn't know what to say. Lily had looked so pale, so shell-shocked, when Anna had come back to the house last night to break the news of what she'd found. She was frightened of getting in touch.

'I'm not sure where they are,' she said. 'They might be with the police. I don't want to intrude.'

'Call her,' Tim said firmly. 'It'll only get harder if you leave it.'

Anna wrapped her arms round Cassie's shoulders and gave her a squeeze. She had such a fierce need to hold her. To protect her. To shield her from all this. She kissed the top of her daughter's head as she released her.

'Cassie, love,' she said. 'I know it's hard. We're all going to feel a bit unsettled for a while. But I think you should come downstairs for a bit and do something else. Haven't you still got homework to finish?'

They headed down to the kitchen together. Anna made a fresh pot of coffee and a hot chocolate for Cassie to take with her into the lounge.

Anna stood alone at the kitchen window, looking blankly out into the garden. She stirred her coffee for a long time, scraping up a softly swirling whirlpool, her mind everywhere. She ought to call Lily. Lily was her oldest, closest friend, and Tim was right, it would only get harder the longer she waited.

But still she was wavering. She wasn't sure she could go through with it. It wasn't only that it was so difficult to find the right words. It was more than that, much more.

She couldn't imagine how much pain Lily must be feeling right now. None of them could.

Anna felt a creeping tide of darkness. A darkness she couldn't understand but which terrified her. A darkness which she sensed would steadily engulf them all.

4

'It's one-way glass. They can't see you.'

The detective gestured for Anna to take another step forward. There were five young men on the other side of the window, all of similar build, each marked by an identifying number.

Anna blinked. She felt horribly exposed. It did feel as if one or two of the men were staring right back at her and that was unnerving. She saw the hard bulk of their muscles, their cold, dead stares, and thought of the menacing note through the letterbox, warning her to keep her mouth shut. She didn't want to be here at all.

'Take your time.'

Anna clenched her sweaty hands. She'd already had a briefing from the detective. He'd been gruff, reminding her to look carefully, no need to rush, to see if she could identify the man she'd seen running from the Taylors' house that night.

She cast her eyes from one face to another. The silence pressed in on her. The detective, close at her side, waited. She closed her eyes and Dr Taylor's twisted features flashed into her mind, the stuff of nightmares. It was an image she didn't think would ever fade. She forced herself to open her eyes and look again. Words from the note passed through her mind as she gazed down the row of burly men in front of her.

Or you're next.

'I don't know,' she said at last. 'It was dark.'

Inside the room, an officer must have given an instruction. The line of men shuffled their feet and turned to face the wall, giving her a side view. This was the profile a young man might present as he turned right out of a gate and headed off down the road.

Anna looked wretchedly from one man to another down the line, then turned quickly away.

'I'm sorry. I really don't know.'

The detective, quietly observing her, asked, 'Do you need more time?'

'No.' She shook her head. 'I'm just not sure. Sorry.'

The detective let out a heavy breath. 'OK. That's it, then.' His features, as he showed Anna out, were tight. They'd be in touch, he said as they parted at the police station doors.

Anna stumbled her way to the bus stop. She stopped now and then for breath, feeling sick. Her hands were slick with sweat. She was letting everyone down. Letting down the Taylor family itself, the kind, loving people who'd opened their doors to her when she was still a child and treated her as one of their own. She boarded the bus back to Otley and sank into a seat, her body trembling. She was so stiff with stress that the vibrations of the engine through the metal felt torturous. She stared unseeing at the passing streets, the parades of shops with their newsagents, cafés and late-night convenience stores.

The world seemed an alien place to her. How could this have happened to Dr Taylor? How could he have died such a sudden and violent death? It was impossible. She gripped the seat rail in front of her until her knuckles blanched.

Memories crowded in. Of Dr Taylor standing in the garden with her father when she was a child, sharing a beer and a joke, while Mrs Taylor watched from the kitchen window. Of Dr Taylor's benevolent smile when she and Lily came careering into the house together and discovered him in his armchair in the lounge, reading his newspaper or working on the crossword. Of all the Sunday afternoons he'd sat at their dining room table with them, books spread across the surface, patiently explaining a piece of maths or science or history homework. She remembered the way his hand, with its long, capable fingers, moved his silver pen slowly, meticulously, across the paper as he taught them. Always calm. Always patient. How could he be dead?

The bus, with its jolting stop-start motion, nosed its way through the clogged city streets and picked up the main road to Otley. The claustrophobia of the congested streets gave way to a patchwork of fields, scored with dry-stone walling. Her eyes blankly scanned the familiar contours of the steep hillsides, thickly coated with trees, rising to the Chevin ahead.

Something seemed to relax a fraction inside her and she found herself sobbing, a tissue pressed against her face, her shoulders hunched, trying not to make a spectacle of herself in the half-empty bus. The pain of the last two days seemed to burst in her as she wept. Dr Taylor. *Murdered.* It wasn't true. It couldn't be. It was impossible.

She could barely remember a time when their two families, the Kings and the Taylors, had been intact and untouched by tragedy. She'd only been a little girl when her mother had died, and Lily and George's mother and father had helped to fill the desperate gap. Now the very last of their parents had been taken. There was no one left to protect them, no one from that older, wiser generation to turn to for support or advice. She felt utterly bereft.

In the centre of Otley, she climbed down unsteadily from the bus and crossed the cobbled market square, past the bank and teashops, past the stone Victorian clock tower, picking her way through the stalls selling Yorkshire cheese and jams, cakes and fancy knick-knacks made by some artist up the Dales. The air around her seemed heavy with the town's grief for Dr Taylor.

She'd avoided reading the local newspapers and watching the regional TV news, but, passing the newsagents, it was hard not to see the headline in the *Yorkshire Post*: *Otley doctor fatally stabbed in bed. Police launch hunt for killer.*

Of course it was making headlines. People weren't murdered, not here in Otley. Theirs was such a small, insular town, stolidly proud of its heritage, of its history stretching back to the Bronze Age and the ancient people who, all those centuries ago, had settled in this same valley, drawn water from the same rushing stretch of the Wharfe and left their mark with carvings still visible today in the rocks high on the top of the Chevin.

It didn't have the glitz and glamour of Leeds with its art galleries, theatres and concert halls. Otley didn't even have its own proper cinema anymore.

It didn't have the gentility and wealth of Ilkley, further down the valley.

Otley was built more on the rough toil of farming than the middle-class professions. Its people were tough but decent. They might not suffer fools – or, sometimes, outsiders – but they knew how to band together to help their own. They valued the richness of the land and the beauty of the natural world around them. They settled, and however far the younger generation might travel, they generally yielded in the end to the firm tug of return when it was time to start their own families. They belonged.

Anna turned, red-eyed, into Riverside Road. She sensed

Mrs MacKay's stout figure looming in her front window, observing the comings and goings. Anna bent her head as she passed. She pretended she hadn't heard when Mrs MacKay lifted a ringed knuckle to rap on the glass and wave at her.

It was rude. She ought to pop in for a chat and say thank you for the homemade soup Mrs MacKay had dropped round the previous day. It had been one of many acts of thoughtful kindness since the night of the party. But Anna knew that if she did go in right now, Mrs MacKay's warmth and sympathy would reduce her to a sobbing mess, and she didn't want to do that to her sweet elderly neighbour. Right now, she just needed to get home and curl up in bed.

Over the next few days, everyone in the street was questioned by police, one by one. Many of them had been at the party.

Anna felt sick about it. She'd wanted the party to celebrate Tim's return. It was a way of announcing a fresh start for him after all the unpleasantness of the past. Now, all those friends and acquaintances had been dragged into something sordid and were being pestered by the police. When they spoke, she sensed their awkwardness. Everyone felt on the back foot. Suddenly, they were being forced to answer questions, to account for exactly where they'd been, what they'd been doing, who else they'd seen.

'It's fine,' Tim tried to reassure her. 'We're all alibis for each other. They just want to know if anyone heard or saw anything unusual, I suppose.'

It was only a few days since Dr Taylor's death but Cassie, plunged back into her daily routine at school, seemed at times to forget what had happened. Anna tried not to mention it more than she needed to.

Then, in the evening, as Anna kissed her daughter goodnight and went to leave, Cassie said in a small voice, 'What if he comes here?'

'Who, sweetheart?' Anna, on the threshold, turned.

'That man. The one who killed Dr Taylor. What if he comes for us?'

Anna went back into the room and perched on the edge of Cassie's bed. Her daughter, pale against the pillow, looked small and vulnerable.

'You're safe here, perfectly safe. We all are,' she said. 'Anyway, he's probably on the other side of the country by now.' She took a deep breath, trying to find the right thing to say to reassure her daughter. 'Wherever he is, I'm sure the police will catch him soon. They're throwing a lot of resources at it.'

'Really?' Cassie sounded so anxious.

Anna waited, sensing that Cassie didn't entirely believe her. 'What is it?'

Cassie gripped the top of her duvet tightly, pressing her fingers into claws. 'I don't want to tell you.'

Anna reached out and gently stroked the hair away from her daughter's forehead. 'Try,' she said. 'Maybe it'll help.'

'You won't be angry?'

Anna tried to keep her face expressionless. 'It's hard to be sure without knowing what it is but I'll try not to be angry, OK?'

Cassie's eyes fixed on her mother's face. 'I've seen him.' Cassie lowered her voice to a whisper. 'Out there.' She stabbed a nervous finger towards the curtained window.

Anna frowned. 'What do you mean, seen him?'

'At night. Across the street.' Her voice faltered. 'Watching me.'

5

For a moment, Anna couldn't speak.

Instinctively, she got up and crossed to the window, peered out at the gloom below. The street was shadowy. She strained to make out a figure in the shadows. 'I can't see anyone.'

Cassie threw back the duvet, hopped out of bed and joined her mother at the window. 'Not now. But I did see him. In the night. I woke up and thought I heard something and when I went to look, he was there' – she pointed across the road – 'under that tree. A man. Staring right at me.'

Anna said, almost to herself, 'Maybe a reporter came back.' Interest had quickly faded in the days immediately after the murder. The cordon had already been taken down. Anna had tried to see that as a positive sign, an indication that life in the street might soon get back to normal. She shook her head. 'I thought they'd given up.'

Anna tried to imagine what her daughter might have seen. It was a spindly tree, the trunk not broad enough to conceal a grown man, the branches broad and leafy. Maybe the limbs had been stirring in the wind and, half-asleep, Cassie had imagined a person, lurking there in the shifting shadows.

She knew better than to share her doubts with Cassie. Instead, she said, 'What did he look like?'

Cassie shrugged. 'Normal. It was dark.'

'Tall or short?'

'About the same as Uncle Tim, I guess. Like I said, normal. I couldn't see his face, not properly. But it was tipped up, staring back at me.' She shivered.

'Just keep away from the window, OK? If it's a reporter, they'll soon get bored. Now come on, back into bed.' Anna shooed her back across the room. 'I know it's scary, what happened. We're all upset. But we're safe now.'

Cassie looked back at her doubtfully. 'But what if he comes back?'

'If you see anyone out there again, anyone at all, you come and wake me up, OK? No matter what time it is.'

Cassie considered this, her face serious. 'What if I'm not quite sure?'

'Even if you're not quite sure. Any time you're worried or feeling scared. OK?'

'You won't be angry?'

'Promise.' She leaned in and kissed Cassie on the cheek. 'Now try to get to sleep.'

She sighed to herself as she switched Cassie's light off and headed downstairs to join Tim. She didn't know what to think.

It could be her daughter's overactive imagination. It could just have been a passer-by, stopping for a quiet cigarette and catching Cassie's eye as they gazed around.

She frowned. She didn't want to consider the alternative. That Cassie was right. That a stranger really was spying on them, late at night. A stranger who might know too much, either about the present or about the secrets of the past.

6

That evening, Anna felt exhausted.

All she wanted to do was collapse onto the sofa with Tim, just the two of them, their TV dinners on trays and a bottle of white wine open on the coffee table.

Usually, he liked to flick through the channels, looking for something to distract them. He had a knack for finding things they'd both enjoy. A fast-paced drama series or some gossipy documentary about the life of a pop singer or actor they both liked. Nothing too demanding. Nothing too long.

But this time, the TV screen was dark. She knew at once that something was wrong. He didn't look her in the eye as he poured her a glass of wine and pushed it across to her. His face was tight.

She didn't need this. 'You OK?' Her tone sounded more impatient than she'd intended.

He didn't answer.

They picked at their pasta in silence. Anna hadn't felt hungry since she'd found Dr Taylor. She forced down what she could but the very idea of eating seemed revolting to her. All she saw in her mind's eye, as she chewed and swallowed, was Dr Taylor's battered body, bleeding out.

Finally, she set down her fork and said, 'What is it?' She shot him a hard look, waiting. 'What's wrong?'

He gave a low sigh, almost too quiet for her to catch, then set down his fork too. 'I'm sorry.' He stared miserably at the half-eaten meal. 'I just... I just can't do this. I mean, how has this even happened? To him, of all people?'

The anger seeped out of her and her face crumpled. 'Same,' she said. 'I know. How can...?'

Tim twisted to her and opened his arms. She leaned into him and pressed her head into his shoulder as the tears spilled.

'Hey.' He pulled out a handkerchief from his pocket, shook it open and dabbed at her face. The cotton smelled fresh, of detergent and ironing. 'I'm sorry. I didn't mean to—'

Anna heard the crack in his voice.

A moment later, he tried again: 'It's just so horrific, isn't it? Pretending to be normal when—'

'I know.'

He took a long, shuddering breath, trying to compose himself. She thought of the way he used to comfort her when she'd sobbed at night after their mother died, missing her so much it made her body ache. He'd only been a child himself, but he'd always struggled to be brave, to be strong for his little sister.

Now, he said, 'It'll be alright. You'll see.'

Still crying, she almost laughed at that. 'That's what Dad always said.'

'Well, there you are then.' He turned her gently round and drew her closer into a firm, clumsy hug. She sobbed into his neck, wet and messy. The handkerchief, balled in her hand, pressed against her face.

He waited until the sobs eased, then moved her back against the sofa cushions and reached for her hot, damp hand.

'You've done so well, keeping it together. I can't imagine. The shock.'

'I keep seeing him. His face. How could anyone—?' Anna dissolved again into tears.

'I know.' Tim squeezed her hand. 'He was like a second dad to us, wasn't he? I keep thinking about when we were kids. After Mum died. We were always over there. He taught me how to play cricket. How to whistle.'

Anna laughed through the crying. 'I know. You drove us all mad with that tuneless whistling, remember? All bloody summer.'

Tim laughed too. 'I was only nine. Well, maybe ten.'

Anna took a shuddering breath. 'I miss Mrs Taylor too. The way their kitchen always smelled of cake. I often think of her when I bake something. She was so calm and patient. Lily and I must have iced a million fairy cakes in there. And she always had things in the cupboard to decorate them. Silver balls and sugar strands. I thought it was marvellous.'

Tim shook his head and put his finger on her lips to stop her. 'Don't. Please.'

They sat in silence. The only sound was Anna's uneven breathing.

Finally, Anna said: 'I'm glad Dad isn't here to see it.' She glanced guiltily at her brother. 'I don't mean that. I mean, of course I wish he was still here, obviously, I just—' She trailed off, thinking of their father.

'I know.' Tim nodded. 'He'd be so upset. He'd struggle with it. With how anything so wicked could happen to such a lovely man.'

Anna withdrew her hand from Tim's, unscrewed the crumpled handkerchief and blew her nose.

'And it's not just that, is it? It feels as if everything is bursting to the surface,' she said, twisting to give him an anxious look, trying to read in his face if he understood. 'Everything we've kept buried all these years.'

Tim shrugged. 'Is it me? Is it the fact I've come back? I've stirred it all up again?'

She peered across the lounge, remembering. 'It's not just that. It's the fact he's died. The fact it's' – she braced herself to say the word, instinctively lowering her voice – 'murder. Everything's going to be pulled apart now. Everything.' She raised her eyes to Tim's, her expression desperate. 'Think about it, Tim. Strangers rummaging around in the past, shining a light into every dark corner. I don't think I can bear it.'

Tim blinked, taking it in. 'I know,' he said at last. 'But I think we'll just have to, won't we? I don't think we've got a choice.'

Anna felt her breathing quicken. 'But they can't! Have you thought? Have you thought what they might find?'

'Stop it.' Tim looked round as if he feared someone might hear. 'Just don't go there, OK? We can't.'

For some time, neither of them spoke. Anna felt the tension burn through the silence between them. Eventually, she got abruptly to her feet, picked up her tray with bad grace and took her half-eaten meal through to the kitchen.

She stood at the window in the shadows, her arms braced against the counter. Her pale ghost-self peered back at her from the black glass. The eyes were large and bright with fear.

'Anna?'

She started. Tim had followed her. She spied him in the reflection. He hovered on the threshold, apologetic, as if he were afraid to intrude.

She turned to face him, eyes sharp. 'What?'

Tim cleared his throat, nervous. 'There's something else.'

Anna felt her stomach drop away. 'What?'

He waited a moment longer, considering, then brought a crumpled piece of paper out of his pocket. 'I found something today. On the mat.'

'What?' She frowned. 'Found what?'

He stepped towards her, holding out the paper. It was a standard white envelope, cheap-looking.

She turned it over in the half-light. The front was blank.

'Why did you open it?' Anna glared. 'You had no right!'

He flushed. 'I'm sorry. I know. It wasn't sealed and I didn't think...'

She pursed her lips. She was angry but it wasn't really with him. It was a sense of what was coming. She couldn't take much more.

'I wanted to give it to you earlier,' he went on. 'I was waiting until Cassie had gone up.' He nudged the envelope with his finger. 'Look inside.'

She slid out a small sheet of paper and unfolded it, feeling suddenly sick.

It was the same crude, block lettering. A simple, stark message.

LAST WARNING. KEEP YOUR MOUTH SHUT. FOR YOUR DAUGHTER'S SAKE.

7

'*Last warning?*' Tim's face was creased with concern. 'What does it mean? That you've had other letters like this?'

Anna's body felt leaden. She leaned back heavily against the kitchen counter.

Tim, watching her, persisted. 'You have, haven't you?' He took her silence as confirmation. 'But who, Anna? Who'd threaten you like this? Threaten Cassie too?'

Anna said quietly, 'I don't know.'

Tim raked his hand through his hair. 'We've got to tell someone. The police, maybe. I mean, when they say "keep your mouth shut," it's about the murder, right? About the fact you're the only real witness they've got? They still haven't found the murder weapon. Doesn't sound like forensics have turned up anything worth having. Frankly, you're the only person with evidence which might actually put someone away.'

'I guess so.'

'Anna!' He took a few steps towards her. He sounded exasperated. 'This is really serious. What if this is the murderer? What if whoever's sending these messages killed Dr Taylor and knows you're working with the police? What if he's watching you and wants to make sure you don't say or do anything that might help him get caught? Don't you get it? He's really dangerous. He's killed once.'

Anna mumbled, 'I get it.'

'So we need to go to the police. Show them the notes. They might even help, as evidence.'

Anna felt her way along the counter to the kitchen table and sat heavily in a chair. Her head ached. It was too much, all of this. Gripped tightly in her hand, the crumpled paper shook.

'But it can't be the murderer, sending these,' she said at last. 'No one here would kill Dr Taylor. I can't believe that. It was a burglar. Some chancer. He'll be halfway across the country by now.'

'What if he isn't?' Tim pointed at the envelope. 'That wasn't sent by mail. It was hand-delivered.'

Anna felt her shoulders sag. Tim slid into a chair beside her and she sensed his awkwardness. There were times they felt so close, the two of them, as if they'd managed to pick up where they'd left off ten years ago, and others, like this, when he seemed to have no idea what to say to her.

He rested his large hands on the table, the fingers interlaced. 'There's another possibility, I suppose.' He didn't look at her. 'What if you're right about the murderer being an outsider? Maybe he isn't the one sending the notes. Maybe it's someone else, who is local, trying to take advantage of what's happened.'

Anna frowned. 'But why?'

Tim's eyes stayed on his hands. 'Because they know you witnessed the murder and they want to upset you.'

Anna twisted sideways. His profile was stern. 'But who would...?'

He didn't answer.

'George?' She shook her head. 'You mean George, don't you?'

He pursed his lips. 'I don't know. I just, well, he hates us, doesn't he? He's got every reason to.'

'Even so.' She hesitated. 'He wouldn't...' *Would he?*

The fridge whirred and buzzed in the silence between them. She wanted to get up, to go back through to the lounge, out of the shadows, but she couldn't move, not yet.

She thought about George. She had worried about how cold he'd been, since Tim had come home. Brittle, as if the slightest jolt might fracture him. Lily had seen it too. Anna had thought all that was behind them, that he'd found a way of moving on. He had kept his distance for some years but gradually, when their paths crossed, he seemed to thaw, especially with Cassie around. It was hard to stay stiff with a child as warm and friendly as Cassie. But now he'd lost his father too, so brutally. She could imagine the floodgates bursting open all over again. Maybe Tim was right. Maybe he was the one trying to hurt them.

Tim, watching her now, said, 'Did Lily say anything about him? About how he's coping?'

Anna didn't look him in the eye.

'Anna? You did talk to Lily, didn't you?' He craned closer, trying to peer at her face, then shook his head, taking her silence as his answer. 'Oh, Anna. I know it's hard but you've got to. She's your best friend. She needs you.' His eyes were full of concern. 'Please. Just call her. Will you?'

'OK. I will. First thing tomorrow.' Anna felt the tension hard in her body, from her pounding head to the tightness of her spine. 'Can we stop talking about all this now? Please?' She set her hands on the table, palms down, and pressed herself to her feet. 'I just want to sit quietly and finish that wine. OK?'

Tim followed her back into the brightness of the lounge and sat beside her on the sofa. She refreshed her glass and took a gulp of wine, feeling it burn through her body. Tim was unyielding. He picked up his own glass but didn't attempt to drink.

'What?' she said sharply.

He looked down into his glass as if he were talking to the wine. 'Look, there is something else. One more thing.'

Anna's fingers gripped the stem of her glass.

He raised his eyes sheepishly to hers. 'It's just that Cassie, well, she's been asking me stuff. About her dad.'

Anna tutted at once. 'When?'

'The other day, when I was helping her with homework.' He sat up straighter. 'I didn't say anything. But I really think you need to talk to her. She said she thought she'd heard something about him. Apparently, some of the older women in the road were chatting when she walked past. She said they stared at her and lowered their voices.'

'They were talking about her?'

'I said maybe she was imagining it, but she wouldn't let it go. She asked me if I remembered him. Who he was. What he looked like. If he was kind, clever, funny or whatever. I didn't know what to say.' He seemed to steel himself for what he was about to say next. 'She seemed to think he'd died. Years ago. Is that what you told her?'

Anna's mouth was too dry for her to speak. She drank off her wine. 'We don't talk about him. She knows that. Off limits.'

Tim persisted, 'So you didn't say he's dead?'

Anna studied the inside of her empty glass. 'She went through a phase when she was little. Five or six, maybe. She kept asking why she only had a mummy and not a daddy, like her friends.' She squirmed, felt herself flush under Tim's gaze. 'I might possibly have said her daddy died years ago, before she was even born.' She lifted a hand in self-defence. 'I know. Maybe it wasn't the best move. It just seemed the easiest thing for her to understand. And it seemed, you know, final. A way of stopping her wondering about him. I made out he'd left her for me as a special present, so the two of us had each other and wouldn't be lonely. She seemed happy with that.' She shook her head. 'She's never talked about him again. Not with me.'

Tim gave her a thoughtful look. 'Well, she has now. I fobbed her off. I said I wasn't really sure and if she had any questions, she should ask you.'

'Thanks a lot.' She leaned forward and topped up her glass.

He frowned. 'I'm sure she knew I wasn't telling her the truth. She's not stupid. It's not fair, Anna. She has a right to know.'

Anna swallowed hard. 'I don't want her thinking about him. Not now, not ever. Simple as that.'

'She's already thinking about him.' Tim spread his hands, trying to be conciliatory. 'Look, I know what happened. I was here, remember?' His tone softened. 'You're an amazing mum. I admire you for that. And for getting your own business off the ground too. It can't have been easy. Especially after Dad died. I want to help, if I can.'

He hesitated, as if he were feeling his way to the words which followed. 'I did alright for myself in the City, you know. Turns out, it suited me. I didn't want to stay down south forever, I missed this place too much, but, look, I'm not boasting, I'm just saying, I made a fair bit of money. I can afford not to work for a while, to help you and Cassie, make up for lost time. And if you need more cash, you know, to grow the business even faster, maybe I could—'

Anna sat up straighter. 'You don't have to do that. I'm doing fine. Business is booming, in fact—'

He lifted a hand to stop her. 'OK, I hear you. That's fine. But the offer's there, if you ever need it. And I mean it, about lost time. This is my chance to step up to the plate and be a proper uncle to Cassie. I want to do more than send her cash in a card every birthday and Christmas. I really want to get to know her. To hang out with her.'

Anna said stiffly. 'You should have come back sooner. You were always welcome, you know that. This is your home too. Dad left it to both of us. You've just as much right to live here as Cassie and me.'

Tim nodded. 'I know. But it's yours now. You've done a great job with the place. I'm grateful to you for letting me stay. It won't be forever. As soon as I figure out—'

'Stop it.' Anna got to her feet abruptly and glared down at him. 'I like having you here. So does Cassie. It's fine, OK?'

'But it's not, is it?' Tim steadied himself. 'I saw the way George looked at me at the party. It hasn't gone away, all the hurt, the bitterness. I could feel it... And then what happened to Dr Taylor. Feels like it's stirred everything up again. Those threats, Anna. They're horrible, whoever sent them.'

'It's still no reason for you to blame yourself. It's not because of anything you've done.'

'Isn't it? I'm not sure George would agree.' Tim patted the sofa cushion and said calmly, 'Come on, sit down again. You look daft, standing up.'

Anna let herself by cajoled into sitting down again.

'Good.' Tim patted her arm. 'Now, what about Cassie? You do need to talk to her, Anna. Properly. Tell her the truth.'

'The truth?' Her voice was incredulous. 'Really?'

Tim swallowed. 'However hard it is, she needs to know. Better it comes from you, surely, than from someone else. You know what the road's like, how people talk. Even if she was wrong this time, there'll be other times, other spiteful people eager to poke their nose in our business. She ought to be ready for it.'

Anna sipped at her wine. 'As far as she's concerned, he's long gone. That's all she needs to know.' She made a point of reaching for the TV remote. 'That's worked pretty well for the last ten years, I don't see why it needs to change now.'

'I do.'

His quiet, sober tone made her turn back to him, suddenly uncertain.

'What do you mean?'

'You can't get away with it anymore. You can't keep lying to her.'

'What do you mean?'

He shrugged. 'Don't give me that look. I'm trying to help.'

'Go on, then.'

'I don't know for sure.' Tim weighed his words, knowing that what he said next would change everything. 'I can only tell you what I've heard.'

'What you've heard?' The glass in her hand trembled.

He steadied his voice. 'Not just once. From several people. Anna, I'm sorry. I know this is going to be a shock.'

'Well, go on then. Spit it out.' She was trying to sound defiant but they knew each other too well for that.

He kept his eyes close on hers, his face serious.

'You said he was long gone. But here's the thing, Anna. He's back.'

8

Later, after Tim finally went to bed and the house fell quiet, Anna pulled on her dressing gown and crept across the landing from her own room into Cassie's. She lowered herself to the carpet, her back against the wall, wrapped her arms round drawn-up knees, and gazed on her daughter as she slept.

Cassie looked younger in sleep. One arm was thrown across her pillow, one cheek pressed into it. The other cheek, striped in shadow, turned to the room. Her eyelashes were delicate and long. Her hair was scattered in a chaotic halo.

Anna sat very still in the silence and listened, finally making out the barely audible rhythm of her daughter's breathing.

You and me, Anna thought. *You and me, little one.* It was something she used to whisper to Cassie when she was a baby, a mantra through those long, solitary nights of feeding and winding, of soothing and cuddling. She remembered studying the impossible fragility of Cassie's skin, almost translucent, showing its map of fine veins, the sweet, milky scent of her body, the tiny, puckered eyes and snubbed nose. Her own miracle.

She thought of all the promises she'd made her daughter then. The vow to be two parents in one, to work hard and succeed so she could provide for her, but to be there too, every moment she could, whatever it cost her. She blinked hard, her mouth twisting as she tried not to cry.

Wasn't I enough, Cassie? Wasn't it enough just to have me?

He's back.

No. She shook her head. She couldn't see him. Never. Cassie mustn't see him, mustn't ever know what had happened between them.

She saw again Tim's earnest, concerned face. He didn't understand. He thought he did, they all thought they knew what had happened all those years ago, but they had no idea. It was too terrible a secret for her to share.

Cassie mumbled to herself in sleep, kicked out a leg, then settled again. Anna, watching her, felt her chest tighten.

Tell Cassie the truth? She couldn't possibly.

It would destroy them both.

9

Lily

In bed at night, I lie, red-eyed and sleepless, and stare at the shadows on the ceiling. Blood throbs in my ears and temples. No amount of time, no amount of sleep, can wash away the memory of him. My father. My poor father.

Dad, how do I do this? How do I carry on without you?

Nothing in reply but silence and emptiness.

George insisted on coming with me to identify the body. I tried to dissuade him, only because I was frightened of how distressing he'd find it. He's not as robust as he pretends. I remember the nights, after our mother died, when I heard him sobbing. I didn't dare creep across the landing to him. The one time I did, he was angry, accused me of spying on him.

But going to the morgue, I was relieved to have him there. We held hands tightly on the way in, clutching each other for comfort, the way we used to cling together as children. George's face was pallid and his palm clammy. I heard Dad's voice, after Mum died: *We need to be strong for one another, look after each other.*

I hardly recognised the cold, white corpse as my father. His hair, grown thin and wispy over the years, had been combed flat across his skull. He never wore it like that. His chin was shaded by a fine growth of salt-and-pepper stubble. The rest of the body was shrouded. *Five significant stab wounds,* they'd said in the *Yorkshire Post.* When I closed my eyes, I saw pools of blood, the carpet stained with it.

Later, we went together to the solicitor's office. An old friend of Dad's, of course, part of Dad's professional set, the local men who played golf together, whose wives met each other for coffee. He must be ripe for retirement now too. George and I perched on sagging chairs in his dusty office while he adjusted his spectacles and read us the contents of the will.

I only half-listened. Most of my mind was drifting, thinking how bald the solicitor had become, how pouched his cheeks were. He used to slip us tubes of Smarties and wink when he and his wife came for dinner. His office window was raised, letting in air and the noises from the market square: the low rumble of traffic punctuated by the sing-song cries of the old man on the butcher's stall, shouting for custom.

I bit my lip hard and managed not to cry. I didn't want to let Dad down. He hated tears.

Afterwards, George and I went back to the house, which had finally been abandoned by the forensics team and restored to us. I made tea with Dad's kettle, Dad's mugs. All ours now. All these scraps and oddments which made up the fabric of our parents' lives, of our lives, for so many years. Now what do we do with them?

I set a cup of milky tea in front of George. He rolled his eyes then dug around in his bag and produced a can of beer, cracked it open, slurped off the rising foam and started to drink in large, open-throated swallows. He had a wild look in his eyes.

I perched on a kitchen stool and sipped my tea, dunked a biscuit. 'Are we going to keep it?'

He took his lips from the can and glanced across. 'Keep what?'

'The house.'

Dad left it to both of us, along with his carefully hoarded savings.

George shrugged, turned his attention back to the beer. He drained the can and crushed it in one hand, set it crookedly on the counter. In a moment, he'd start searching for more. Beer in the fridge, if he was lucky. Spirits in the cabinet. I sensed his mood start to change as the alcohol kicked in. He became different when he drank. Volatile, even dangerous.

I swivelled round on the stool and gazed through to the lounge. Dad's chair, the cushions still carrying the imprint of his weight. The newspaper, folded open to the cryptic crossword, waiting on the side table, a pen resting on top. It would wait a long time now. No one else could finish it. My chest tightened.

Crack! An explosion of noise, a crash of shattering china. I jumped, heart thumping, eyes widening with shock.

The mug I'd set in front of George had smashed against the far kitchen wall. Coloured fragments lay on the floor tiles in a pool of cooling tea. The lipped curve of the base. The handle, broken off but still intact.

George's face was red. His fist tense from the throw.

I didn't move, hardly dared to breathe, waiting out the rage.

'Whoever did this, I'll make him pay.' He forced out the words through gritted teeth, his jaw tight. 'I'll track him down and, God help me, I'll make him sorry.'

10

Anna

Anna steadied herself before she opened the front door.

She knew who was waiting on the other side. Usually, she'd have torn the door open and Lily would have come rushing in, all energy and excitement, the two of them already talking non-stop.

This time, she and Lily just stood there, on either side of the threshold, looking at each other. Lily's eyes were puffy and red with crying. Her skin was grey with tiredness.

Anna couldn't find words. She had practised in her head, as soon as Tim had warned her that he'd been on the phone to Lily and that she was coming round. Anna had planned to say that she was sorry. That it was silly, this awkwardness, that it was her fault, she needed to get past it.

Finally, Anna just opened her arms and Lily stepped into them, pressed her face into Anna's shoulder and gave a shuddering sob.

Anna held her close. 'I'm so sorry,' she whispered. 'So, so sorry.'

. . .

In the sitting room, Lily hunched forward in her armchair, her shoulders rounded. She had an embroidered handkerchief balled in her hand and she fiddled with it as they talked, smoothing it out and staring at it as if she couldn't quite place it, then dabbing her nose and eyes and scrunching it again in her fist.

Tim quietly brought in mugs of tea and a plate of biscuits. 'Is there anything we can do?' He took a sip of tea, awkward. 'Have you had a chance to think about, you know, the funeral arrangements? I can do some phoning round if you like. If it helps.' He paused. 'I know it's a lot to organise.'

Lily's eyes were fixed on her handkerchief. 'I've made a start,' she said. 'But we can't set a date yet.' Her voice was small and miserable. 'Because he was' – she searched for a form of words she could bring herself to say – 'because it wasn't natural causes, it'll take longer to release the body.' Her lips puckered. 'It's so strange in the house. Everything's there, just as he left it. On the counter, there was' – she swallowed – 'a dirty plate and glass. Like he was right there.' She breathed hard. 'It's sort of all unreal.'

Anna couldn't look her friend in the face. 'It's early days.'

'Every time I tell someone what's happened, it sounds ridiculous,' Lily said shakily. 'I feel as if I'm lying, making it all up. I nearly phoned him yesterday. I had Dad's number up on my screen, ready to hit call when I suddenly realised what I was doing. Then I thought maybe I should delete him from my contacts but I couldn't. It seemed so final.'

Anna saw the tremor in Lily's hands. 'Are you managing to eat anything? Are you getting any sleep?'

Lily shrugged. 'Not much.' She gestured at her untouched mug. 'I've been drinking a lot of that. Too much.' She grimaced.

'Sorry. Everywhere I go, people push cups of tea at me as if it'll help.'

'Have a biscuit.' Tim jumped up and offered her the plate. 'You've got to eat.'

Anna waited as Lily bit half-heartedly into a plain biscuit and chewed. 'Have they got any further, the police?'

Lily looked up. 'What, finding who did it? I'm not sure. They keep saying they'll catch him but I can't see how, really. They still haven't found the weapon, the knife or whatever, did you know that?' She shuddered. 'I mean, why?' She looked round helplessly. 'Why would anyone kill Dad? Everyone liked him. Loved him, even. You should see the letters and cards we're getting. Everyone's got a story to tell. Not only about what a great doctor he was but something kind he did for them, something beyond the call of duty. He touched people's lives in ways even I didn't realise.'

Tim murmured, 'He made a real difference, Lily. You should be so proud of him for that.'

Lily blew her nose, gathered herself together again. 'You know what the police keep banging on about? They keep asking if Dad had any enemies, someone with a grudge against him. Dad!' She shook her head. 'I thought George was going to explode.'

'They don't know your dad, that's all,' Anna said. 'They just don't get it.'

'I suppose they've got to ask,' Tim said gently. 'But maybe it was exactly what it seemed, a burglary gone wrong. Some random guy on drugs who thought the house was empty and then panicked when he realised your dad was there.'

Anna closed her eyes, seeing again Dr Taylor's contorted face and the blood congealing on the carpet.

Tim went on, 'They'll get him. Even if it's not right away. They'll have his DNA, won't they, from the house? He'll get arrested for something else and they'll get a match. Don't give up hope.'

Lily swallowed. 'George and I went to the solicitor's this morning. They went through the will.'

'Is it all straightforward?' Anna asked.

'Well, yes and no.' Lily spread out her sodden handkerchief on the knee of her jeans and flattened out the wrinkles. 'He's left the house and most of what he had to the two of us.'

'Of course, he has,' Tim put in. 'You'll have to have a think about the house – I mean, what you want to do with it.'

'I know. I don't think I could sell it.' Lily blinked at him. 'Is that what you mean?'

Anna gave Tim a quick, hard look. 'Maybe you could move back in, once all this is over. Maybe George could too.' She'd felt the same about this house, after their father had died. It was such a powerful link to him, to their mother, to her own childhood. She'd always felt so rooted here, in Riverside Road, in the community. The idea of passing their home on to strangers was unimaginable. 'You'll bring new life to the old place, Lily. You've never really liked that flat of yours, have you? Now you can save on rent. Maybe George too? Besides, it'd be great for us to have you back across the road for good.'

Lily's face was thoughtful. 'You're mentioned in the will too, Anna. He's left some money to you and Cassie. Ten thousand. I guess the solicitors will be in touch but I thought you might as well know.'

'Oh.' Anna, stunned, didn't know what to say. It was the last thing she'd expected. *Ten thousand pounds?* 'No, I mean, that's OK. That's your money. You and George.'

Lily pulled a face. 'No, we want you to have it. You know how fond Dad was of you. He thought of you as family, well, all of you. You could put it into the business.' She tried to smile. 'And you know what you're like with money, you'll have turned that ten into fifty thousand by the end of the year.'

'I don't know.' Anna frowned. 'It just doesn't feel—'

'It's really kind,' Tim said quietly. 'If Lily and George are OK with it, maybe you should be too. Lily's right. You and Dr Taylor were always close. Maybe it's not about the money, it's about telling you that, you know?'

'What money?'

They turned. Cassie was there in the doorway, home from school, her face tense. Anna didn't know how much she'd heard.

'Come and say hi to Auntie Lily.' Anna reached out an arm for her and Cassie approached stiffly.

She crossed to Lily and stood by the side of her chair. Anna could see her daughter looking Lily over, taking in the sallow skin and heavy eyes.

Cassie said, 'I'm sorry. Really sorry.'

Then her young face crumpled and Cassie burst into noisy tears.

11

Maybe Cassie's outburst was the most honest response of the lot.

Anna found herself dissolving into tears as she watched the two of them, woman and girl, comfort each other. Cassie squashed onto the chair beside Lily and they wrapped their arms round each other as Cassie sobbed into Lily's neck.

Later, when Cassie had recovered and disappeared back upstairs with a drink and a biscuit, Anna murmured, 'How's George doing?'

Lily grimaced. 'Not great. You know George. It's hit him hard.' She gazed vacantly across the lounge. 'It was always complicated, wasn't it? Him and Dad? Firstborn and only boy and all that.'

Anna knew exactly what Lily meant. George had always seemed to disappoint his father. She'd seen it happening ever since they were kids. Dr Taylor's awkward attempts to turn George into the sports fanatic he was himself. It had never worked. Then there was his ill-advised determination to persuade George to follow in his footsteps and study medicine when it was clear to everyone that George just wasn't that academic, not like his father. It had simply made George feel more of a failure.

Then, of course, there was Mrs Taylor's death. George and his father had barely spoken to each other for months. George's grief had been so explosive and charged with fury, such a contrast with Dr Taylor's idea of quiet dignity. Anna didn't blame George. He'd had every reason to be angry.

But his father had refused to listen. It was an accident, he'd said, and he wanted no more said about it. Anna remembered the way Lily, struggling under the weight of her own grief for her mother, had been caught between the two warring men, father and son. In a way, she always had been.

'About the funeral...' Anna nodded discreetly towards the kitchen, where Tim was clattering about at the sink, washing up. 'I think Tim wants to come and pay his respects. He was very fond of your dad. But do you think George...?'

Lily pursed her lips. 'I'll talk to him. Of course he should come, if he wants to.'

Anna was sure it wouldn't be an easy conversation with George. 'Cassie wants to go too. She was so close to your dad. I said I'd think about it.' She hesitated, remembering Cassie's tear-streaked face as she'd pleaded to be allowed to go. 'She's young, still. I'm not sure she can cope.'

Lily didn't answer. She frowned slightly, her eyes on the carpet.

Anna, watching her, waited. She knew her friend well enough to know she was bracing herself, getting ready to say something she might find difficult. Anna just didn't know what.

'About Cassie,' Lily said at last. Her eyes stayed pinned to the carpet. 'There's something I need to tell you.'

Anna tensed. 'What?'

'Mike's back. Did you hear?' Lily raised her eyes at last and gave Anna a careful look.

Anna felt her stomach twist. 'So?' She managed to give a

tight shrug, pretending nonchalance. 'Nothing to do with me. Water under the bridge.'

Lily was still staring at her. 'It's something to do with Cassie though, isn't it? You know what people are like. Small town and all that.'

'People should mind their own business.'

Lily shifted in her chair. 'I know. I'm on your side, you know that. But even so. Someone might say something.'

'So what if they do?'

Lily looked pained. 'You can't keep a lid on it forever, Anna. It's not just about you, is it? It's about her now too.'

Anna glowered. 'You sound like Tim. You two been comparing notes?'

'Don't be paranoid.' Lily turned away. 'Maybe we both just happen to care about you. And Cassie.'

Anna reached out to grab Lily by the arm. 'Sorry. It's just—'

'I know.' Lily hesitated. 'Look, I didn't know whether to tell you but, well, the thing is, he wants to see me.'

'Mike?' Anna frowned, taken aback. 'Why?'

'I don't know, exactly. He'd heard about Dad. He sent a card to the house, giving his condolences and all that. He said he needed to talk to me.'

Anna felt her face burn. She twisted to the kitchen to check that Tim couldn't hear them. The low rumble of voices on the radio drifted through, interspersed with chopping as Tim made a start on their evening meal.

Anna said in a low hiss, 'Why didn't you tell me?'

'I haven't exactly seen you, have I?' Lily hissed back. 'There've been one or two other things going on for me, Anna, if you remember.'

Anna bit her lip. 'Of course. Sorry. It's just weird, that's all. So, you got this card and then what, you called him?'

Lily looked affronted. 'I didn't, actually. I just put it on the pile and thought I'd get round to it later, after, you know, the funeral and everything.'

'So that's it?'

'Not exactly.' Lily could hardly look her friend in the eye. 'I went into school the other day to check in with the head. I think I saw him outside. Hanging around. I'm pretty sure it was him. I think, maybe, he was waiting for me.'

'How'd he even know where to find you?'

Lily shrugged. 'It said in the papers that I'm a teacher. It wouldn't take a genius to figure out which school it might be, right?'

It was true. There was a tiny private school half an hour's drive away but most people in the street sent their kids to Mountbank, the main state primary school where Lily taught. The same school that she and Lily, Tim and George had all attended and where Cassie went now.

'Did you talk to him?'

Lily shook her head. 'I avoided him. Slipped out the side entrance. Don't look at me like that or I won't tell you any more.'

Anna raised her hands in a gesture of submission. 'Go on then.'

'He said in his card that he's come back to support his parents. His mum's got Alzheimer's, apparently, and his dad's nearly eighty and not managing too well... Then he asked about you. If you were OK, if you were still here, what you were doing now. He said he's been phoning you but you wouldn't pick up.'

'Quite some card.' Anna twisted away from her and stared across the road towards the trees. She thought of the recent barrage of calls and voicemails, all deleted. 'I don't answer the phone to anyone, not if I don't know the number.'

Lily raised a sceptical eyebrow. 'Well, anyway, I just thought you ought to know. He seems pretty persistent and, well, I can't avoid him forever.'

'I don't see why not.'

Lily rolled her eyes. 'Anna, come on. What if he asks about you? About Cassie? What am I supposed to say?'

'How about, "Mind your own business"?'

Lily shook her head, her eyes sad, and Anna looked away.

Anna was trying hard to sound tough but inside she was shaking. She couldn't do this. She couldn't see him again. She couldn't bear it.

She said quietly, 'It's not that hard to find me, is it? I'm right here, same place I've always been.'

Lily said, 'Maybe it's tough for him too.'

Mike. The anguish hit her right in the stomach like a fist. The memories. They'd been so young, teenagers, falling in love for the first time. His arms, warm round her. His kind, handsome face. She wondered what he looked like now. She knew how much she'd changed in the last ten years. Maybe he wouldn't even recognise her.

She remembered the way he used to pull up outside the house in his mum's car, right there in the street. He'd had his own signal, two sharp blasts on the horn. Her body felt again the heady, nervous excitement which had always gripped her as she'd piled out of the house, slamming the front door behind her, and gone running across to pull open the passenger door.

'It's not just about you,' Lily said. 'It's about Cassie, too. He's her dad and if he wants to see her—'

'Who said he's her dad? I didn't.' Anna shook herself, dragged herself back from the past. 'He'll have to take me to court if he wants to prove that. Good luck to him.'

Lily looked at her in dismay. 'Think about it. Please. Cassie deserves—'

'Don't,' Anna flared. 'Don't start lecturing me on what my daughter does or doesn't deserve.'

'Fine. I haven't got the energy to fight. Not right now. Let me concentrate on burying my murdered father first and then get back to you.' Lily got to her feet and headed for the door.

Anna heard the scrape of the front door as it opened and closed behind her.

Sitting there, remembering, time seemed to warp and compress.

All the times. The long afternoons when she and Lily were children and ran, helter-skelter, to and from their houses, coming to call on each other to play out. Then, when they became teenagers, the evenings when they sauntered across the road, self-conscious now in public even for that short distance, to hang out in their bedrooms, to talk and listen to music, to revise for exams, side by side, to get ready for nights out, fussing and fretting as they did their make-up and assessed each other's outfits.

And Mike. Anna felt her chest tighten. She'd tried so hard to lock away all those memories of Mike. If she let them out now, even after all this time, she was frightened they'd overwhelm her.

All the times.

Her stomach tightened. How young they'd been. How much in love.

She wrapped her arms round her stomach and pressed them down hard, easing the hurt. It had just been Cassie, after that, filling her world. She'd learned to tamp down any hope that he might come back, that she'd ever see him again. And now?

She jumped up and ran to the front door, tore it open. Lily had already crossed the road.

'Lily!' Anna hollered. She didn't care who heard. Let them. 'Wait!'

Lily didn't turn. Her shoulders were tight, her head bowed, her body offering a glimpse of the elderly woman she would someday become. She ducked into the police tent which shrouded the front of the house and disappeared abruptly from sight.

Anna stayed there for some moments, looking after her.

The truth was, even Lily, her dearest, closest friend, didn't know the truth. She only thought she did.

12

Lily

I worry about Cassie. I always have.

I try to keep my distance in school. I know it's complicated when someone who's practically a member of your family is also a teacher. I made sure, of course, that when she reached year five, where I'm a class teacher, she went to Mr Swithin's form instead of mine. It would be too much like teaching my own daughter.

She and I had a chat about it when she first started at Mountbank, about how we should behave around each other when we were at home and when we were in school, how we'd manage it.

'We just have to be sensible,' I told her. 'When we're at home, I'm Auntie Lily and we can mess about and do all the normal, crazy things we've always done. But when we're at school, I'm a teacher and you'll have to call me Miss Taylor. Sound OK?'

She smiled up at me, eyes shining. She was smart. She got it straight away. Better than that. She revelled in the subterfuge.

If I passed her in the corridor, she'd say primly, 'Good morning, Miss Taylor,' then catch my eye and dissolve into silent giggles. Once or twice, when I was on lunch duty and she needed help – forgot her lunch money or got into an argument with some other girl or whatever – she sought me out. I always took her side, as she knew I would. But quietly, keeping it just between the two of us.

It probably wasn't the right thing to do, to be so partisan. The headteacher mightn't think so. But frankly, I didn't worry too much about that. The day a school teacher can't slip some lunch money to someone who's practically her daughter, it's time to call it quits, that's what I think.

And besides, I've been besotted with Cassie since she was a few seconds old. I was there in the delivery suite when she fought her way out into the world, red-faced and angry, mewling, tight fists flailing as they cut the cord, wrapped her round in a white cloth and weighed her.

I look a sight in those first photos, not only because of the stupid plastic gown and hairnet they made me wear but because my eyes are red and puffy from crying. I was overwhelmed. I was only eighteen, just months older than Anna. I'd had to plead with my dad to let me be in the delivery room at all. He only gave in because he was sorry for Anna, I suppose. And we'd so recently lost Mum, he barely knew which way was up anyway.

Anna was my anchor, despite everything. She was the one I clung to in those dreadful, lost days after the accident. She was suffering too. We were there for one another.

When she asked me to be her birth partner, I understood at once. It wasn't only the fact that she was so alone. There was her father, of course. We knew he'd be there at the hospital with us, but she wanted him to stay outside, mainlining coffee and wearing out the shiny floor of the corridor. She didn't want him to 'witness the gory bits', as she put it. That felt too weird.

But it was a sign too to me that, despite everything that had happened, we were as close as sisters, not just friends but family. We were both victims, after all, not perpetrators of the terrible things that had happened. That mattered.

I'd never seen a baby being born before and Anna wasn't the only one who was exhausted by those long, grey hours of labour.

And then, there she was, Cassie, bursting into the world with such vigour, such power, this scrawny, yowling scrap of humanity, patches of dark hair plastered wetly against her skull, her skin papery. Until that moment, when they placed her in Anna's arms and I leaned in too and touched her cheek with my fingertip, marvelling at her, I hadn't known why women fussed and cooed over babies. But it crashed over me, a tsunami of feeling, protective, wondrous, passionate, catching me unawares, stealing my breath, wetting my eyes. I looked from her miniature scrunched-up face to Anna's and saw the light shining there.

'Hello, beautiful,' she whispered. 'I'm your mummy.'

Anna's mouth crumpled and she bit down on her lip. She couldn't say any more. It was all too much.

'And I'm Auntie Lily,' I told her baby quietly.

I didn't see enough of Cassie in those early years. I did my best. I'd made a promise to Anna to help, and I tried to keep it. I went to university nearby, in Leeds, coming back every weekend to hang out at home.

At first, my father complained that he hardly saw me during those visits. I was always across the road at the Kings' house, hanging out with Anna and little Cassie. In the end, he gave in and adopted her too, in his own way. Cassie filled the chasm in both our hearts. As she grew, my father started keeping a stock of sweets and bright plastic toys in the kitchen cupboard for Cassie to search out when she came to visit.

It made my heart swell to come home from university one

Friday afternoon and find Cassie, two or three by then, kneeling up on a chair at the kitchen table, supervised by Dad. She had a voluminous apron tied round her waist. The tip of her tongue protruded from the corner of her mouth as she concentrated, poking the currant eyes and buttons into a baking tray of ginger-bread people, just as I remembered doing myself at that age. George said it took the pressure off the two of us to produce grandchildren because, in her own way, Cassie had already filled the gap.

During post-grad teacher training, I pulled hard on what-ever strings I could find back home to get a placement in Mountbank and did my best to make sure they loved me.

The following year, Cassie and I started at Mountbank together. I was a newly qualified teacher starting my first proper job, still nervous, still not quite able to believe I was in charge of my own class. Cassie charged into reception with far more confidence.

I have struggled over the years not to intervene now and then and give Cassie special treatment. She went through a rocky period in year four when she was drawn into a threesome with two other girls, an intense friendship which, it seemed to me, verged on bullying. I tried to keep an eye on things more than Cassie could ever know, developing an antipathy for the girl I saw as the ringleader in the group, a stocky, bossy girl with a mean streak. Mostly, Cassie could handle it herself, but I saw the confusion in her face when the third girl, a weaker charac-ter, was the butt of jokes and dissolved into tears.

It was never bad enough for me to have a word with the staff concerned. That might not have been appreciated. But I did give Cassie gentle talks at home, now and then, about remem-bering to be kind and standing up to those who weren't.

Last year, when Cassie reached year five and, like others her age, was afforded the privilege of walking to and from school by herself, I added my own voice to the general talks on safety bestowed by the head. About being careful of the traffic and not letting herself become distracted on the way home, about sticking to the main, busy thoroughfares and avoiding the short cut through a dingy alley. About telling me at once if she had any reasons to be nervous or frightened, any at all.

I wasn't too worried. She was one of the smart, sensible ones.

Now, since my father's death, I'm concerned about how upset Cassie is. I invite her to come and see me at the house after school and, once or twice, she does, appearing at the back door, a still shadow against the glass, giving a soft rap with her knuckles.

We agree from the start. Whatever we say in these times together stays with us. She needs to know it won't go any further.

Once, she asks me about my father, suddenly, out of nowhere.

'Do you miss him?'

I consider and nod. 'Yes.' I try to find the right words. 'There are some people who are so important in your life, so central, that it's hard to imagine carrying on without them. But we can, if we really have to.'

She frowns. 'I don't think I could carry on without Mum.'

'I know.' I nod. 'Your mum's young and healthy. She'll be here for a very long time, I'm sure. You don't have to worry about that until you're much older, and by then, you might have a family of your own.'

She shakes her head. 'I'm not getting married. Not ever.'

'Well, wait and see. You might change your mind if you meet the right person.'

'My mum didn't.' She lifts her eyes to me, her gaze frank and searching. 'You didn't either.'

I don't know what to say to that.

Cassie has asked me once or twice over the years why her

mum didn't marry her father and I'm never sure what to say. I'd be happy to chat to her about Mike if Anna weren't so set against it. I liked him. He seemed warm and funny, as well as good-looking, and he really seemed to care about Anna. They were good together. A natural fit.

And Anna adored him. I watched her fall in love almost despite herself, heavily and hard. It was such a shock when he dumped her the way he did, heading off to university with barely a backwards glance. It was only after he'd gone that Anna's period was late and, terrified, the two of us had shut ourselves in the bathroom with a pregnancy kit. When it was positive, she refused to tell him. Just too proud to write to him, after all he'd done, and break the news.

'Is my mum scared of my dad?' Cassie pipes up.

I blink, taken aback. 'I don't think so. What makes you say that?'

Cassie picks up a piece of apple and munches on it, her eyes thoughtful. 'I just wondered. It sort of makes sense. I mean, I thought maybe that's why she told me he was dead. He's not, you know.'

She's trying hard to be casual but I can see the way she's observing me from the corner of her eye, checking my reaction.

I shake my head carefully. 'No, he isn't dead.'

'And he's come back.'

'Back? Did your mum say that?'

She narrows her eyes a fraction, trying to assess how much I really know.

'The ladies in the road were talking about it. They said there was trouble ahead.' She shrugged. 'Then they saw me and went quiet.' She reaches for another piece of apple and chews.

I bide my time.

Finally, she carries on. 'Did Mum tell you about the nasty notes? I heard her talking to Uncle Tim about them.'

'Nasty notes?'

'Threats. Someone wants to hurt Mum. And me. I think it must be the murderer, coming to get us next because Mum saw him.'

I feel myself blanch. 'Oh, Cassie, that's awful. You mustn't—'

'It could be anyone. Maybe even my dad,' Cassie says, her voice lowered.

I'm too shocked to speak, even to open my arms to comfort her. She seems barely aware of me. She just furrows her brow and I realise how much weight is resting on those narrow shoulders.

13

Anna

'Mum!'

Anna had to fight her way towards the surface, her brain fogged with deep sleep.

Someone was shaking her shoulder, pulling at her.

'Mum, wake up!'

'You OK?' Somehow, Anna managed to prise her eyes open and sit up. Sleep clung to her, her mind thick and clotted with it. Her hand raised the duvet, making space for her daughter to climb in beside her. Cool air ran across her skin.

A bad dream? Cassie often used to have them when she was younger, and then she'd climb into Anna's bed for a hug before she could settle again. That hadn't happened for a while, though.

'Wake up! MUM!'

'OK, OK.' Anna sighed and said resignedly, 'What time is it?'

'He's here. That man.'

Anna shook herself awake and slid her feet out of bed. 'Who's here?'

Cassie's face shone pale and pinched in the half-light. She pointed a trembling arm towards her bedroom. 'Outside. Watching me.'

Anna jumped up, reached for her daughter's hand. 'You sure you weren't dreaming?'

Cassie shook her head. 'I woke up because I needed the toilet. I only looked afterwards, when I got back. He's there, Mum. Really, he is.'

Anna took Cassie's hand and walked her back into her bedroom. The house was silver with shadow. Cassie drew her quietly to the window.

Anna lifted the edge of the curtain and peered out, her heart hard in her chest. She couldn't see anything out there. The street seemed emptied and calm, the whole road deep in sleep.

Then, a movement in the shadows caught her eye. She peered closer. There, across the road and a little further down, a figure was standing by the tree. As she looked, the low street-light flashed on something in his hand as he turned.

Cassie was right. He was looking this way, staring up at her window. He was casually dressed, in a dark, baggy top, a loose sweatshirt or hoodie. Too far away for her to make out his features.

'I'm going to get my phone,' she whispered. 'Take a photo.'

Cassie kept close to Anna's side as she hurried back to her bedroom, unplugged her phone from where it was charging on the bedside table and rushed back with it to the window. It couldn't have taken Anna more than a minute, but by the time she pulled back the curtain again and lifted her phone to focus, the man had disappeared.

'Did you get him?' Cassie pressed against her, trying to see. 'Did you?'

'Too late.' Anna scanned the deserted street, then let the curtain fall. 'He's gone.' She scooped up Cassie's hand and led her back to her own room, trying to sound more cheerful than she felt. 'Come on, you can sleep with me, if you like. It's late.'

Cassie cuddled up next to her under the duvet, the way she used to when she was younger. Her icy feet pressed against Anna's calves. Anna lay still, listening to the pace of her daughter's breathing as it gradually slowed and settled into sleep. Her own heart raced.

She felt suffocated, made breathless by panic. She stared at the shifting shadows on the ceiling, eyes wide. A net was closing around her, around her daughter, she sensed it. The sins of the past were stirring and boiling, ready to break out into the open. She didn't care what happened to her – she'd suppressed the truth for so long, maybe she deserved what was coming – but Cassie, she was innocent. She had to protect Cassie.

She turned her head, this way and that, struggling to think. She didn't know whether to trust the police. She was losing faith in them. There were still so many glaring holes in the investigation. The local newspapers had started to criticise the fact that no one had been arrested yet and, despite a search of the house and the surrounding area, they still hadn't found the murder weapon.

The detective had seemed cool when she'd taken the two threatening notes to him. He'd laid them together on the worn table in the interview room and sucked his teeth.

'You've no idea where they came from?'

She'd shaken her head.

'They were both delivered by hand but you never saw anyone approaching or leaving the house at the time?'

She'd bitten her lower lip. His tone, laced with incredulity, had brought back so much, so many painful memories.

'I'm sorry,' she'd said stiffly. 'I thought you'd want to know, that's all.'

She'd made to get to her feet, reached a hand towards the two scraps of paper to gather them up.

He'd shot out his own hand, large and thick-fingered, and placed his palm squarely on the notes.

'I'll keep hold of them, if that's OK.' He'd said it as if it were a challenge. 'Let me know if you get any more, will you?'

She squeezed her eyes in the darkness, seeing it spangle. Beside her, Cassie kicked and stirred in her sleep. No, not the police. Not this time.

She strained to visualise the vague details of the man they'd seen. A stranger, she was sure. Not anyone from the street. She tightened her arm around Cassie, holding her close. She was clearly terrified by the thought that this man, silently spying on them in the darkness, might be the murderer, come back to warn Anna, perhaps, to keep her mouth shut.

She clenched her jaw.

Whoever it was, they didn't know her very well if they thought they could frighten her off.

Anna knew how to take care of the people she loved. She'd do what she had to do, whatever the cost, just as she had in the past.

14

Lily

Anna's just been round. God bless her. She's looking out for me now as much as she did after my mother died, even when her own family was almost as split into pieces as mine.

She's been such a practical help. She's somehow extricated herself from the shops, so she can focus on helping me. They've been pretty understanding.

Some days, I do OK. I'm never free of it – *how could I be?* – but I get through. It's an almost out-of-body experience. I can see myself going through the motions of being alive – boiling the kettle and buttering toast, forcing my jaws to chomp and my throat to swallow. I stand under the shower and feel water cascade down my skin and I try not to think too much.

It astonishes me that the rest of the world is carrying on, almost as if nothing has changed. The crisis continues to unfurl in the Middle East, there's some upheaval in Brazil and, closer to home, students are protesting in Manchester. It's as if they don't know. My father has been brutally murdered and the world is oblivious.

I've given notice on my flat. I wasn't sure about it but Anna persuaded me. *It's silly,* she said, *wasting good money every month when you and George have got the house. Even if you do decide to sell, it'll take time. You've got to get probate and, even when that's through, it might take months to find a buyer. Think how much you could save.*

It isn't only about money. She's mentioned several times how special Riverside Road is, what a close community, that she wouldn't ever leave, even though she and Cassie could afford to now. She hasn't spelled it out but it's clear that she's keen for me to move back and settle across the road from her again, like old times.

Some days, I think she's right. Maybe I could make this a happy home again, a house teeming with love, with children tearing in and out, as we once did. Despite the horror of recent days, I don't want to leave it. I don't want to leave my childhood behind. Anna, fresh from finishing her own renovations, is full of ideas about how George and I could modernise this place and, with the money Dad's left us, we could just about afford it.

So, the great purge is underway. The chest of drawers and the wardrobes in my parents' room stand empty but the bedside tables, both of them, are still crammed. My mother's, in particular, is a time capsule, a chaos of old photographs, cards and letters in spidery hands, the ink long since faded, from friends who are probably dead themselves, receipts for goods she bought decades ago, tattered programmes for events I don't remember her ever attending.

I toss much of it straight into the recycling. Now and then, I unfold a piece of paper or open an envelope and I'm ambushed. A note in her neat handwriting. An echo of the perfume she liked to wear. It slays me. I crumple and sob like a child. I can almost sense her, just out of sight, out of range, watching me. I half-expect to feel her arms around me, her hand stroking my hair. Then I blink and the shadow lifts and I remember, all over again.

I find, in Dad's drawers, a copy of the order of service for Mum's funeral. I sit for a long time, numb, staring at the picture of her on the front. I'd forgotten. It's from a life before mine started. She looks so young and pretty, sitting in the open, surrounded by trees and wild bushes. An outing in the Dales or on the Chevin. Her eyes shine and her hair flows in loose waves around her neck and shoulders, her spirit free. No wonder my father fell in love with her.

He was never a man to show his feelings. I don't remember him crying after her death. He busied himself with organising and planning and with us.

I open the order of service and scan the hymns, the readings. My father had added some quote from William Ross Wallace on the back.

Every man dies. Not every man really lives.

I'd forgotten about that. I hadn't thought anything of it. I'd assumed it was Dad's way of paying tribute to her. But George was incensed when he saw the proofs. He cornered me, his jaw hard, his eyes furious, and accused Dad of belittling Mum by choosing that quote. Dad was poking fun at her for being a homemaker, George insisted, for giving up her own career as a nurse to look after the three of us. I just didn't see it that way.

At her funeral, my father's body bore the grief his face refused to express. It stooped and bowed under the weight of it. He clenched his jaw as he stood at the door of the restaurant after the service, all propriety, stiffly greeting and thanking the people who'd come to pay their respects.

He made us both, George and me, stand at his side in a ragged receiving line. I struggled not to cry, eyes swollen, as the characters who had formed the fabric of our lives passed by: the teachers and business owners, the friends and neighbours, the hordes of my father's grateful patients who'd turned out to show support in our time of grief. They clasped my hot hand or patted my arm, murmuring condolences. I was seventeen. Too young to lose a parent. Perhaps every age is too young.

Then and always, we struggled to be what our father wanted us to be. We knew from infancy that we were part of a proud, upstanding family with standards to maintain. We grew up, both of us, knowing what was expected. We were lucky and we should know it and be grateful. It wasn't only the fact that we were more prosperous than most people in Otley, the farmers and traders and shopkeepers and stall-holders. It wasn't only the fact that we could afford foreign holidays and a smart car.

We were significant. We were well-known. Our father was one of Otley's doctors, after all. All-knowing, a discreet guardian of the community's secrets. At Christmas, he would come home with subtle tributes: bottles of wine and whisky, chocolates, hampers and gift vouchers.

I close the fading order of service and set it aside. I feel my father watching over me, not unkindly but sternly, judging me. In this final act for him, his own funeral service, we must do him proud.

Eventually, after hours of searching and much crying, I settle on a photograph of him for the front of his order of service. He's a young man, younger than I am now, raising a glass to the camera. I don't know the occasion. He was a young doctor, freshly qualified. A bright young thing.

He's dressed formally, in a suit and tie, smiling broadly. His life is gathering and blossoming and all ahead.

Impossible, then, to imagine the horror of its end.

15

Anna

For a while, life picked up its old, familiar rhythm. The clock, rewound, fell to ticking again.

Cassie seemed once again to become absorbed in the everyday business of school: the triumph of a win in the weekly football fixture, the stress of mounting homework and the jokes she heard at school and dashed home to try out on her mother and uncle.

Anna kept across work emails, but nothing seemed to crop up that the shop managers couldn't handle. For now, while she could, she focused her attention on Lily, across the road, and Cassie. Lily still seemed mired in grief. Often, when Anna went to visit, Lily slouched to the door in baggy sweatpants and an oversized hoodie. Her hair was messy and unwashed, her face drawn. The kitchen sink became piled with dirty dishes.

Eventually, Lily reported that her father's body was being released and she was making progress on plans for the funeral.

There was no more mention of Mike. Anna started to tell herself that maybe the gossips had got it wrong. Maybe he'd just visited his parents for a few days and left again. She dared to breathe.

One evening, Cassie finished an early tea then disappeared upstairs to start on homework while Anna cooked for herself and Tim. She had the radio on low in the kitchen. The background chat and laughter of a news quiz washed over her as she gathered up peppers from the fridge and, standing at the counter, large knife in hand, split them open and started to strip out the seeds.

CRASH!

'What the—?' Anna fumbled the knife, dropped it on the wooden board on top of the peppers. Blood soared in her chest, her ears. She stood stock still, shocked, listening. The only sound was the babble of the voices on the radio. Some joke about the state of the health service, met by audience laughter.

Tim, in the lounge, was suddenly on his feet, running for the stairs. Dazed, Anna shook herself, followed him. It was here, then. It was in their house. An explosion. A bomb. A—

She stumbled up the stairs, two at a time, tripping and stubbing a toe in clumsy haste. Her voice, flying ahead of her, was thin and reedy. 'Cassie? You OK?'

It was nothing, surely. Sounded worse than it was. Cassie had just dropped something, smashed a glass. That was all.

Tim, in Cassie's doorway now, ahead of Anna, muttered, 'Oh, no.' He disappeared inside.

Anna threw herself across the landing after him. One step inside the room and she stopped dead. Froze.

Cassie was sitting on the floor, her back against the bed. Her legs were loosely drawn up, her arms wrapped round her body, her eyes wide with shock. Her skin – legs, arms, face, neck – was stained with fresh blood, bright and dripping. Above her, the shattered window was a broken mess of jagged edges, blowing cold air into the room. It couldn't be Cassie. How could it? She looked like a shrapnel victim, something from a war zone.

Tim, pressing in, bent over Cassie, examining her face, arms, legs. 'Can you move?'

Cassie stared up at him, barely able to understand. She started to shake.

Tim helped her gently to her feet, plucked a fleece from the chaos of clothes on her bed and wrapped it round her shoulders.

'Take it slowly, OK?' He held Cassie and walked her carefully towards the door. Glass crunched under their feet. 'We need to get you to hospital. You're going to be fine. We just need to get you cleaned up.'

Cassie's face had drained of colour. Anna flattened herself against the wall to let them pass. She couldn't speak. She didn't understand, her mind struggling to catch up with what had happened. Why had the window collapsed? What was going on?

As she turned to hurry after them, her eyes ran over the debris strewn across the carpet where the shards of smashed glass had scattered. Then she saw the rock. A heavy chunk of stone which had come to rest there, by the bed.

Any fleeting thought that perhaps this had been some kind of freak accident was quashed.

No.

Someone had done this deliberately.

Someone had pitched that rock at Cassie's bedroom window.

Someone had just targeted her beautiful ten-year-old daughter.

Why? What do they think I know?

16

The uniformed police officer dwarfed the small plastic chair, his legs splayed, his body thickened by a bulky stab vest and pockets bulging with kit. He frowned at his notebook as he asked Anna and Tim questions and wrote down their answers with care.

They were sitting in a clinical side-room of the hospital emergency department, spare, cool and buzzing with bright light. Cassie was lying on her back, sedated. The adults had clustered at the foot of her bed, speaking in low voices.

Tim was doing most of the talking. 'It must be related to the murder case. Don't you see? My sister's the key witness. She's had threats. Threatening notes through the door. Plural.'

The officer looked up. 'Have you reported these threats?'

Tim nodded. 'We told the police team in Leeds.' He turned to Anna for support but she didn't speak. 'One of the notes specifically mentions Cassie.'

The officer looked over his notes. 'Did they give you a case number?'

Tim grimaced. 'I don't know. Probably.' He turned again to his sister. 'You know anything about a case number?'

Anna shrugged without looking round. Tim didn't know everything. She hadn't told him about the mysterious man in the shadows who'd watched their home and frightened Cassie. She hadn't told him that there'd been a third warning, one she hadn't shared with either Tim or the police, just ripped up and hidden in the bin.

The officer look resigned. 'That's OK. I can look it up.'

Anna's eyes went back to Cassie's face. She still wondered if she needed stitches. That gash on her chin. It wasn't long but it had bled a lot. The doctor who'd treated Cassie had laboriously cleaned the cuts, stemmed the bleeding and then applied dozens of butterfly strips, white criss-crosses up and down her injured skin, holding the wounds closed. He'd said they were less likely to cause scarring than stitches.

Anna's eyes filled. Cassie was too young to be scarred. It was all her fault. If only she'd minded her own business and hadn't crossed to the Taylors' house that evening. If only she hadn't seen. This would never have happened, she was sure of it.

'I don't want anything more to do with the case,' she said softly. 'I'm done with it.'

The officer looked up from his notebook, confused.

Anna cleared her throat and said more loudly, 'I don't want to be involved from now on. I've been questioned and made a statement. That's all I've got to say.'

The officer seemed confused. 'Which case?'

'The murder investigation. Dr Taylor's murder.' Anna reached over the bars which caged the sides of the bed and enveloped Cassie's hand. 'Can you tell him that, please? Tell the detective in charge.'

The officer looked doubtful. 'Well, you'd really need to go into the station and talk to him yourself.' He shuffled on his chair. 'He'd be the best person to discuss your concerns.'

'I don't want to *discuss my concerns*.' Anna's expression

hardened. 'I'm sorry about Dr Taylor. I really am. But I must put my daughter's safety first.'

The officer looked from Anna to Tim and back again, his brow furrowed. 'Ms King, I understand you're upset. But don't let's be hasty. We don't have any evidence yet that this incident in your home' – he glanced at Cassie – 'has any relationship to Dr Taylor's murder. They could be unrelated.'

Tim bristled. 'It's one heck of a coincidence.'

The officer flicked back through his notebook. 'Your daughter could just have easily been the victim of teenage vandals. Kids messing around.' He leaned forward, conspiratorial. 'Last Saturday night, a gang of local youths put in several shop windows off the high street.' He seemed to think he'd proved his point. 'I'm afraid we do have unruly elements, even here, who are more than capable of antisocial behaviour of this sort.'

Anna watched Cassie. Her face was pale. She'd turned her head and was staring without expression at the giant electronic screen on the wall as it dissolved from one image to another: sunset over water, a path through woods, a verdant pasture dotted with wildflowers. Images from another, calmer world.

'You're sure there's nothing going on at school?' the officer went on. 'No bullying? Fights on social media?'

'No,' Anna said flatly. 'She's not allowed on social media. She's too young.'

The officer sucked the end of his pencil. 'You'd be surprised how often some spat online breaks out into the real world. Not all parents know what their kids are getting up to on those screens.'

'I do.' Anna glared. 'My daughter is ten. This is not some spat with a friend at school.' She took a beat and collected herself. 'Look, I've tried to help the police. But if I've put Cassie in danger...' She shook her head. 'Just tell them, would you? I'm withdrawing my cooperation.'

The officer raised an eyebrow. 'I'm sorry but that's a conversation you'll really need to have with them yourself. Now, if we could just get back to...' He poked the pages of his notebook again.

When the police officer finally left, he almost collided with the young doctor who'd been treating Cassie. The doctor made his way quickly round the side of the bed and checked over Cassie's injuries, then scanned the figures on the monitors which were quietly pulsing and whirring beside her.

'I'm happy for you to take her home,' the doctor told Anna at last. His manner was brisk, but his eyes were dull with tiredness. 'She needs to rest. Give her Calpol if she needs it. It's going to take a while for those cuts to heal.' He indicated the map of criss-crosses on Cassie's skin. 'Any change, if she has a fever or if the wounds become inflamed or productive, oozing or weeping, bring her back in.' He seemed unable to look Anna directly in the eye. 'I'm sure she'll be fine.'

Fine? Anna looked away. *Nothing about any of this is fine.*

17

Later, back at home, Tim tacked a piece of hardboard over the smashed window as a temporary fix and hoovered the carpet, throwing a rug over the top until they could go through it carefully, checking there was no more broken glass. Meanwhile, Anna dosed Cassie with paracetamol and put her to bed.

Anna sat for some time on Cassie's bed, her hands folded in her lap, her eyes on Cassie's torn face.

The hardboard made the darkness more intense. The low shine of the streetlights penetrated round the edges and gleamed on the white butterfly strips on Cassie's cheek and the pale arm which trailed along the duvet. Cassie's breathing steadied into sleep.

Anna's nerves were strumming. She cursed herself for ever crossing the road that evening, for pushing her way into Dr Taylor's house and finding him there. She'd done this. She'd put Cassie in danger. If someone had tried to hurt her daughter once, how could she make sure they didn't do it again? She bit down on her lower lip so hard she tasted blood.

Tim appeared at the door, a heavy, leaning shadow. He whispered, 'Asleep?'

Anna nodded.

'Come downstairs. You need to eat.'

Anna shook her head. She wasn't hungry. She wasn't sure she'd ever be hungry again.

Tim went across to her, lifted her hand from her lap and tugged. 'Come on. It's an order.'

He'd finished off the pasta sauce which Anna had started hours earlier. It seemed like another lifetime. Anna let Tim sit her down at the kitchen table and she made a show of pushing the pasta round her bowl, pretending to eat.

Tim said, 'I had another look downstairs when you were up with Cassie. There's more I can do, if you like, to make this place more secure. Better window locks, for a start. Do you even use them?'

She shrugged. 'Sometimes.'

'Doesn't look like it. Well, we should, from now on. At least until this is over. And I'll put another bolt on the front door, if you like.'

'I suppose so.' She felt her heart quicken. How had it come to this, that they needed to barricade themselves inside to stay safe? How could she live like that?

Tim, watching her, said, 'I still feel it's my fault.'

'Yours? Why?'

He hunched his shoulders. 'Maybe if I hadn't come back...'

'Don't start that again. I'm glad you're here.'

Tim didn't answer for a moment, then said, 'We need to keep things as normal as possible for Cassie. However worried we are, not let it show.'

They sat in silence for some time. The kitchen clock pulsed. Noises drifted in from outside. The high-pitched yowl of a cat in a neighbouring garden. The distant revving of a motorbike.

'She wants to go to the funeral,' Anna said. 'I'm thinking maybe not. I don't want her upset.'

Tim said, 'She's upset anyway.'

'She's only ten. It's awful, seeing a coffin for the first time. Seeing everyone cry. It's frightening for anyone but especially if you're young and sensitive.'

Tim hesitated, remembering. 'I was nine at Mum's funeral. It was awful. Obviously. I was scared. Imagining her inside the coffin. Seeing Dad cry...' He took a deep breath, steadying himself. 'But I'm still glad I was there. It felt important. I needed to be part of it.'

'I know. I was seven. But she was our mum. That's different.'

'Well, that made it worse, didn't it? More traumatic. Anyway, you know best. But if Cassie really wants to be there, I'd say you should think about it. He was the closest thing she's ever had to a grandparent.'

'Maybe.' She paused. 'I asked Lily about George. If he'd be OK about you coming to the funeral. I assume you'd want to?'

He winced. 'I don't want trouble, Anna. It's his dad, after all. If he doesn't want me there...'

Anna shook her head. 'Lily says she'll handle George.' She hesitated. 'It was a long time ago, Tim. We need to move on. All of us.'

Tim didn't answer. She saw the set of his shoulders, his head bowed under the burden of the guilt he still struggled to bear.

'Were you serious,' Tim said at last, 'about telling the police you won't cooperate with them anymore?'

Anna shrugged. 'They can't make me.'

Tim looked anxious. 'I'm not so sure about that.'

Anna looked up, wary. 'What do you mean?'

'Well, it's a murder investigation. And you're their key witness. Their only witness, as far as we know.'

Anna frowned. 'I've given them a statement, haven't I?'

'But they might need more than that. If they charge someone, if it ever goes to trial, they'd need you to give evidence in court, surely?'

Anna felt herself stiffen. She put a piece of pasta in her mouth and tried to chew, force it down.

'You think they can force me to testify?' she said at last. 'Even if I don't want to?'

Tim looked pained. 'Well, yes, actually. I think they can... You might face contempt of court. That's really serious.'

Anna set her fork down with a clatter. 'Contempt of court? You can go to prison for that.'

Tim didn't answer. He carried on slowly eating, going through the motions while she sat, her spine stiff and straight, thinking.

A rush of fear broke over her. Prison. The thought of it terrified her. She didn't know how she'd survive. Then a fresh horror struck her: what about Cassie? Anna didn't think she could bear the thought of her daughter being so alone, so vulnerable. She turned to Tim, her stomach cold.

'If it came to that, you'd look out for Cassie, wouldn't you?'

Tim tutted. 'Stop it. Of course, I would. You know that. But that's not going to happen.'

Anna put her elbows on the table and sank her head into her hands, her food forgotten. Her mind was whirring. She saw again Cassie's pale, cut face at the hospital. The sight had nearly broken her. She had to protect Cassie. That was all that mattered. If she had to risk being sent to prison, well, maybe she just had to find the courage to do that.

'You saw those notes,' she said at last. 'That's what tonight was about, wasn't it? Pretty clear. Keep your mouth shut. Don't talk to police or else there's worse to come.'

'I think so, yes.' Tim's voice was quiet. 'Thing is, it's not just about breaking the law, is it? Have you really thought this through?'

She lifted her face and gazed at him through the sieve of her fingers. 'What are you getting at?'

'Lily and George and Dr Taylor,' he said softly. 'What about them? Don't we owe them justice as well? How would they feel if a case against the man who killed their father fell apart because you refused to testify?'

'But what about Cassie?' Anna let out a sob. 'What am I supposed to do?'

18

Lily

Mike comes looking for me again. This time, I'm certain that it's him.

It's my first week back at school after losing my father. I'm glad to be back, to be surrounded by noisy children again and distracted by teaching.

School has just let out and the building's settled into that calm quiet which comes at the end of a hectic day, disrupted only by the low hum of activity in after-school clubs along the corridor. I clear up the classroom, then make a cup of tea and settle at my desk to tackle some marking. I've been struggling to concentrate in the house this week. Too many memories. Besides, this avoids the need to carry bags of exercise books home.

I've reached the end and stacked them away in the store cupboard when I happen to glance out of the window and there he is. He's sitting on the wall just beyond the school gates, hunched forward, tapping a phone screen.

Instinctively, I take a step backwards into the classroom to avoid being seen. I feel my face flush. *Mike.* Here again. It's so odd to see him. Why is he so determined to talk to me? It must be about Anna. As I watch, he twists back to look, almost as if he can feel my eyes on him. I shrink against the wall, out of sight.

I remember the hardness in Anna's face when I mentioned that he's back. If he's tried to contact her directly, he won't have got far. I remember what Cassie asked me, about whether Anna is afraid of him. An odd question. It's stayed with me.

When I'm ready to leave, I stride out with confidence across the empty playground and through the gates and say, 'Hello, stranger.'

He jumps up. He seems nervous.

'Lily!' He recognises me, then. 'It's me. Mike.'

'I know. What are you doing, loitering outside school? You can get in trouble for that, you know.'

He flushes, embarrassed. 'I heard you were teaching here,' he says, gabbling slightly. 'I didn't know how else to catch you. Sorry. I mean, I don't have your number or anything.'

I consider him. He's aged, of course, but he's still handsome. I always liked him. When we were teenagers, I thought he was good for Anna. He gave her confidence and, although he was attractive, he never messed her around. He only had eyes for Anna, from the day they met. I liked that about him. I dreamed of someone looking at me the way he looked at Anna.

'Did you get my card?' he presses on. 'I was wondering, could I take you for a coffee? I need to talk to you. Just as friends, I mean.' He realises how clumsy that sounds and flushes again. I already know what he's trying to say: *Don't worry, I'm not hitting on you, I just want some information.* Presumably about Anna.

'When? You mean *now*?' I make a show of looking at my watch, as if I might struggle to fit him into my busy schedule. In fact, all that's waiting for me at home is a proof of the order of service for Dad's funeral and a list of emails to send to people who might want to attend. Nothing that can't wait an hour or two.

'Well, if you're free.' He hesitates, trying to read me. 'I won't take up too much of your time.'

I let my shoulders relax and smile at him, making the decision to be nice. 'There's a new place round the corner that'll still be open. Come on. You can buy me a pastry as well, if you like. I'm starving.'

He falls into step beside me as I lead him in the direction of the café.

'I'm really sorry about your father,' he says as we walk. 'I can't imagine.'

I watch the steady back and forth of my black pumps and his tan brogues on the pavement. It's easier to offer condolences when you're not face to face, I understand that. Easier to accept them too. And sympathising with someone after a murder is apparently a lot harder than after a natural death. I've seen one or two family friends actually dive into a different aisle at the supermarket when they've seen me coming, just to avoid having to deal with it.

'Thank you,' I murmur. 'I appreciate it. It's not exactly easy, right now.'

After that, we fall silent and barely speak again until we're settled at the back of the café, two large coffees and two cinnamon buns on the table in front of us. I take the chance to look him over.

He clearly looks after himself. He was broad-shouldered and muscular as a teenager and that hasn't changed. His hair is closer cropped and already, though he's still young, showing signs of receding above his temples. He's dressed smartly – casual in jeans and a dark blue shirt but they're well cut and pressed.

I launch in with a question as soon as he sits down,

pretending I haven't already heard some of the answers on the grapevine. It isn't always accurate.

'So, you said you've come back to see your parents? It's been a long time.'

He looks down at his coffee as he stirs it, his eyes on the swirling chocolatey foam.

'It has,' he says simply. 'They're struggling. Mum needs a lot of looking after now. She's not bad physically but mentally, you know, she's not doing so well. Dad has pretty much taken over, shopping, cooking and washing and everything, but he's not in great shape.' He takes a deep breath, steadying himself. I sense that he finds all this hard to talk about. 'He had a coronary bypass last year. He needs to take it a bit easier.' He looks up, his eyes piercing. 'They were pretty old when they had me. Dad's not far off eighty now.'

I nod. I've never met his parents but Anna has described them, his mother especially. A stylish middle-aged woman who gardened and held dinner parties and played tennis. They had one of the bigger, posher houses in Otley, a converted farmhouse near the Chevin with stunning views over the Wharfe valley. Anna didn't much like them or perhaps she was just intimidated by them. It all seems very inconsequential now and sad.

'I'm sorry.'

He shrugs. 'Well, maybe it was time to come back anyway. I liked London but it never felt like home, not really. Now I'm here, I wonder what took me so long.'

I quietly check his left hand for a wedding ring. He isn't wearing one and there's no white mark where one might have been. Even so, I wonder if there's another, more personal reason that he's abandoned London and come home. A broken heart, perhaps. I don't know him well enough to ask.

'So are you back for good?'

'Yep. For good.' He sounds resolute. 'I'd been with the same company since uni, in their London office. It was a good job, I learned a lot, but I started to realise I was never going to get beyond middle management, however many years I put in. I'm not great at office politics.'

'So now what?' I reach for my cinnamon bun, break it into sticky quarters and start to eat it.

'I've joined a small firm in Leeds, builders' merchants. Anderson's?' He looks at me hopefully as if he expects me to know them. I just give a non-committal nod and let him carry on. 'Totally different business, much more rough and ready, but growing rapidly. I really think I'm getting in on the ground floor. If they grow, hopefully I'll rise with them. I just need a bit of luck. Well, and a lot of hard work, obviously.'

He grins sheepishly as if he isn't used to sharing his plans and feels awkward about it, wary of sounding boastful. He's talking a lot. I hardly know him and I don't really care about systems management or accounting or whatever it is he does.

He sips his coffee. 'So, how's teaching?'

I shrug, chewing, speaking through crumbs. 'Pretty good. I'm never going to get rich, I know that, but it's what I always wanted to do.'

He smiles. 'I remember.'

'And it's a good school. Nice people. The kids keep me on my toes.' I smile too, thinking about one or two of the more challenging children in my class this year. 'It's funny though, being Miss Taylor all day. I feel like someone's elderly aunt.'

He starts to eat his bun too. He's just being polite, asking about me. I get that. My teaching career isn't the reason he's sought me out and bought me coffee. I realise I'm wary of him without quite knowing why.

I swallow down the food in my mouth and wipe off sticky fingers on the paper napkin, getting down to business. 'So,' I lean forward slightly, giving him my full attention, 'you wanted to talk to me about something?'

'It's a bit...' His eyes flick up from his plate to mine, checking something.

I jump in, impatient: 'Is it about Anna?'

He nods. 'I don't want to put you in an awkward position, you know, betraying a confidence or anything, but I have tried to make contact and she won't talk to me.'

I raise an eyebrow, reach for more bun. 'Well, that's up to her, isn't it? I mean, you two...' I choose my words with care. 'It's water under the bridge. She's moved on. You can't expect her to roll out the welcome mat, just because you've decided to pitch up again.'

'I know. Of course—'

'You had a choice, didn't you?' I feel myself becoming more emphatic. 'She didn't, not really. She wanted to go to university too, you know. And she might someday, I'm sure. Once Cassie's a bit older. She's very smart.'

He says meekly, 'Of course, I know that. She has every right.'

'You know about the shops?'

He gives an indecipherable blink. If he does know, he must sense that I plan to tell him anyway.

'She's got two now and she's looking at opening a third. Remember Johnson's, the jewellers and watch repair place, off the market square? That's hers. She's really turned it around. It wasn't much when we were kids. You should see it now. And the second one's in Guiseley, on the high street. She's amazing. All that, plus being a single mum. Most days, she's there for Cassie after school, then catches up on paperwork in the evening. I don't know how she does it.'

He stares at his plate. 'I always knew she was smart. You don't have to tell me.'

'She didn't exactly have an easy start, did she? Schoolgirl mum and all that. If her dad hadn't supported her, in that first year, I don't know what she'd have done.'

I reach for my coffee. That came out more forcefully than I'd intended. I suppose I've waited a long time to tell him what I think about the way he dumped her.

There's a long silence. His eyes are downcast, studying his cooling coffee. I eat the rest of my bun. I don't really want it now. The sudden surge of anger, of disappointment about the way everything turned out, has left me feeling sick, but I don't want him to see that.

When he finally raises his eyes to mine, he looks stricken. 'I had no idea. About Anna, that she was... that she was going to have a baby. She didn't tell me.'

I snort. I want to say: *What did you expect? You'd just walked out on her. She had some pride.* I swallow it down. He looks genuinely upset.

'Since I've been back, I've heard a lot of loose talk around town. Gossip. About Cassie being mine.' He seems to struggle to form the next two words: 'My daughter.' He's lowered his voice and I have to lean closer to catch the words. 'One of my mum's old friends hinted that too. Is that true? Is she? Can you tell me that at least?'

I take a deep breath. 'That's something you need to ask Anna, not me.'

He shakes his head. 'I want to. I'm trying. She won't talk to me.'

He's right, of course. She won't talk to him. But what am I supposed to say? I don't want to be the one to break the news.

'You knew her best, Lily.' He's groping for the words, feeling his way. 'There wasn't anyone else, was there? Anyone else in her life, someone who might possibly be Cassie's father?'

I close my eyes and regroup. The food in my stomach churns. 'If there was, she never told me about him,' I say at last. 'Just you.' *Then and ever since*, I think.

'And what about Cassie? Does she know about me?'

I think about the bright, beautiful ten-year-old and all the questions she's asked over the years, all the blanks she's received in return. Then I think about her furrowed brow and the fear in her eyes as she tried to make sense of who her father might really be, her instinct that he could pose a threat to her and Anna.

'Not really,' I say. 'She wonders. She asks about you. For a long time, she thought her father was dead.'

'Dead?' He looks horrified.

I shrug. 'What did you expect Anna to tell her? She thought that was easiest.' I don't condone the lies but, at the same time, I can understand them. 'So even if you are her father, which is not what I'm saying by the way, that's between you and Anna and no one else.' I take a deep breath, gathering my thoughts. 'But, speaking hypothetically,' I hesitate, conscious of how closely he's studying me, 'even if you were, you might want to ask yourself what good it would do, raking all this up. OK, you're back. I don't blame you for being an absent father all these years. What else could you do if you didn't know Cassie existed? But she's ten now. You can't turn the clock back and start again.'

Around us, the café has fallen silent. The only sound is the wet slap of the manager's cloth round the inside of the glass cabinets as he cleans, ready to close up.

I focus back on Mike. 'So just stop and think, will you? What are you planning to do? To stir things up? To go chasing after Anna for the truth and then tell Cassie you might indeed be her long-lost dad? You'd blow their world apart. So would that be the right thing to do, a kind thing?' I pause, my eyes boring into his. 'Or just plain dangerous?'

19

Anna

'That's mine!'

Cassie snatched at the phone in her mother's hand. Her fury made her clumsy and Anna yanked it away. Anna took a step backwards, bumping into the edge of the kitchen table. She'd been too shocked by what she'd seen to realise that Cassie had quietly come into the kitchen and caught her.

'Mum!' Cassie's voice was a wail. Her body was rigid, her hands in fists at her sides. 'That's private.'

Anna glared. 'What's this? This message. Don't you think—?'

'Why are you checking my phone?'

'I was doing that update for you, remember? You agreed. And I saw this.'

She brandished the screen in front of her daughter's face. An unread message showed there.

Great to finally see you! Message me any time.

The sender's name was stored simply as Mike.

Cassie flushed. 'You're spying on me.'

'No, I'm not!' Anna forced herself to breathe out hard, trying not to lose her temper. 'Who's Mike?'

Anna bumped down into a kitchen chair and pointed Cassie to the one beside her. Cassie hesitated, frowning, then slid gracelessly into a chair and stared at the table.

'Well?' Anna's heart drummed. The fact Cassie seemed so guilty only made matters worse.

Cassie gave a vague shrug. 'A friend.'

'A friend? Right.' Anna looked down at the phone again. She wanted to think she was jumping to conclusions. She wanted it to be some other guy called Mike, some boy Cassie knew at school, perhaps, or a crush. She just didn't think so.

'So, who is he? How do you know him?'

Cassie had only got her first phone earlier in the year, when she'd started walking to and from school on her own. Part of the deal was that there were no secrets. Anna knew the passcode and could check it now and then, if she felt the need. Mostly, she hadn't. She'd trusted her daughter.

Cassie hesitated, refusing to look Anna in the eye. 'It's no big deal.'

'Really?' Anna sensed her daughter's discomfort. 'So tell me. How long have you known him?'

Cassie rolled her eyes. 'Stop it, Mum. This is exactly why I didn't tell you.'

The silence stretched. Anna felt her initial flare of anger mutate into something else. Fear. She set down the phone on the table between them. Cassie's hand snaked out at once and grabbed it, hid it under the tabletop.

Anna forced herself to soften her voice. 'Look, Cassie, I'm sorry, I know you're old enough to choose your own friends. It's not that. It's just, if this is who I think it is, I need to know. He's no right contacting you behind my back.'

Cassie kept her eyes on the table.

'OK.' Anna took a deep breath. 'I had a boyfriend called Mike, years ago when I was still at school. I haven't seen him since we broke up but I've heard he's back and he's been asking questions about you and me. Is this the same person?'

'Yes,' Cassie mumbled.

Anna felt her insides contract. 'So what does he mean, "great to finally see you"? Has he spoken to you?'

Cassie nodded dumbly.

'When? How? This is important.' The clock ticked through the seconds as Anna waited. 'Please, Cassie.'

'He said hi after school, that's all.'

'He said hi?'

Cassie squirmed. 'He said he used to know you but you weren't talking to him. He said I looked like you.'

Anna struggled to keep her voice level. 'You do realise how wrong that is. A grown man hanging around the school gates to see a ten-year-old girl.'

Cassie banged her fist on the top of the table. 'Mum! Stop it!' Cassie shook her head, as if it were pointless trying to explain. 'He was just, you know, nice. Friendly. He walked me home, that's all. He talked about you, mostly. About what you were like when he used to know you. It sounded like' – she sounded embarrassed – 'like he was really into you.'

Anna tried to imagine Mike ambling along at her daughter's side, flattering Cassie and appealing to her sense of long-lost romance. 'Oh, Cassie.'

'What?' Cassie's eyes flashed. 'What's so awful about that, anyway? That's all it was, OK?'

'And he asked you for your number?'

'Yeah. Why not?'

Anna felt suddenly bone-tired. She sagged against the table. 'And you don't think that's a bit, well, weird? He's a grown man. Why would he need your number?'

Cassie didn't answer. Her mouth fixed in a tight line.

Anna rubbed her eyes then ran her hands over her face. She sensed herself hover on the brink of tears. She had to tense to stop her mouth from puckering.

Cassie scraped back her chair. 'Can I go now?'

'No! We're not done yet.' Anna reached out and placed her hand on her daughter's. 'Things happened years ago, things you don't know about. Things you can't understand.'

'Maybe I would if you'd tried to explain.' Cassie tipped back her head. Her expression was defiant. 'If you'd actually talked to me about him instead of lying.'

'What's that supposed to mean?'

'You know.'

Anna's mind hovered, wheeling as it tried to comprehend. Then the realisation broke over her like a shock of cold water. Her eyes widened. 'No, Cassie! He didn't say—'

'Yes, Mum!' Cassie jumped to her feet. She looked so brittle she might snap. 'My dad didn't die, did he? He just didn't know I existed. How could you do that?'

Anna shook her head. 'You don't understand.'

'And now he's back. And he's not scary, he's actually really cool. He just wanted to say hi. That's all. That's why he gave me his number. Because he cares about me and he actually wants to get to know me.'

'But he can't... He's got no...' Anna was too stunned to form the sentence.

'He tried to do it through you. He told me. He wanted to. He said he's phoned you, like a million times, and you never pick up. That he's left messages begging you to call him back and you never have. I believe him. Even Auntie Lily and Uncle Tim are frightened to talk to me about him. They're frightened you'll flip your top. So, yes, he gave me his number – so we might actually have the chance to talk to each other sometimes.'

'Oh, Cassie, you don't—'

'And you're trying to ruin it!' Cassie stormed across the kitchen, phone clutched in her hand, her voice shaking. At the door, she turned for a final salvo. 'I just don't get it, Mum. I mean, really? What's so terrible about wanting to get to know my own *dad*?'

She turned and ran from the room. Anna, left alone at the table, heard her daughter's feet pounding up the stairs, then the crash of her bedroom door slamming shut.

Oh, Cassie, she thought wearily. *My poor, naïve girl. You have no idea what you've done.*

20

Lily

I don't time it well. I don't want to be late. That would be a disaster. But, as a result, I arrive at the crematorium far too early.

Already though, groups of mourners are strolling down from the car park in sombre overcoats and dark suits, making their way along cinder paths between carefully tended rose bushes and border shrubs. I glimpse them from a distance as I park. They greet each other with handshakes and tentative smiles, awkward and tense and pleased to make polite conversation to fill the time.

There are so many of them. I identify former colleagues of my father's, a large group of staff from the local doctors' practice. One of my father's early partners is with them. He looks older himself now, with grey hair and stooped shoulders. Many of the people gathering here are former patients who've seen him often over the years, each generation slowly giving way to the next.

They're families whose secrets he kept with such care.

Mostly, they were secrets of the body: the leaky bladders and heart murmurs, the infertility problems or complicated pregnancies, then measles, eczema and asthma and other afflictions of children who have now grown to have children of their own. But in many cases, they were also personal secrets of the heart which spilled over into his surgery, appearing in the form of depression and sleeplessness, of high blood pressure and migraines. He was a wise man and a good listener and he often understood the underlying causes: bereavement, disappointment, failed marriages. These were so much harder to treat.

Some of my colleagues have turned out too. I see two of the office ladies step briskly through the gates of the crematorium, alongside four or five teachers. My eyes fill. I hadn't expected that. Clearly, it's going to be a large crowd.

There's a general, gentle drift down the slope towards the main building and, once I've locked the car, I purposefully head off in the opposite direction, taking a path which circles round the top flowerbeds and beyond towards the memorial gardens which stretch away from the back of the building.

I need to keep walking. My body's tense and, if it slackens, I'm in danger of starting to sob. That can come later. For the next hour, I need to hold myself together. I owe it to both of them, my father and my mother. It's what they deserve.

I pick my way past rows of polished granite remembrance stones. I pause to read one or two. *Much loved wife, mother and grandma. Always in our hearts. Sorely missed. Until we meet again in heaven.*

When we were young, before we knew what it was to grieve, George and I would have made fun of sentiments of that kind. How naff, we would have said, rolling our eyes, feeling ourselves superior. I don't feel that now. It's a comfort of a kind, reading the plainly worded inscriptions. I've already lost my mother and now I'm here to bury my father. And I'm in good company. Here they are, these rows upon rows of lost souls, mourned by the people who loved them, the people they left behind. I blink hard and bite down on my lip.

Stop it, for heaven's sake. Don't get maudlin. Save that for later. You just need to get a grip and get through this.

I find a tissue in my pocket, one of many stowed there as a precaution, wipe off my eyes and blow my nose hard, then turn on my heel and head smartly back down the path towards the front, a fixed half-smile on my face, ready to play my part.

I stride up to the loose group gathered there. Concerned faces windmill to me, hands reach to touch my elbow, my upper arm, making physical contact to show their support. Murmurs wash over me as a collective whispering of 'sorry, so sorry'.

George appears on the far side of the crowd, unfamiliar and awkward in an ill-fitting dark grey suit and black tie. I hate it. It looks so wrong on him, so shot through with death and grief. My insides twist and my lip quivers. The last time he wore it was to our mother's funeral, I'm sure. He catches my eye. He looks lost, alone.

I find myself pushing my way through to him and slip my hand through his arm, pressing close against him. His body is sturdy and solid against mine. We can do this, together. We can get through this.

He looks past me and his expression shifts to a fearful nervousness. I turn to see. The hearse has slid quietly down the slope and into position. As if by common consent, the crowd around us turn and move swiftly through the large, wooden entrance doors of the crematorium to take their seats. The funeral directors, calm and unhurried, take control, checking with a few low words that we're ready, then rolling out the coffin, topped by the brightly coloured wreath I chose a week ago from the undertaker's album. None of this is real. This is not my father. It's impossible.

Without my permission, my mind reaches for memories of him. The broad warmth of his arms and lap when I snuggled into him as a young child for a story or just a cuddle. The man whose homecoming each evening was so special, so long-awaited. The rough tweed of his jacket against my cheek when he came home from the surgery and I went running through the hall to be lifted up and kissed. The faint smells it carried of the outside world, a male world, of petrol fumes and cigarette smoke, of antiseptic and bleach.

The chief undertaker gives a discreet cough, drawing us back to proceedings, and they start to process, these burly men. George and I follow on behind, hand in hand, like two lost children.

I spend much of the service with my eyes and jaw clamped tightly shut, pretending to myself that I'm somewhere else, anywhere else, breathing hard and struggling not to cry.

Somewhere behind us, a woman warbles her way through the hymns loudly and slightly off-key, straining painfully for the higher notes. I don't trust myself to turn round to see who it is. I'm grateful to her for the diversion and for filling the gaps. I don't trust myself to sing.

My eyes, when I feel I can open them again, fix on the coffin. All I can think about, as the officiant says the final words and the curtains twitch and swish and begin to close, is of the sight of my father's murdered body, the paleness of his stubbled cheek and the horror of his cold, lifeless skin.

I stagger and stumble against George, clutching his arm to keep myself on my feet, to anchor myself in the mist swirling through me. I'm not sure I can do this. I don't know how to stay whole when everything I am is collapsing into pieces.

As I file out, head bowed, still catching my breath, I see Cassie.

It takes me a moment to register that it's her. She's standing alone in the entrance, pressed back into the door-frame, her eyes fixed on something happening outside. She seems such a tense, forlorn figure, so different from the energetic child I know so well. She's dressed differently too, enveloped in an old-fashioned buttoned coat, her hair combed back neatly and fastened in place by a plain black headband. Puzzled, I look past her for a glimpse of Anna or Tim but there's no sign of either.

The hall has already almost emptied, people hastily spilling out ahead of me into the weak sunshine. Their comments drift back to me: *What a lovely service, so moving.* The sort of platitudes my father would have hated.

I hurry towards her, worried about why she's alone. Maybe I was wrong. Maybe Anna was right and Cassie is too young to be here. 'Cassie!'

She doesn't seem to hear me. Her attention is too focused elsewhere.

I reach her. Her cheeks are pallid. Is she ill?

'Cassie, are you OK?' I touch her arm, concerned.

Numbly, without looking at me, she shakes her head.

I turn, confused, trying to see where she's looking. Then, as soon as I do, I gasp. And everything breaks apart once again.

21

Anna

As soon as they'd arrived at the crematorium, Anna had walked Cassie straight through the gathering crowd at the entrance. She couldn't talk to anyone. She was too tense. She didn't know how people could stand there, chatting in low voices and even smiling. She steered Cassie by the shoulders into the main hall.

It looked as if the previous funeral had only just ended. An expressionless man in a long, black coat was moving between seats, picking up stray orders of service to take away. She glimpsed the photograph on the front: a middle-aged woman with a sweet smile. Some other poor soul. Some other sad parting.

Anna led Cassie into a row about halfway down. Tim followed quietly behind and fussed over Cassie as they both took off their coats and settled. They were almost the first to take their seats. Anna scrutinised the photo of Dr Taylor on the front of the order of service. A younger version of him, only faintly remembered from her childhood. He'd been handsome, she realised. It was odd to see his younger self with her own adult eyes.

She opened it and scanned the contents. Lily had been the one behind all this. A simple, straightforward service, not too sentimental. Now, reading the details, she nodded to herself. Good choices. Dr Taylor would have approved. Cassie glanced sideways at her, nervous, and Anna reached over to squeeze her hot hand.

She hadn't wanted Cassie to come. She didn't want her to be upset, that was the main reason, but she sensed another, more selfish motive as well. Having Cassie here added to the pressure she already felt inside herself, an anxiety that she might sob or do something equally embarrassing, that she might make a spectacle of herself. She bit the inside of her cheeks and took deep, deliberate breaths.

The seats were slowly starting to fill. It was an impressive turnout. Anna tried to focus on the building, warm and carpeted, as inviting and comfortable as a crematorium could be. A plain wooden cross stood to one side of the lectern at the front. It was the only nod to religion that she could see. The stained-glass windows at the far end showed a striking image of yellow, orange and red streaks exploding from an orb. The sun, she supposed.

'Alright?' She leaned in close to Cassie and instinctively lowered her voice to a whisper. 'Not long now.'

Cassie didn't answer. Her cuts were healing well, the wounds already shrinking and starting to knit. There was still a chance of scarring, the doctor had warned. The skin never forgets.

Anna felt a memory bubble up inside her, passing through her like a chill. A dank, shadowy church and eyes turning to stare as she followed her mother's coffin down the aisle. Her father, head bowed with grief, walked ahead of her, and Tim trailed, eyes vacant and lost, at her side. She'd been too young to lose her mother; they both had been.

It was almost time. Cassie fidgeted with the handkerchief in her hand, balling and crushing it in her palm. Only Tim seemed calm, flicking briefly through the order of service, then facing the front as if he were deep in thought.

She turned to watch when the opening music sounded and they carried the coffin in. She didn't want to see it, she was afraid of the sight, but she couldn't help herself. As it passed, shouldered by the undertakers' men, she saw again Dr Taylor's staring, terrified eyes, his body slumped against pillows, his blood draining. She shivered.

Behind, Lily and George processed slowly, side by side. Lily's face was white. She seemed unaware of the people around her. Anna sensed what all this had done to her. Not just the loss, but the violence and the horror of it – it had changed her.

Anna sucked in her cheeks and tried to close down her mind as the service began. She couldn't go back to the night she'd found Lily's father. Not now. She wanted to remember the kind, clever man he'd been.

Afterwards, once the service had ended and the curtains closed on the coffin, the energy in the hall changed. It was as if a collective tension, a general withholding of breath, had been released.

Anna bent close to Cassie. 'Well done,' she said. 'Are you OK?'

Cassie shrugged. She seemed shrunken inside herself. Anna's forehead tightened, looking at her daughter, wondering what she was feeling, how this might affect her. Anna still thought she was young for her first funeral but at least, if it had to happen, this one hadn't been too traumatic.

The officiant, a soft-spoken woman in late middle-age, her short hair peppered with grey, had given a thoughtful address about Dr Taylor's life, from his happy childhood in the Peak District to the importance of his marriage and family and, finally, the contribution he'd made to Otley, to so many of the families gathered here today to say goodbye. There was no mention of the violence which had so abruptly ended his life and the ragged uncertainty it had left in its wake.

Around them, people were murmuring, gathering up coats and bags, shuffling down the rows towards the exit. Anna turned to look back towards the main doors.

Then she saw him. For a moment, she couldn't breathe. *Mike.*

Heat flushed through her. She knew him in an instant. There. He was getting up from a row near the back, nudging his way gently into the exiting stream of people.

She snapped her head back to the front, blood pounding in her ears. Thinking she was going to cry, she bit down hard on her lip. *Mike.* She'd known he was back. She'd sensed, as he'd made contact with Lily, then with Cassie, that he was closing in on her. Even so, she somehow hadn't prepared herself for being confronted with him, with seeing him again. She tried to steady her breathing.

She didn't know what she'd expected. He looked so much the same. Older, that was all, and more smartly dressed. The last ten years had matured him, led him through the creeping change from a youth, leaving his teens, to a man.

Thoughts pressed in on her in a confused tangle. He must have sneaked in late, after everyone else was seated. She'd been too busy holding herself together, eyes forward, to notice. But he would have seen her, from where he was sitting. He must have seen her clearly. She imagined his eyes on the back of her head, on her neck, on Cassie beside her, all this time. Her stomach was hollowed out.

Why had he come? After all, he'd hardly known Dr Taylor.

His family had attended a different surgery. He and Lily hadn't been friends, not really. Was it to see her?

She turned again and searched for him in the crowd. He was almost at the doors, hemmed in by doughy figures, padded with winter coats, funnelling slowly through. Her eyes were fixed on him, her hands shaking. She didn't know what she wanted. For him to disappear or to wait there for her. She knew, as soon as the thought formed, that he would wait.

She hurried out of the far end of their row, leaving Cassie behind with Tim, and navigated the less crowded outer aisle towards the exit, pursuing him. She didn't stop to think why.

She emerged with the crowd into the watery sunshine and looked nervously around.

There. He stood slightly back from the path, a still, solitary figure alongside the moving stream of people, scanning the emerging faces. He saw her. There was no mistaking the moment. His eyes fastened on hers and didn't leave them. His mouth twisted in a tense half-smile.

From behind, a middle-aged woman bumped into Anna, then apologised and extravagantly steered round her. Anna realised that she'd stopped, smack in the middle of the crowd, in everyone's way.

She looked down at her feet, self-conscious now, embarrassed, and let the momentum press her forward towards him. When she reached him, she stepped out of the flow to join him there on the grassy verge.

He stared down at her shyly. 'You haven't changed.'

She dipped her chin, hiding her face from him, painfully exposed, and said, more brusquely than she'd intended, 'Of course I have. A lot's happened.'

He didn't answer, and when she took a quick glance up at his face, his expression was soft.

'I heard your parents aren't doing so well,' she said, finding her feet again. 'I'm sorry.'

He seemed to recover himself, becoming polite and a little distant. As she looked at him, a succession of thoughts tumbled through her head, unbidden, chasing each other into shadows. People were watching.

She should never have followed him out here. It had been over, long ago, their intense teenage romance. This was absurd. Then another voice, a younger, sadder one: *I loved you so much. You have no idea. The last time I saw you, my heart broke so badly, I thought it would never heal. Why are you here? Why did you come back?*

'Thank you.' He cleared his throat. 'Yes, it isn't easy.'

There was an uneasy pause. She sensed their need to relearn how to speak to each other. They were almost strangers now, after all. Acquaintances. But all she could think about was their old intimacy, the endless animated conversations they used to have when they were together, driving in his mother's borrowed car, her hand resting always on his thigh, or walking for hours side by side across the moors. It had never been awkward. Never like this.

It was an effort to pull herself back from the past. She countered it by throwing out a challenge: 'I didn't expect to see you here.' They both knew why he was here, and it wasn't for Dr Taylor or for Lily and George.

He swallowed. 'Awful. Poor Dr Taylor.' He couldn't look her in the eye. 'Awful for all of them.'

She shook her head and frowned, reminding herself that she needed to say something to him. 'I heard you've been asking questions about me.' She forced herself to stand erect, to confront him. 'My daughter says you approached her, after school?' She didn't sound like herself. Her voice swelled as anger came. 'You took her phone number. You messaged her, didn't you? What the hell? She's ten years old, Mike. Really? I've a good mind to report you. Did you think I wouldn't find out?'

Mike held up his hands as if he were warding her off. 'I wanted you to know. I wanted to make contact. We need to talk, Anna. Please. I need to know—'

'You OK?' Tim's quiet voice sounded in her ear. His hand warmed her shoulder.

She was too tense to calm down, not yet. She twisted away, shaking her brother off, focused still on Mike. 'Don't go near Cassie again, I'm warning you.'

Anna sensed movement around them. Something shifted. People nearby were drawing back. A low murmuring. *They're listening in,* she thought. *They can't help themselves. They're drawn to the tension in the air.*

'Anna?' Tim's voice was tight.

Mike's eyes shifted from her face to somewhere behind her. His forehead knotted in concern.

Anna blinked, wrong-footed. Something was happening but she didn't understand what. She started to turn, to look over her shoulder and see for herself.

A uniformed police officer, thickened by a bulky stab vest, was approaching her from behind. He reached her side. His stern eyes were on hers.

Something inside her shrank and chilled, frightened of what was about to happen.

'Ms King?' His voice was hard. 'Would you come with me please?'

'Now?' Anna felt a bubble of panic rise. 'Do I have to?'

Tim, pressing close to her, said, 'Has something happened?'

The officer reached for Anna's arm, as if he intended to use force if she resisted.

Behind him, there by the side of the road, Anna glimpsed a waiting police car. A second officer sat at the wheel, his face turned to them, watching.

'Anna King, I am placing you under arrest,' the police officer said, loudly and carefully, as if he were making a public proclamation.

Mike took a step towards them. 'Arrest? What for?'

The police officer ignored him. His eyes stayed fixed on Anna's. 'I'm arresting you in connection with the murder of Dr Philip Taylor.'

He started to intone a formal caution. Anna saw the movements of his thick, dry lips. The dead words swirled around her. Everything seemed to slow.

This is it, then, she thought.

As the police officer led her past the main entrance to the crematorium, she saw Cassie, slumped against the door-frame of the entrance, her thin face pale and frightened, and, beside her, Lily, open-mouthed, stunned and helpless, watching her best friend be marched away.

22

Lily

I don't know how I survive the wake.

All those people, touching my arm and nodding sympathies, the syrupy voices and murmured condolences. My father's former patients, many I don't even recognise, press in, eager to tell me personal stories about Dad's kindness, anecdotes about his comfort or support. It's so hot and stuffy in here, I feel sick. My head's reeling. When I glance at myself in one of the large, gilded mirrors, I see startled eyes and a pale face. I look so ill.

Someone pushes a cup of tea into my hands. The teaspoon rattles in the saucer as my hands shake. I can't drink it. I just nod, numbly, as a grey-haired woman I can't place tells me how sorry she is for my loss, what a wonderful man my father was, how he touched so many lives.

I stare at her. This isn't a normal funeral. This isn't a normal death. My father was murdered and that changes everything. I can't focus on her. All I can think about is the shock on Anna's face as she was marched away to the waiting police car. I heard what they told her, that she's been arrested for Dad's murder. But why? Anna? It's ridiculous. Anna wouldn't kill a soul.

So when Mike comes across to me, concerned but hesitant, as if he fears he's overstepping the mark, and asks in a low voice if I'm feeling OK, if I'd like him to drive me home, I simply nod and say yes and leave George and his mates to their drinking and the last stragglers to finishing off the crustless curling sandwiches and fingers of cake.

'She didn't do it. They're wrong if they think she did.' Mike blurts it out as soon as we're both in the car. He flushes, defying me to disagree. Clearly, the thought has been burning in his mind since Anna was arrested. She may have shouted at him just before she was arrested, but Mike clearly feels he still knows her.

'I know.' I'm calmly dismissive, watching the hedges and trees slip past as he drives. 'Anna wouldn't hurt a fly.'

Mike nods, his brows still furrowed. 'Then why?' He shakes his head at the road. 'What have they got on her? It makes no sense.'

I can't answer that. He's right. It makes no sense.

Something deep in my gut twists and sours. All the hurt, all the anger that's damaged our two families. I was just starting to hope, with Tim's return, that it was behind us.

Please don't let this rekindle it all over again.

George's behaviour frightens me. I can't predict him. He still struggles with what Tim did. He doesn't talk about it, but I see it in all the evenings he drinks too much, in his meaningless rages, in the girlfriends he dumps as soon as they get too close.

It was a relief when Tim left for London and George no longer ran the risk of seeing him in the street, in the pub. But all that was a very long time ago. I learned to forgive. I thought, given time, he could as well. But now this?

As Mike turns into Riverside Road, I point across at the Kings' house.

'I want to see them. I want to check on Tim and Cassie. I want them to know I'm standing by them, that I don't believe she did anything wrong.'

He pulls in at the side of the road, behind Tim's car, kills the engine, then hesitates. His knuckles, tight on the steering wheel, whiten.

'I'd like to come in with you.' He breathes hard. 'If there's something I can do, anything...'

I shrug. The only person who'd object to that is Anna and she's not here. 'Sure.'

Tim opens the door, his face harrowed. Behind him, Mrs MacKay pops her head out of the lounge as she checks who's arrived.

I touch Tim on the shoulder as I pass him. I can't quite give him a hug, even now. Mike makes a show of pointlessly wiping his feet on the mat. If Tim minds him being here, he doesn't show it. He's in such a state, I'm not sure he's really taking in who it is.

I press ahead into the lounge and the men follow. The four of us stand there, awkward.

Mrs MacKay is the first to break the silence.

'Fancy a thing like this. I can't believe it. At your father's funeral too. No respect.' Mrs MacKay shakes her head. I see she's got her coat on. 'I was just leaving.' She adds in a lower voice to me: 'I popped round to see how they were bearing up. But now you're here...'

I manage to say, 'That was kind of you.'

She starts to leave, then pauses, remembering, and turns back to me. 'Lovely service. You did your father proud.'

Mike takes it upon himself to see Mrs MacKay home. His gentle voice murmurs from the hall, then the door closes behind them.

I turn to Tim. 'So? Any news?'

He looks dazed. 'Not really. I've been calling the police

station, but they won't tell me much. I spoke to a legal helpline. They can hold her for several days, apparently, because it's murder.'

I frown. 'Has she been charged with anything?'

'I don't think so.'

I pace back and forth across the carpet. We should be doing something. I just don't know what.

'What about a lawyer?'

'I phoned one.' Tim flushes. 'The ones in Bridge Lane, you know. Bendons. They're sending someone down.'

I give him a sharp look. Yes, I know Bendons. The same firm who represented Tim, all that time ago. I shake my head and let it go. Now isn't the time. 'Where's Cassie? Is she alright?'

Tim runs a hand through his hair, distraught. 'Not great. I haven't had time to talk to her properly, to be honest. Too busy ringing round, trying to work out what to do.'

I point to the ceiling, assuming she must be upstairs. 'Can I go up?'

He just nods. He doesn't seem to know what to do with himself.

Mike comes back. I know it's him from the sounds of nervous foot-wiping in the hall.

As I pass Mike, heading for the stairs, I whisper, 'Make him a cup of tea, would you?' and leave them to it.

Upstairs, Cassie's bedroom door is half-open. I give it a cursory knock as I head inside.

Cassie is hunched on her bed, her knees drawn up. Her face is blotchy, her nose wet, her eyelashes encrusted with dried tears.

'Cassie?'

I sit beside her and open my arms, and she crawls into them at once, presses her wet face into my neck. She sobs. I stroke her back in rhythmical circular motions and feel the vibrations shake her, feel the wetness of her tears on my skin. I touch my lips to her hair and hold her close and think of all the times, all the hurts, since she was a baby. She used to cry on me such a lot when she was tiny, when she was disappointed or frustrated or just tired. I loved the fact she trusted me. I loved it when she lifted her arms to me and I bent down and scooped her up. I loved the cuddles. Now she's growing up and it's been a while.

When the sobbing abates, she gives a long shudder. I ease her off my shoulder now she's quieter and reach for a tissue, wipe off her face.

'What if she goes to prison?' Cassie's eyes are wide with fear. They bore into mine, looking for reassurance. 'What if I can't see her again?'

'She won't go to prison.' I try to sound more certain than I feel. 'She's done nothing wrong, Cassie. We know that, don't we?'

She frowns, gives a cautious nod. At the age of ten, she has more faith in the infallibility of the justice system than I do, and I'm not going to disillusion her.

She says, gulping, 'But why did they take her away like that? It was so awful. In front of everyone.'

I nod. 'I know.'

Cassie's fingers reach for the edge of her duvet and she plucks at the cotton. 'If she does go to prison, I'll be sent to a children's home, won't I?'

'Oh, Cassie, of course not.' I give her a hard, quick hug. 'First of all, that's not going to happen. But even if it did, you've got Uncle Tim and me. We'd look after you. Right? You'd stay right here.'

She considers this. A small part of the burden she's carrying, here in her room with her own thoughts and fears, seems to lessen.

'Uncle Tim is trying to find out what's going on,' I say carefully. 'It's clearly some sort of mix-up, you'll see.'

She sits very still for a while, her head bowed. The only

movement comes from the nervously plucking fingers. Finally, she says, without looking me in the face, 'Would you and Uncle Tim really look after me? After, you know, everything that happened?'

'What do you mean?' I'm trying to sound light, to reassure her, but the words sound strangled. It's not something any of us talk about. She knows that.

Her neck flushes scarlet. She doesn't speak for a while. I reach out my hand and grasp hers, hold it tightly. I want to tell her it's OK. That I won't be angry. That I can be brave and try to talk about it, if she can be brave about Anna.

She mutters, barely audible, 'Someone at school said something. She said Uncle Tim should never have come back here. Because of what he did.'

I take a deep breath. 'I can try to tell you, if you like.' I keep tight hold of Cassie's hand. 'It was all a long time ago. Your mum and I were only seventeen. She was pregnant with you. She'd only known for a few months. Anyway, I persuaded her to come along to a party with me. She wasn't keen. It was December, not long before Christmas. Freezing cold.'

I break off, look at her eyes, focused intently now on mine. I'm not sure I can go on. I'm not sure I can tell her without crying, without breaking down. I don't want her to see that.

I look away at the litter of pencils and half-finished drawings, plastic trinkets and books strewn across her carpet.

Why are we talking about this, today of all days? The day I cremated my father.

I feel her soft pressure on my hand and turn back to her, feel her waiting.

Maybe that's why. Maybe that makes it exactly the right day to remember.

23

THEN

Lily stood at the open wardrobe in Anna's bedroom, scraping coat hangers back and forth as she scrolled through the clothes there, pulling out some loose-waisted jeans and one of Anna's favourite goth tops.

Anna, sitting on the end of her bed, shook her head. 'I can't. It looks awful now.'

Lily held up the top, thoughtfully. 'Try it on.'

Anna sighed. 'I'm telling you. It only looked good when I was skinny. Now—' She gestured at her stomach. She wasn't quite four months pregnant yet but her flat stomach had recently started to swell and was round enough to make her self-conscious in her old crop tops.

Lily threw it at her. 'Go on.'

Anna threw off her baggy sweater and pulled on the top, then spread her arms in an ironically dramatic gesture to demonstrate how badly it sat. 'See?'

Lily gave her friend's figure an appraising glance. 'Hang on, then.' She turned back to the wardrobe.

'Look, I'm not going.' Anna shook her head at her friend's back. 'You don't need me. You'll be flirting with Raj all evening.

And what's the point, really? I can't drink. And I'm not exactly on the pull, am I?'

Lily was still rummaging. 'Try this one.' She pulled out a soft denim shirt, one Anna hadn't worn for a while. 'Let me see.'

Anna reluctantly tried it on.

Lily tipped her head on one side, considering. 'Yeah, that works.' She held up the jeans. 'Do these still fit?'

'I really don't fancy it, Lily. You go. I'm going to have a long bath and get to bed early.'

Lily raised an eyebrow. 'It's Saturday night. What are you, ninety? Get dressed and let's do our make-up.' She unzipped her make-up bag and started to set her things out on the edge of Anna's desk.

'Besides, it's freezing out there.' Anna looked through the window without enthusiasm at the low mist softening the bare branches of the trees.

Lily was unimpressed. 'I thought you had the car tonight?'

'It's Tim's turn.' Now she'd also passed her test, the two of them had to fight over who had access to their father's battered old car. Saturday nights were always a choke point. 'He's going too. So, if we do go, he'll give us a lift.'

'Cool.'

Anna had felt closer to Tim in the last few months than she had for years. For a while, after he'd left school and started work with their father at the bank, he'd seemed aloof. For the first time, he had money in his pocket and had started saving for his own place. She was still a schoolgirl.

But he'd changed towards her since he'd found out she was pregnant. Become more gentle, more protective. He made a quiet effort to look after her, apparently more aware than their father of how much Anna had struggled in the last few months with sickness and tiredness.

'What about George?'

Lily pulled a face. 'He won't come. Some big match on TV. You know what he's like.'

Anna let herself be cajoled into pulling on the jeans and stood, side on, in front of her mirror, trying to see how her stomach looked.

'You can't tell, honestly.' Lily, starting on her foundation, was keeping an eye on her.

'Maybe he'll find a girl who likes football,' Anna said. 'Someone whose idea of a great Saturday night is watching the match.'

Lily gave her an old-fashioned look. 'Well, he won't find her if he never goes out, will he? I've told him.'

'Bet that went down well.' Anna raised her eyebrows.

They grinned at each other.

'Come on,' Lily said, scooting up to make room. 'Get some lippy on. You never know what the night will bring.'

'Right.' Anna looked at her tired, pasty face in the mirror. The first trimester had taken its toll. She was hoping the second would be easier. 'Actually, I think I do.'

In the end, it wasn't a bad party.

Lily and her new boyfriend, Raj, spent the night dancing wildly, their eyes locked. Anna smiled, watching them. Lily had been worrying that Raj wasn't really into her, but he clearly was. Already, Lily had whispered to Anna not to wait for her at the end of the party. Raj had asked to take her home. Now his hands strayed to her waist, pulling her close.

Anna had settled into a dark corner and perched on a stool there, her legs splayed for balance, sipping a can of Coke. She liked to shrink into the shadows nowadays, to observe anonymously without being seen. It suited her mood, separate and a little melancholy.

The house was impressive. It had a large, open-plan lounge

and, by pushing the furniture back against the walls, they'd opened up a decent area for dancing. It was already dense with gyrating bodies. The music, pumped up high, vibrated through the floorboards and into her legs. The air smelled of cigarette smoke and male sweat, of teenage perfume and hair lacquer.

The overhead lights were dimmed to a faint glow. A plug-in disco ball was sending multi-coloured swirls across the ceiling, painting the plaster with flashes of purple, green and orange. The window behind Anna, propped open a few inches, wafted waves of chill onto her back. It made her shiver but she was grateful for the way it cut through the fug.

As she watched the waving arms, the bouncing bodies, her thoughts drifted to Mike. They always did. She wondered where he was right now. If he was at a party. If he was dancing with someone. If he was happy. If he ever thought of her.

She'd loved dancing with him. They knew each other so well. They moved intuitively together, mirroring each other. When their eyes met, the rest of the world melted away and all she could see was him, the only solid, real thing in this shifting, spinning world. The memory was so intense, she could almost smell him, almost feel his heat warming the air between them.

She blinked and sipped another mouthful of Coke. *Stop it*, she told herself. *Rear-view mirror.*

She rested a hand on the mound of her stomach and thought about the tiny person growing there. About the size of a turnip now, according to the books. With its own unique set of fingerprints. She smiled to herself as a new track started – a fast-paced favourite – and swayed as she listened.

Lily appeared in front of her, face flushed. She pulled the can from Anna's hand, set it on a table and heaved Anna to her feet.

'Come on!'

Anna let herself be dragged into the centre of the room. Some of their friends greeted her with whoops and cheers as she joined the dancing. Most looked slick with sweat and alcohol. They banged into each other as they shouted out the words of the chorus in unison, arms flailing.

Someone hollered, 'Go, girl!'

She and Lily took each other's damp hands, boyfriends forgotten, and swung each other around, giggling and exuberant, playing out the moves they used to practise in their bedrooms when they were younger girls.

A shockwave of icy air hit them, careering down the hall from the opened front door and breaking over their hot bodies. It must be bitter outside. Well below zero. The mist had turned to ice.

Anna stopped dancing, suddenly hyperaware. She'd felt something. A new sensation, deep inside. It wasn't what she'd expected, not a kick but a tiny shift and release, as if a bubble had been burst. Maybe it was just the Coke. She pushed her hand under her baggy shirt and pressed it flat on the smooth round of her skin. There it was again.

It was a faint sensation but there, definitely. It was starting to become real, finally, this miracle of a person growing inside her.

Lily leaned in and bellowed in her ear. 'You alright?'

Anna smiled. She looked round the reinvented lounge, at the shadowy chairs and tables against the wall, at the jumping, writhing teenagers and the flash of coloured lights. She felt very still, very separate from the rest of them, as if she were reaching already towards another life, a world bounded by a different form of love.

A slow track followed. Raj appeared at Lily's side to reclaim her and the two of them wrapped their arms around each other and drifted away. The crowd was thinning, the dance floor dominated by clinging couples.

Anna checked her watch. It was just after eleven. She was suddenly dog-tired. Around her, people were groping for coats and jackets in the messy pile and starting to leave. Those without their own transport needed to catch last buses, last trains or face long, numbing walks in the cold.

Anna went in search of Tim. He bumped into her in the hall, already pulling on his jacket. He smiled and jingled car keys at her.

'You ready?'

Anna nodded, then stalled and scrutinised his face. It was hard to see clearly in the darkness of the hall but something made her pause. His eyes were so bright, they seemed almost feverish. 'Are you OK?'

'Fine.' He zipped up his jacket and waited for her to sort herself out. 'No Lily?'

'No, she's doing her own thing.' Anna fastened her coat, her good winter one. It would get tight soon, too tight to button up at the front. She imagined herself with a large bump, waddling. She'd expected to mind that, but she didn't now, not so long as the baby was OK. Her feet ached though.

They spilled out into the night, slapped at once in the face and hands by the sharpness of the cold. It snatched her breath from her mouth. The pavement glittered with frost.

She glanced again at Tim. 'You're sure you're OK?'

Tim shrugged. 'Well, not great,' he said, his tone matter of fact. 'Don't worry. It's not booze. I've only had one beer. Must be something I ate.' He hesitated. 'I threw up in the loo earlier. Nice, eh?' He rolled his eyes. 'Well, you did ask.'

He made light of it, but she sensed how embarrassed he was. He hated to be ill.

'Join the club,' she said with a wry smile. 'I've been throwing up for months.'

She took his arm as they slithered down the road to the car, holding each other up on the frost-slick tarmac. They climbed into the car, blowing on their hands. The engine coughed into life. Tim tried to turn up the heating, weathering the blast of cold air in their faces. The car nosed its way carefully into the empty street.

'Soon be home,' he said, adding in a silly imitation of their father's voice: '*Nice cup of tea.*'

They smiled at each other, brother and sister, side by side. Their father was absurdly uncool but still loving, still comforting.

The main road was almost deserted. The large houses, whose drives ran back from the pavements, lay in darkness. The only light came from the hazy yellow circles of the streetlamps and the flash of the car's headlights on the reflectors down the middle of the road. The beams caught a hare, scut shining, dashing across their path. She thought of the frosted grass, the iron-hard earth, solid with ice, and felt sorry for it.

'Minus one,' Tim read off the dashboard. 'Feels worse.' He reached for the heating controls and fiddled with them. 'Soon as I make my first million,' he said, 'I'm buying Dad a fancy car. With heated seats.'

'Just a heater that works would be a start.' Anna hunched lower in her seat, shivering. She wondered if the baby was distressed, if it was affected by the sudden drop in temperature. Their father would have gone up to bed by now. If he'd put the heating off, the house would be freezing. She might make herself a hot drink when they got in. Warm herself up. Her ears buzzed with cold.

They slid down a side road, taking a short cut. The pavements were deserted, gleaming eerily in the cold. Theirs was the only car in sight.

She said, 'It's so quiet.'

'It's the cold.' Tim shrugged. 'And it's not exactly party central round here, is it?'

She smiled. Now and then, a downstairs window flickered blue from a television but most of the houses were shrouded in darkness. Upstairs curtains were drawn closed. She imagined the families inside, huddled under duvets, trying to get warm. She thought of her own bed. If she made herself a cup of tea, she could use the rest of the water for a hot water bottle. *Don't worry, turnip*, she told the bump. *We'll soon be warm again.*

The road veered right. It was a tight turn and even as the brakes engaged, nothing seemed to happen. Tim let out a strangled noise, his eyes widening. The tyres started to skid, sliding sideways, out of control.

Ice. They must have hit a stretch of black ice, secreted there along the side of the road.

Anna's mouth opened. Wordless. She couldn't breathe.

The car, out of control, shot violently across the icy surface. The tyres hit the kerb, the momentum carrying them forward. They mounted the pavement and ploughed towards the bus stop. It all happened in a fraction of a second and yet later, when she remembered, every moment seemed to last forever. The stuff of nightmares.

There, ahead, right in their path, lit by the sudden dazzling glare of the headlights, was a solitary figure. A woman stood stiffly, waiting for the last bus, shoulders hunched against the treacherous cold. A phone glowed faintly in her hand.

Oh, God. Anna couldn't speak but something formed in her mind. *Please. No.*

The beam hit the woman full in the face, blinding her. Her eyes shone with reflected light, then squeezed shut. In all the rush of movement, only she was statue-still, too dazed to move.

The car crashed into her. She seemed to fold, her head flopping forward in a grotesque bow. Then she disappeared abruptly from sight. There was a thud, a bump, as the car passed over her, dragging her body under the chassis, crushing the life from her chest.

The car, ploughing on, struck the stone wall on the far side of the pavement. The front of the bonnet crumpled with the impact as they came, at last, to a halt.

Anna was thrown forward. Her ribs were gripped with bruising force by her seatbelt, knocking her back into her seat. Her head seemed to ricochet on her shoulders, wrenching her neck. Stunned, she couldn't move. Dimly, she sensed Tim beside her, shocked into silence. A low hiss came from the front of the car. The engine had cut. The air was jagged with silence.

Mrs Taylor's mobile phone, thrown wide in a graceful arc, spun on its back on the pavement. The screen faded quietly to black. Lily and George's mother was gone.

24

Anna, concealed by the wall, watched from her bedroom window on the day the sleek black hearse slid up outside the Taylors' house.

The Taylors came slowly down the path from the back door. It was a ragged, fragmented family now. Dr Taylor, sober in his black greatcoat, shoulders hunched, followed by Lily and George. George, head bowed, scuffed his feet.

As Lily made to get into the hearse, she paused and lifted her gaze, looking across towards the Kings' house. Anna ducked back against the wall, not sure if she'd been spotted. When she dared to look again, Lily had disappeared. The hearse was making its stately way to the far end of the street, then turning right into the traffic.

Anna's father had sent flowers to the church. They'd spent a long time deliberating over what to do, how to word the message. Attending the funeral was out of the question, her father had said, his face grey with strain. He'd looked meaningfully at Anna as she'd opened her mouth to object. For all of them, he'd added.

Tim shut himself in his room. Their father was never a

vindictive man, but it was clear that he couldn't bear to look at his son. Anna remembered the anguish, the wretchedness in their father's face when the police had driven them home. Their father, roused from sleep, hadn't shouted. He'd just stood there at the top of the stairs, a sad, ageing figure in a shabby dressing gown. Blue light from the police car outside strobed the hall.

In the lounge, he'd listened in silence as Tim had stuttered his way through what had happened.

He'd shaken his head when Tim had come to the end. 'Oh, son,' he'd said at last in a broken voice. 'How could you?' It had been his only pronouncement but he didn't need to say any more. Their father's crushing disappointment in his son cut Tim to the quick, Anna knew.

Now, Anna lay on her bed, hands behind her head, and listened to Chopin, music that helped her cry. She thought about Mrs Taylor and imagined her in a coffin, imagined the slow procession down the aisle, the quiet sobbing.

She'd been like a second mother, after Anna had lost her own. A still, calm presence in the Taylors' house, quietly organising and supporting, cooking and baking. She'd always seemed to have time. She'd been the only one in the house, perhaps the only one in Anna's life, who listened more than she talked. Anna had no idea how they'd carry on without her.

Some weeks later, Anna watched Lily leave the house. Lily looked tired, her steps slow. Anna knew exactly where she was going.

An hour later, Anna was standing on the pavement outside the music school, waiting. It was cold. She kept watch determinedly, hands thrust into her pockets, nose red raw with biting wind.

Lily saw her at once, as soon as she stepped out onto the pavement after her piano lesson.

They simply locked eyes, weighing each other up.

I wouldn't blame her, Anna thought, *if she turned her back on me and stalked off or if she screamed at me, if she told me to leave her alone, said she never wanted to see me again. Maybe that's what I'd do too, if it were the other way around.*

Lily ducked her head. Her hand swept back a lock of falling hair and tucked it behind her ear, such a familiar gesture. Then she carefully crossed the road to Anna.

'I thought I'd take a coffee down to the park,' Anna said. Her ears thumped with blood. 'Want one?'

Lily shrugged. 'Alright.'

She fiddled with her phone while Anna stopped off at a local café and bought two takeaway coffees, then they fell into step, walking in silence, warming their hands on the cups, passing the new mothers with slings and prams, heading down to the weir.

There, they huddled together in the cold on a bench, overlooking the fast-flowing water. The river was in spate, the water hurtling past, crashing across the stones in a flush of foam. Further up the river, the humped snake of Otley's medieval bridge crossed the water.

'I wasn't sure you'd come.' Anna's breath made steamy puffs in the cold air. Dragon's breath, they used to call it when they were children. It mingled with the rising steam from her coffee and dispersed lazily.

'Neither was I.'

Anna swallowed hard. 'How are things?'

Lily gave her a caustic glance. 'Bit of a stupid question?'

Anna flushed. 'OK.'

Lily couldn't answer at once. Finally, she said, 'Not great.' She bit down on her lip. 'It's grim. Not just for me but Dad. George. Everyone cries all the time.' She gulped in air. 'I miss her so much.'

Anna reached a hand and put it on her friend's arm. 'I'm so

sorry. Really. We all are.' She said gently: 'I wanted to come to the funeral. Dad wouldn't let me.'

Lily shook her head, numb with remembering. She put the coffee cup to her mouth and tried to steady herself to drink. The plastic lid juddered on her teeth.

Anna said, 'Tim's in such a state. He's so sorry, you know that, don't you? He loved your mum. We all did. If we could only—'

'But we can't, can we?' It was a bitterness Anna had never heard in her friend's voice before.

They sat in silence for a while, side by side, watching the angry torrent of the river. Beyond the weir, ducks flew in low, riding the currents of air, then landed, legs extended, with a rush. Behind them, in the park, the shrieks drifted across of an excited young child throwing food for them.

Lily said, 'George hates him. Tim. I'm sorry.' She raised her eyes to look across the water. 'Sad, isn't it? They were such good mates.'

Anna didn't know what to say. Fear bloomed in her chest. She hardly knew this Lily, so cold and hard. It wasn't like her.

Lily said, 'George wants Tim to pay for it. Prison, ideally. He was furious when the coroner said accidental death. He stormed off and got drunk.' She hesitated, her eyes focused far off on the churning foam. 'He and Dad aren't speaking. Dad says we have to accept it was an accident. That blaming Tim won't help anyone. His way of coping, I guess.'

Anna tried to breathe. 'What about you? Do you think he should go to prison?'

Lily shrugged. 'Well, Dad's right. It won't bring her back.' She sipped at her coffee, her eyes on the rushing water. 'I try to think what she'd say. She loved Tim. You know how big she was on forgiveness, turning the other cheek. So, no, I don't see the point in ruining another life. It's bad enough already, isn't it?'

Yes, Anna thought, *it's bad enough.*

She thought back to the night of the accident. There were things she would never tell Lily. They were just too raw.

Anna remembered shivering in the darkness, crying, holding Mrs Taylor's limp fingers in her own and stroking her matted hair, while Tim had stood beside her, white with shock, his eyes glazed. He'd realised before she had that it was too late, that there was nothing they could do, that she was dead.

It had seemed so long before the police and ambulance arrived. They'd been tight-faced, angry, as if they too needed someone to blame. They'd put Mrs Taylor's body on a stretcher and covered it with a sheet. Their attitude to Tim had been strangely formal, as if they were already in court. They'd talked about his rights, breathalysed him. Even though he'd been in tears, he'd volunteered everything he could, willingly talked them through the whole thing, there and then. The black ice, the skid, the struggle to regain control. It had been a tragic accident, pure and simple.

The following morning, he'd been taken in for questioning, bundled into the back of a police car in full view of the neighbours. Anna had seen Mrs MacKay at the window, gawping. Afterwards, she couldn't help hearing the gossip on the bus, in the shops.

Some blamed drugs or drinking. She knew that wasn't true. Tim hadn't felt well that night. He'd had one small beer, that was all. Even if he'd been well, he'd never drink and drive. Their dad had always drummed that into them. And he never did drugs. Ever. Tim was just too responsible.

For a few days, they'd thought he'd be charged with death by dangerous driving and face jail. Their father had hired a lawyer from Bendons to represent Tim. Soon, it sounded as if the prosecution might have shifted its ground to the still serious but lesser charge of death by careless driving. Finally, once the coroner's verdict was announced, the idea of a formal prosecution was quietly dropped for good.

That's when, in its place, the informal prosecution had started. The shouts and whispers in the street, the harassment, the angry letters to the local paper about a teenage driver getting away scot-free when he'd taken an innocent woman's life.

Tim had held his head up and tried to weather it all. He'd carried on going to the bank each day as usual, ignoring the taunts, coming home alone and shutting himself away in his room.

But, days after the coroner's verdict, Tim had gone out to one of the pubs in the centre of town, a popular hangout with the teen crowd, and hadn't come home.

By midnight, long after the pubs had closed, Anna and her father, really worried now, had started to ring round his friends. They'd all had the same story: Tim had been in for a few drinks, then decided to head home. He'd never made it.

They'd found him, finally, slumped by the side of the road. His nose was crooked and his lip bloody, one tooth broken and one knocked clean out. All he would say was that he'd been jumped from behind. No idea who they were. He seemed almost resigned, as if he felt he'd deserved the beating, as if he felt cleansed by it.

They hadn't involved the police. Tim kept saying he didn't want trouble, as if it were still possible to avoid it. He didn't want to make things worse.

Now, Lily stretched out her legs and gave Anna a searching look. 'Look, I heard what happened to Tim. It wasn't George. You know that, right? He was home all evening.'

Anna didn't look at her. She wanted to believe her. She just wasn't sure she could.

25

Anna and Lily slowly fell back into being friends. There was a new wariness between them for a while. A fragility. It wasn't easy. If Anna went across to the Taylors' house, George hardly spoke to her. If Lily came to Anna's, she ignored Tim.

Anna watched Lily grieve. Once, she found Lily crouched on the floor of her parents' wardrobe, holding her mother's coat and dresses to her face, inhaling the traces of her still caught there in the fabric, crying, then afraid to cry in case she washed them clean of her. Lily wanted to keep everything: her mother's shoes, dresses, blouses and skirts, trousers and jumpers, right down to her scarves and gloves, every piece.

Anna knew too that the only person really capable of comforting Lily, of setting her broken-hearted seventeen-year-old daughter back on her feet, was the person she'd just lost. Her mother's own death was the first hurt in Lily's life that her mother couldn't love her through. Dr Taylor seemed to withdraw into himself, spending long hours at the surgery, then burying himself at home in practicalities. Anna and Lily tried to help as he struggled to manage all the domestic tasks Lily's mother had once performed with such quiet competence: the laundry, cleaning, shopping and cooking.

They sensed Mrs Taylor's presence every time they stooped to the freezer to lift out one of her carefully labelled meals or loaded dirty clothes into the washing machine. It was as though, if they could turn quickly enough, they might just catch her there, smiling as she watched.

As for George, he was lost to them, angry, largely absent and often drunk.

Anna was the one who tried to step in to save Lily. She sat in Lily's room with her for hours. Despite her cumbersome movements, increasingly pregnant with Cassie, Anna sat beside her friend on the floor, hunched against the bed, for hours, her arm firmly round Lily's shoulders, patting her, stroking her, soothing her. It was as if she became a mother to Lily, a pale substitute, before she became one to Cassie.

Some weekends, Anna forced Lily to go out with her, just to take a walk on the Chevin or down by the weir. They lost themselves in gazing on the churning, frothing waters.

Once, Lily turned to her with red-rimmed eyes and said, 'I'm so sorry. I didn't know. I didn't understand.'

Anna knew what she meant. They'd both been children when Anna's mother died. Of course, Lily hadn't understood the pain of it. The sheer physical pain of grief.

By May, their end of school exams loomed. They took to studying together, side by side, in one of their bedrooms. Anna, only weeks from her due date, struggled to get comfortable. On the eve of their first paper, they revised in Anna's room. Neither of them could concentrate.

Anna looked up from her books. 'Tim's going away.'

Lily considered this. 'Away? Where?'

'London.' Anna could hardly believe it herself. 'As soon as the baby's born.'

Lily gave her a careful look. 'Why?'

'He hates his job in the bank. He says he'll get something better down there.'

Lily didn't reply to that. They both knew that his job wasn't the real reason Tim wanted to leave. It had been brewing since the accident.

Anna understood too that Lily would be relieved. Lily had tried so hard not to hate Tim. She'd tried not to blame him. But she still didn't want to see him, there, across the street, day after day. The reality was inescapable: he was alive and Lily's mother was dead and, accident or not, he'd killed her.

'Ow.' Anna reached for Lily's hand and placed it on the hard mound of her stomach.

Lily felt the kicks and smiled. 'Definitely a footballer.'

'She'd better stay put until the exams are over,' Anna said. Lily's hand was warm and comforting on her bump. 'It'll be strange without Tim. Just be Dad and me. And the baby.'

Lily shook her head. 'And me.'

They smiled at each other.

'And you,' Anna said.

Lily's eyes fell to her books. She was sick of revising. The words started to blur. She sensed that Anna too was struggling to concentrate. She thought instead about the baby.

'Are you really not going to tell him?' she said quietly. It was a risk, even mentioning him. It was just hard not to. Anna and Mike had been so close. He'd always seemed devoted to her. Lily still found it hard to believe that he'd broken it off with Anna so abruptly in September, right before he'd left for university. She wondered if his parents had something to do with it. His mother, especially. Lily had the feeling she'd never approved of Anna.

Anna said sharply, 'We're not in touch. I've told you.'

Lily leaned in closer. 'Even so. He's got responsibilities.' She saw Anna's face cloud but ploughed on regardless. 'And even if you two aren't in touch, well, he still needs to know he's a dad.'

'I don't want to talk about him.' Anna glared. 'And neither should you.'

She turned her eyes to her books and gently stroked her bump, thinking about the baby who, she was determined, must never know her father.

26

NOW

Anna

Anna came home late the next day.

The path, from gate to front door, seemed impossibly long. Her hand shook as she fumbled with her key in the lock, rattling it against the metal.

From inside, Tim appeared, pulling the door open, and she stumbled inside.

'You alright?' Tim held her by the shoulders, studying her.

She saw the concern in his face and realised how she must look. The throbbing in her head spiked. She thought she was going to cry, then she made an effort and collected herself.

He drew her properly into the house and closed the door. 'What happened?'

She shook her head, waving the question away, at least for now. 'Is she OK?'

'Cassie? Fine.' He helped her through the hall to the bottom of the stairs. 'Up in her room.'

Anna went straight up. Cassie's door was propped open and, for a few seconds, Anna paused on the landing and looked in on her daughter, unseen. Cassie was lounging about in her cat onesie, sitting cross-legged on the floor, her back against the edge of the bed, hair falling forward over a book. Something in Anna's body softened and relaxed. This was what mattered, Cassie. Nothing else.

Cassie suddenly became aware of the shadow on the landing and she looked up and jumped. 'Mum! You scared me.'

Anna went in to sit beside her on the floor and reached an arm round her daughter's shoulders, drawing her close.

'I thought you weren't coming back!' Cassie, letting go, burst into noisy tears. She buried her wet face in Anna's shoulder. Anna imagined the strange smells she must have carried back with her from the police station. Disinfectant and cheap, sour coffee, stale sweat and fried food.

'Of course, I came back. I always come back, don't I?' Anna rocked her as she cried. 'You never have to worry about that.'

'But why?' Cassie struggled to speak through her sobs. 'Why did they take you away like that? Are you going to prison? I've missed you so much.'

'It's OK.' Anna tried to keep her voice steady. 'Everything's going to be fine.'

Cassie pulled away and turned red eyes to her. 'Promise?'

She forced a smile. 'Promise.' What else could she say? 'You need to settle down and get some sleep.' Anna smoothed her daughter's hair. 'Come on, now. It's late.'

She fell to stroking Cassie's back through the duvet with slow, rhythmical rounds. It was the way Cassie had loved to be soothed to sleep when she was little and couldn't settle. Gradually she felt Cassie's muscles slacken and her breathing stretch and deepen.

When Cassie was calm, Anna kissed her goodnight and traipsed wearily downstairs to find Tim bustling about the kitchen.

'Have you eaten?'

Anna shrugged. 'Half a stale sandwich, if you call that eating.'

Tim didn't answer. He lifted a pan off the stove and drained the pasta.

Anna looked round and saw a bowl of grated cheese, beaten egg and chopped ham standing on the counter, ready to add. She shook her head. 'Look, I'm not sure—'

'You need to try,' he said, pre-empting her. 'You don't have to finish it.'

She let her shoulders fall a little. It was a relief to have someone take care of her.

She stood in silence, too tired to move, as he tossed it all back into the pan and stirred it vigorously over the heat. She wondered when he'd learned to cook, even basic dishes like this one. If some girlfriend in London had taught him, someone he'd never talked about. It hadn't been in this kitchen, anyway.

Their father had tried so hard in those first years after their mother died. She remembered him struggling to make home-made pizza or pancakes at the weekends and, on Christmas Day, to produce a proper turkey dinner with all the trimmings. It was done with so much love but she'd sensed his frustration that he'd never measure up, that he could never be both parents to them, never replace their mother and everything she'd been. He'd seemed always on the brink of despair.

In the end, he'd given up in the kitchen and they'd lived on sandwiches and ready meals until Anna had started to learn to cook at school and taken control.

'I've opened a bottle of wine,' Tim said as he spooned the pasta into two bowls. 'Thought you might need a glass.'

'Maybe, just one.' Any more than that and she'd be asleep.

They carried it all through to the lounge and she did her best to eat, conscious that Tim was surreptitiously observing her.

Finally, he asked, 'Can you talk about it?'

She rested her fork against the edge of the bowl and thought of the detective's stern face in the interview room, his piercing brown eyes barely leaving hers. Of the interview room itself with its shabby, institutional chairs and stained table and pulsing artificial light. That had been as bad as his probing questions.

'They haven't charged me. That's something. I'm on bail. I've got to go back tomorrow.' She swallowed hard. 'They locked me in a cell, Tim.'

'Oh.' He stared at her.

'Is that what they did to you? You never said.' She felt her mouth tremble. 'You never talked about it.'

Tim shook his head. 'Never mind about that. That's history. Tell me what happened.'

'They seem to think there are inconsistencies. In my statement.'

Tim frowned. 'Inconsistencies?'

'I don't think they believe me.' It was frightening, saying that aloud. It had been the thought in her head all the time she'd been there, during the long waits in the locked cell and in the interview room itself. *They don't believe me. They think I'm lying.*

'What don't they believe?' Tim looked confused. 'I mean, you told them everything already, didn't you?'

'Of course, I did.' The tines of the fork drummed against the crockery. She set it down on her tray with a clatter. 'But they kept going over and over the details. Interrogating me. I thought I'd never get out of there.'

Are you sure, Ms King? You're quite sure that's what you saw? And then what happened? Think carefully now. Tell me again. Is there anything you'd like to add, anything at all?

'Was the lawyer any use?'

She nodded. 'Thanks for finding him. He sat in with me. He thinks maybe they're just stumped and trying to get me to come up with something else. But there isn't anything else. They already know it all.'

Tim pushed his bowl away, clearly unsettled. 'But what sort of inconsistencies?'

She looked lost for a moment. 'I don't know exactly. That's just what the lawyer told me.' She looked round the room at the framed photographs of Cassie as a baby, as a toddler, as an infant in brand-new school uniform. At the picture she loved of her father with a young Cassie on his lap. It was all so familiar, so safe. It made her want to cry. 'Apparently, there's no trace of the man I saw running away.'

Tim snorted. 'That just means they can't find him. Their bosses must be putting the screws on.'

'Maybe.' She didn't know how much to say. She was too frightened. 'The lawyer said there were people waiting at the bus stop round the corner, in Richmond Road. They've spoken to some of them. They should have seen him run past.'

'And they didn't?'

She shook her head. 'They didn't.'

Tim pulled a face. 'It's hardly conclusive, is it? It was dark. Maybe they didn't notice. People don't. Maybe the bus arrived just before he came out and they missed him.'

'Maybe.' She sipped the wine and felt the alcohol spread, warm, through her body. 'There's a CCTV camera too, outside Brown's on the next corner. That didn't show him either.'

Tim opened his mouth to speak, then closed it again. Finally, he said, 'Don't let them rattle you, Anna. They've just hit a dead end.'

Anna took a deep breath. 'And they can't find DNA in the house. I mean, from anyone apart from me and the family and the cleaner. They went on about that.'

'So? He wore gloves. He's a burglar, for God's sake. He'd know better than to leave his DNA all over the place.' Tim leaned in and touched her hand. 'Anna, don't look so frightened. It sounds to me as if they're stuck and trying to shake you up, just in case there's something else you can dredge up that might help. It's what they do. Remember?'

They exchanged a tight look. Yes, of course she remembered.

He went on. 'You've nothing to feel guilty about. It's just bad luck that you saw something strange over there and headed into the house. I wish to God you hadn't, believe me. You were just trying to do the right thing. They should be giving you a medal, not frightening you.'

'I know.' In her mind, she saw again the shadowy bedroom, the spilled blood, the horror of Dr Taylor's face. It was a scene she wished she'd never witnessed. 'It just' – she glanced across at her brother, feeling his eyes on her – 'it just brings it all back, you know? Being back in that awful police station. The way they look at you, as if they know something you don't. The sense of helplessness.' She paused, remembering. 'You know what I mean, you of all people.'

Tim's brow furrowed. 'They didn't bring any of that up, did they?'

She shook her head. 'It's there in our records though, isn't it? Yours, anyway.'

He shrugged. 'It's never really gone away, has it? I thought, if I came back now, that people would have moved on, that I could make a fresh start. But...'

She frowned. 'Not everyone's like George.'

'Maybe they are, though.' Tim gazed down at his hands. 'I've applied for so many jobs, Anna. All kinds, in shops and restaurants and local businesses. I'm over-qualified for most of them. Some are minimum wage. But I'm not even getting interviews. Maybe I'm not going to.'

Anna's forehead creased with concern. 'It's tough out there. I know it's hard. You've just got to keep trying. Something will come along.'

'Maybe.' He didn't sound convinced. He raised his eyes to her. 'Honestly, you don't think I should just leave? I won't blame you if you do. I feel as if I've jinxed you and Cassie, brought all these bad things into your lives. What with the murder and then those threatening messages and Cassie getting hurt and now this, this detective harassing you. It's not right.'

Anna leaned over and gave his arm a squeeze. 'You're not leaving,' she said. 'Don't say that again. Please. We need you right now, both of us.'

More than ever, she thought.

He turned away from her but she saw him wipe his eyes roughly with the back of his hand.

'What if it's all going to fall apart?' he said, his voice shaking. 'What if they start digging for dirt, bringing out files on us both, investigating all over again? I don't think I could stand it.' He turned back to her with a look of desperation on his face. 'What if they find out? Then what, Anna?'

27

Lily

I rarely check my phone during the day.

It's against school policy, and even if it weren't, it's too much of a distraction when I'm at school and need to focus on teaching. So it's only at lunchtime, when I'm in the staff room, that I switch it on and find the missed calls and messages.

Tim has always been such a calm person, even as a teenager. Steady and reliable. I've rather envied Anna for that. George was always moody, even before the accident. It's only been more recently, when I've looked back at those troubled years with adult eyes, that I've realised how desperately he grieved for Mum. Those late nights, the drinking, the fights were more than just a normal part of growing up, they were a sign of a young man struggling to cope with emotional pain.

Now, though, in his message, Tim sounds frantic.

Please could you call me? Sorry. His voice is breathless. I imagine him walking briskly as he speaks. *We've had another threat. First thing this morning. About Cassie. Anna was going to take it to the police but then—* He breaks off. In the pause which follows, I can make out the blare and rumble of traffic, the quick blast of a horn cutting through. He picks up the thread again: *Anyway, I just wondered, could you, you know, keep a bit of an eye on Cassie? I've just followed her in, she's got to school OK, but I'm worried. And if there's anything, you know, anything unusual, please, well, just make sure she's safe, would you? And call me. If you can.* Another pause, then a final, hasty: *Sorry.*

He picks up as soon as I dial his number.

'Lily?' He sounds panicked by the fact I've called. 'Is Cassie OK?'

I blink. 'I think so. I mean, she's in school, isn't she? I can check on her, if you like.'

'Would you? Please?' His voice has a strange echo.

'Where are you?' I get to my feet, abandoning my salad and coffee, and head for the staff room door, away from listening ears.

'Leeds. In the police station.' He's lowered his voice, suddenly muffled, as if his hand's cupped round the receiver. 'Anna's in there, with her lawyer. I haven't been allowed to see her. I don't know what's going on.'

I hunch against the doorway, struggling to hear, my brain trying to catch up. 'They're still questioning her?'

'Yes.' His hard breath reverberates down the line. 'They don't believe her. That's what Anna says. What she said about walking in on your father, about seeing that guy run off. I don't know. It's the truth. Of course, it is. But they're picking holes in it, putting pressure on her.'

My food churns in my stomach. 'But why wouldn't they believe her?'

'I don't know.' He stops. He seems to need to collect himself. 'Do you think they're, you know, punishing her?'

'Punishing her?' Two teachers pass me with mugs of tea, heading out to playground duty. I shrink into the wall. 'Why would they do that?'

'To teach her a lesson?' He sounds all over the place. 'Because she said she didn't want to help with the case anymore. She said she might not agree to testify if they charged someone and it came to trial. Maybe they're putting pressure on her, showing her who's boss.'

'They can't do that.' I find myself shaking my head to the wall. My eyes fall on the thin cracks in the paintwork. 'That's harassment. Tim, I'm sure they wouldn't—'

'Why, then?' He sounds desperate.

I don't know. I try to imagine him, sitting hunched on a plastic chair in a corner of the deserted waiting room, a police officer at the desk keeping a wary eye on him.

'Maybe you should go for a walk,' I tell him. 'Go and get a coffee. You need to keep calm, OK? That's the best way to help her.'

There's a long pause. Finally, he says, 'And Cassie – you'll keep an eye on her? We've had hate mail. Did Anna tell you? Threatening letters, targeting Cassie as well. I'm worried. No one can get to her while she's in school, can they?'

'Of course not.' I turn and look over the sleepy staff room, the teachers, several close to retirement, sitting over their cross-words and books, their mugs of tea and sandwiches. The only sounds are the low murmur of chat from a couple of teachers huddled by the tea-making area and the distant hum of the play-ground, punctuated by the shrieks and screams of a tribe of young children let loose.

'I'll go and find her right now and make sure she's OK, alright?'

Tim says at once, 'You'll call me if—'

'Yes, but she'll be fine. Honestly. You worry about Anna. I'll look after Cassie.'

Some of the panic seems to fall from his voice. 'Thank you.'

I think ahead. 'How about I walk home with her after school? I'll take her for a treat somewhere.'

'Would you?'

'Of course.'

After we've ended the call, I clear up the remains of my lunch and head off to find Cassie. It doesn't take long. There she is, hanging out with a group of other year six girls, tearing round the playground, swerving and skidding.

She looks pleased when I go over to her. She likes it when I treat her as more than just another pupil. It makes her feel special.

Her eyes shine when I ask her if she'll come to my classroom when school ends and hint that maybe we could head off to a café together.

That's the easy part done. I send Tim a quick text, confirming that Cassie is safe and well and that I've arranged to take her out somewhere later, then I'll personally see her to their front door.

I switch off my phone and stow it away in my desk, then try to turn my mind to the lessons to come.

I can't concentrate. My hands shake as I stack the piles of exercise books.

My head is bursting with thoughts of Anna, imagining her confused and frightened, being forced to answer questions in some dingy interview room. I think about Tim, trapped in the no man's land of the drab waiting room, frantic but powerless to help her.

I know them both too well. I know what a painful price they'll both be paying, how much of the past horror of the accident all this will now be reawakening.

The exercise books topple and crash to the floor.

I grope my way to the staff toilets and am violently sick.

28

Cassie is all smiles when she comes into my classroom at the end of the school day.

I'm in the process of stashing some creative writing books in my bag to mark later and making a final circuit of the empty classroom, picking up discarded pieces of paper which haven't yet made it to the bin and gathering up any stray work which needs to be kept.

I've also just checked my phone. Tim sent me a text during the afternoon to say Anna's been allowed home and he's taking her back now.

Cassie sits on the edge of my desk and swings her legs, humming to herself. Usually, I love this time of the day. A faint smell of board marker and glue, of felt-tipped pens and wax crayons hangs in the air. There's a special feel to a classroom which has been full of children all day and is now at rest. The room seems to carry an echo of all that energy, slowly releasing it into the quiet.

Today, though, I can't feel it. There's no peace. Somehow, I got through the afternoon, my stomach roiling with acid, my head dull, my nerves jangling. If the pupils were aware that I wasn't myself, they didn't comment. Now all I really want to do is to crawl home, draw the curtains, switch off my phone and sink into bed. I suddenly feel so weary, body and soul. *The long day's task is done and we must sleep.*

'Where are we going?' Cassie beats her heels lightly against the wood. 'Are you still Miss Taylor or can I call you Auntie Lily now?'

'I think Auntie Lily, don't you?' I gather up another abandoned pencil and push a handful of them into the nearest plastic tray.

Cassie nods. 'We are still in school,' she says, debating the issue with herself. 'So technically, I suppose you are still a teacher. But on the other hand, the school day is over and we are going out, aren't we?'

'We are.' I reach for my coat and shrug it on. 'Come on, then.'

She jumps off the desk and bounces lightly on her heels, full of energy, beating me to the door.

I try my best to pull myself together. 'So I thought maybe a coffee for me and for you – a milkshake?'

She claps her hands in glee. 'Yay!' Her eyes sparkle as she sees how far she can push me. 'With whipped cream?'

'Sure, why not?'

Tim's anxiety has infected me. I reach for Cassie's hand as we walk and hold it tightly. She leads me to the new burger and ice-cream place which has just opened on Crossgate, midway between the school and home. I love treating Cassie. It's one of my great pleasures in life, spending time with her, seeing how her eyes sparkle when she's excited.

Cassie chooses a place at the front counter, facing the street, and clambers up onto one of the tall stools there while I place our order: the chocolate chip milkshake, piled with whipped cream, for her and a coffee for me.

'So, how was school today?'

Cassie wields her straw and long-handled spoon furiously. Already, her lips are smeared with traces of chocolate milk, and a blob of cream decorates the end of her nose. 'Fine.'

I wait. Cassie never responds well to questioning. I've learned to bide my time and be patient until she decides she wants to talk.

Once she's made inroads into the milkshake, she chatters about how much homework she has and the part she really wants in the school play but doesn't think she'll get. Then about the lad in her class who was cheeky, then, later, threw his pencil sharpener at another child and was sent out of class. She makes a show of being sorry for the teacher for having to deal with such naughtiness, but I catch a gleam of delight at the drama of it all.

I recognise that. It's the same barely disguised glee, the same titillating delight in someone else's tragedy that I've seen in the faces of the people who've gone out of their way to walk their dogs past our house in the days following my father's death. From the window, I watch their pace slow as they approach, peering carefully, shaking their heads and murmuring together.

Murdered!

In his own bed, apparently.

I heard it was a burglary gone wrong.

Awful! Poor things.

They pretend to be shocked and sympathetic when, all along, their eyes hold the same glint as Cassie's now.

Later, Cassie's appetite sated, we sit on for a while, watching the street. The traffic's building, the rows of cars stretching back from the traffic lights, first from the school run, now because office workers are starting to head home.

Cassie says quietly, 'I've met my dad.' She pauses, then says proudly, as if his name is a hoarded secret, 'Mike.'

I stare. 'You've met him?'

She turns her eyes to the milkshake, coy with excitement, and nods. She can't stop herself from grinning.

'When?' I can't help adding: 'Does your mum know?'

She manages to pull her features into a more sombre expression at that. 'Yeah, Mum found out. He asked for my number, see, and messaged me and she saw. She wasn't too pleased.'

My heart pounds. I can just imagine. Anna must have hit the roof.

'That's not cool, Cassie.' I give her a stern look. 'You shouldn't have gone behind your mum's back like that. And neither should he.'

I think about the way Mike hung around the school gates, waiting to waylay me. Pestering me like that is one thing but a ten-year-old girl? I frown to myself.

'He's nice,' she says simply. 'He tried to go through Mum but she wouldn't talk to him. He just wants to get to know me, that's all.'

That's all. Right. 'You need to listen to your mum on this one, Cassie. Really. She's got enough to worry about at the moment.'

Cassie slides her eyes round to check mine. 'You mean the police stuff?'

'Yeah, the police stuff.'

She turns her attention back to her milkshake. I fix my eyes on a young woman outside, struggling along the pavement with a screaming baby in a buggy and a toddler riding on the backboard, his head and shoulders between her pushing hands, as straight and perky as a meerkat.

'He's my dad, right?' Cassie says at last. 'He just wants to be friends.'

I sigh. I don't want to be caught in the middle of all this. 'It hasn't been easy for your mum, you know. Being a single parent. She's always put you first. Maybe you need to respect how she feels about this.'

Cassie pulls a face. 'Can't you just tell me about him? Please. No big deal but, like, how they met and stuff?'

I try to imagine what she's feeling. All these years, she's been told her father was dead, then suddenly Mike turns up and flatters her with his attention and no one will talk to her about him.

'Strictly between us, right?'

She nods solemnly.

I take a deep breath. 'Well, your mum met him at a disco,' I say. 'I was there too. We were sixteen. He and his friend came over to chat us up, ask us to dance.'

Cassie's eyes light. 'Just like that?'

I nod, remembering. 'Just like that. He and your mum hit it off at once. I never saw his friend again. He said he'd call me but then he didn't.'

'Sorry.'

I laugh. 'That's OK. He was nothing special.'

'But Mike was?'

I think back to how young we were then, how naïve, how full of hope for the future. 'Your mum really liked him. They started going out together and, well, they just clicked. They enjoyed the same things, you know. Going for long walks on the moors and seeing films and, I don't know, talking. They were always talking...' I hesitate, remembering. 'They just seemed very happy.'

'Were they, you know, in love?' Cassie cranes forward, listening closely.

I nod. 'Yes, I really think they were.'

She lets out a held breath. 'That's so cute.' She thinks it through. 'Why didn't they stay together, then? Was it, you know, because of me?'

'You mustn't think that. They were just very young,' I say, treading carefully. 'You know how old your mum was when she had you?'

'Seventeen.' Cassie has it off pat. 'That's not young.'

'It's pretty young to be a mum. She was still at school when she found out you were on the way, and Mike, well, he'd just gone off to university. It wasn't the right time for either of them to settle down.'

I wait a moment, judging her reaction. She's frowning slightly to herself, taking it all in.

I say, 'It was a surprise, when she found out she was going to have a baby.'

I remember the panic when she missed her period. I went with her into Leeds to buy a pregnancy test at the big chemist there. I sat outside the cubicle in the public toilets while she used it. When she came out, brandishing the stick with its blue line, she was white with shock.

I look at Cassie. She's watching me closely.

I carry on. 'But, right from the start, she wanted you so much.' It's what Cassie needs to hear but it is also true. It wasn't what Anna had planned but she was fiercely protective from the beginning of her tiny, growing child. 'She was determined to look after you, even though she knew it wouldn't be easy. And that's what she did. Your grandpa helped. And I tried to help too, when I could.'

Cassie looks puzzled. 'Why didn't Mike help? Didn't he want me?'

I sip my cooling coffee and stall for time. 'That's where it gets really complicated,' I say at last. 'He didn't even know about you. All these years until now, he didn't know you existed.'

'That's what he said.' Cassie turns on me, her eyes intense. 'It's true, then. Mum didn't tell him. No wonder he never came to see me. Why didn't she tell him?'

I focus on the kaleidoscope of passing people sliding to and fro on the pavement outside the window. It's a question I've pondered many times in the last ten years, one Anna always refused to discuss: *Why didn't she tell him?*

'Only she knows for sure,' I say. 'Maybe she'll talk to you about it when you're older, when she feels ready.' I take a deep breath. 'You know what I think? I think they'd just broken up and she was sad and hurt, too sad to want to talk to him. But she's never told me that. I might be wrong.'

'That's stupid.' Cassie considers this. 'If they'd stayed together, my whole life would be different.'

I reach out and put my hand on her shoulder. 'Relationships are complicated,' I say. 'Love can be messy. Sometimes, people make mistakes and box themselves into corners and can't get out of them again.' I try to tell from her expression if she understands. 'It's hard to explain.'

She doesn't answer. I sense her mind working, trying to figure it out.

I push my coffee cup aside and make to climb down from the stool.

'I think we'd better head home, don't you?'

'But what about now?' Cassie doesn't move, her forehead puckered. 'Do you think they still love each other?'

The question feels like a blow to the stomach. Cassie has a way of striking right at the heart of things, sometimes. Is it possible that there could still be something there between them, after ten years of hurt, ten years of silence?

I don't know Mike well enough to read him. Maybe. Maybe not.

And Anna? I'm just not sure. She felt deeply about him once, I know that. But she's stubborn. And she's suffered, struggling to care for a child she kept secret from him. She's more than proved herself capable of providing for Cassie, building up her retail business as well as being a great mother, but it hasn't been easy. I know that, more than anyone.

'I don't know, Cassie. It was a long time ago.' I scramble for her school bag and hand it to her. 'But I know one thing for certain – your mum loves you to bits. And she always will. That love's not going anywhere.'

On the way out, I say, 'You won't tell her, will you, that we talked about all this stuff? She might be cross with me. OK?'

Cassie nods, her face troubled. 'I'm worried about her. About Mum.'

Something in the quiet intensity of her tone stops me in my tracks. 'Are you? What makes you say that?'

'I think she's frightened.'

My heart skips a beat. I want to tell her she's wrong, she's imagining things. But it strikes me that she's right.

I say, as evenly as I can, 'Why would she be frightened?'

'I don't know.' Cassie frowns. 'But I think it's something to do with—'

She breaks off and I see the embarrassment in her face, the sudden awkwardness as she realises what she's about to say. I sense it's about my dad. My poor father and the brutal, senseless way he was killed.

I steady myself and say gently, 'Something to do with the person who killed my dad?'

'Yes.' She nods gratefully. 'Sorry. But yes, something to do with him.'

29

Tim

The next day, Tim took the car out early and drove off into the Dales. The sky was heavy with rain and the muddy paths along the River Wharfe were deserted. He strode out, filling his lungs with the cold moor air. The wind buzzed in his ears, a low backdrop for the sound of the stumbling, bleating sheep he passed in the steep fields, rising steadily from the water, and the occasional splash of landing ducks.

The smells of bracken and heather, of scrub grass and damp sheep's wool took him right back to his teenage years. He and George used to mess about in the Dales together for hours, cycling out into the villages, then hiking and climbing and, when the weather was half-decent, picnicking. It was strange, coming back. It felt at times like bumping into his younger self, as if he'd found a familiar friend. The intensity of remembering was both painful and comforting.

When the drizzle started, he headed back to the car and started the drive through the gently undulating hills back to

Otley, stopping off at the supermarket on the edge of town to stock up.

Riverside Road was calm and quiet when he returned around lunchtime. He parked outside the house and started lifting out the groceries, gathering them on the pavement.

He let his thoughts wander. He was looking forward to having the house to himself for the rest of the day, with Cassie at school and Anna back at work today.

The managers in her two shops had done a brilliant job while Anna had been distracted by Dr Taylor's death and all the drama which had unravelled since. But she needed to get back there now, to sit down with the staff, one by one, go through the books and address whatever problems might have bubbled up in her absence. It would do her good, he thought. She was a smart businesswoman and, besides, she needed a dose of normal life.

He heaved the last bulging carrier bag out of the boot and made for the front door. A cat streaked past, flattening itself against the paving stones. He watched it jump the fence and tip down the other side, disappearing from sight.

I'll cook tarragon chicken, he thought as he let himself in, kicking the door closed behind him. He made himself a coffee, put the radio on, then set to work, washing the mud off the leeks and celery, then starting to dice them.

He still had the large kitchen knife in his hand when the front doorbell rang and he went to answer it.

'Is this a bad time?' Mrs MacKay squinted at the knife with concern. 'I won't be a minute.'

He managed a smile. 'Not at all,' he lied. 'Come on in.'

Mrs MacKay perched on the edge of the sofa cushion like a bird, hands folded in her lap, lightly twisting her wedding and engagement rings on her finger. He hardly remembered her husband. He'd died when Tim was still a young boy. He thought how long she'd lived alone now, a widow.

'Can I make you a cup of tea?'

She shook her head. 'I won't stay.' She seemed agitated, her eyes on the window, avoiding his face.

He waited, wondering what she had to say that could be so difficult.

'I don't like to tell tales, you know that,' she said at last. Her eyes darted to his, checking his reaction before she continued. 'I did pop round earlier but no one was in. It's probably nothing but if something has happened and I didn't mention it, well, I'd never forgive myself.'

Tim said gently, 'Mention what, Mrs MacKay?'

She let out a heavy breath. The rings sparkled as they turned. 'Cassie. This morning. I can't quite put my finger on it. But something was definitely off.'

'Cassie?' Tim felt his chest tighten. He'd told Anna he should follow Cassie in again that morning, just to keep an eye on her, but Anna had argued that they needed to keep things normal, that if Cassie spotted him, he'd just freak her out. He struggled to keep his tone even. 'She's at school today, Mrs MacKay.'

She tutted. 'I know. But, the thing is, I always see her safely down the road. From the window, I mean. I like to stand there with a cup of tea around eight and just see what's what in the street, all the comings and goings, and I always look out for Cassie. She's always on time, bless her. About ten past, hurrying past with her little rucksack to get the bus.'

Tim imagined Mrs MacKay in her window, watching the clock and twitching her curtains, taking note of the street. He looked at her pouched skin and neat, permed bob, at the carefully applied lipstick and powder, and thought of her keeping watch over them all.

'She's such a dear little thing,' Mrs MacKay was saying. 'And I do worry, after all these awful events, Dr Taylor's murder and that nasty rock through her window. I was in my sitting room, you know, when it happened. Heard it as clear as day.'

'So what happened this morning?' he prompted.

'She wasn't herself.' Mrs MacKay looked embarrassed. 'It's hard to explain. Normally, she's in a world of her own, you see. She talks to herself or sings, maybe. I can't quite hear. Sometimes she skips. But today, she seemed, well, agitated. Tense. Not her usual self at all. She kept looking round, as if she thought someone was following her.'

Tim frowned. 'Was anyone following her?'

'I don't know. Not that I could see.' Mrs MacKay looked flustered. 'But that's not all. At the end of the street, she always turns left, to get the number thirty-seven towards school. The bus stop is right there.'

Tim looked confused. 'And...?'

'And this morning, she turned right.' Mrs MacKay hunched forward, her shoulders tight. 'Towards the centre of Otley. She's never done that before.'

Tim locked eyes with her. A sense of foreboding chilled him. 'You're quite sure about that?'

'Completely sure.'

Tim tried to tamp down a rising sense of panic. They were talking about the far end of the street. This lady, close to seventy now, might not have seen clearly. Or there could be all sorts of reasons that Cassie might vary her route a little.

'Maybe she wanted to buy something before school,' he said.

Mrs MacKay raised her eyebrows. 'Where would she do that?'

He nodded slowly. Mrs MacKay was right. There were no shops along that road, not until you reached the market square.

Mrs MacKay said quietly, 'I thought maybe someone was waiting there for her, on the other side of the junction. Someone could have called her across to them. Someone she knew.'

Tim raked his hands through his hair. 'Wait.' This was too much. 'Let me call the school. They can confirm she's OK. That'll put our minds at rest, won't it?'

He searched for the number on his phone and called the main office. It took a few minutes for the office lady, grumpy about being disturbed, to check the computer. She stalled for a while about releasing personal information to Tim, rather than Cassie's mother, then begrudgingly confirmed that no, Cassie wasn't in school today, she was marked on the class register as absent.

Tim ended the call. Mrs MacKay, her eyes on his face, didn't need to ask.

His mind raced. He dialled Cassie's mobile but the number rang out, unanswered. He sent her a short text, asking her to call him back, to say she was OK. It stayed unread.

Anna. He'd have to call her. Maybe she'd know where Cassie was. He shook his head. He doubted she'd have any more sense of why Cassie hadn't arrived at school than he did. She'd have told him if they had something unusual planned.

'There's another thing.' Mrs MacKay looked anxious. 'It might not mean anything. I don't want to get anyone into trouble. But I have been wracking my brains.'

'What?' Tim leaned in closer, all attention.

'Well, George, you know, George Taylor...'

'What about him?'

She lowered her voice to a whisper. 'He was acting very oddly last night. I saw him parked round the corner, half-hidden under that clump of trees in the avenue. It was about seven because I was just upstairs closing the bedroom curtains. I always like to do that before I settle down to watch television. I thought it was strange that he'd stopped there because the downstairs lights were on in the Taylors' house. I saw Lily going in earlier.'

She gave him a knowing look. 'Anyway, I kept an eye on

him. I've got a bird's eye view from up there. He waited until Lily went out, then hurried quietly round on foot and let himself into the house at the back. He was only in there maybe twenty minutes. He came out carrying a bag. A sort of kit bag. Canvas. Then he dashed back to the car and drove off again.'

Tim frowned. 'Maybe he just needed to collect something?'

Mrs MacKay shook her head. 'Then why go to all that trouble to hide until Lily had gone out?'

Tim shrugged. 'Maybe they'd had a row?'

Mrs MacKay pursed her lips. 'I'm telling you, he was up to no good. I saw his face when he passed under the streetlight. It had guilt written all over it. And then Cassie, this morning, acting so nervous...' She heaved herself to her feet. 'Anyway, I'll leave it with you. Let me know, would you, about Cassie? I'm very fond of that little girl. She's a love.'

Tim closed the door behind her and stood in the quiet of the hall, thinking.

If Mrs MacKay was right, why would George act so strangely? What might he have retrieved from the house after dark that he didn't want Lily to see? He stiffened. Could Mrs MacKay be right that it was linked to the fact that Cassie had now, apparently, disappeared?

Something slid horribly into place. He steadied himself against the door-frame. George had never forgiven him for his mother's death, he was sure of that. Tim had never been sure who'd jumped him from behind that night, not long after the accident, and beat him up, but he'd always suspected George.

Since he'd moved back here, he'd been braced for some sort of confrontation with him. Some fight. There'd been nothing. When they'd found themselves in the same room, George had simply acted as if Tim weren't there.

But maybe George was smarter than he used to be. Maybe he'd just been biding his time and he'd plotted another way of getting at Tim. By targeting one of the people Tim loved most in the world.

Tim thought of the crude warning notes through the letter-box, the rock through the window. Anna had assumed they'd come from the murderer. But what if Tim had been right in suspecting George of being behind them, taking advantage of the confusion and trying to punish Tim for what he'd done?

Tim reached for his coat and his car keys.

Anna didn't need to know yet that Cassie was missing from school. She'd go out of her mind. Maybe he had a chance of finding Cassie first and rescuing her.

If it wasn't already too late.

30

Anna

A giant hand was wrapped around her throat, squeezing.

Anna couldn't breathe. She fumbled her key in the latch, burst into the empty hall and ran through the house, calling, 'Cassie! Cassie, where are you?'

Silence. Dead and chilling. She raced upstairs and tore through the rooms. Her own crazed face, hair flying, leered at her from the bathroom mirror.

Back in Cassie's room, Anna stood by her daughter's rumpled bed, panting. She was at a loss. She'd sensed at once, as soon as she'd entered the house, that no one was here. She just hadn't wanted to believe it.

She staggered back downstairs. In the kitchen, groceries were strewn on the counter. A heap of vegetables lay by the chopping board, some already diced. She looked round, confused. Where was Tim? She pulled out her phone and tried his number again but, like Cassie's, it just rang out.

She'd been with the shop staff when the school office had called. She hadn't understood at first.

Just checking, they'd said. *Just wanted to make sure every-thing was alright.*

It had taken several moments for her to grasp what they were saying: that Cassie wasn't in school, that Tim had called them, asking about her, sounding anxious.

Standing there, in the empty kitchen, she felt the hand round her throat tighten. Cassie and Tim. The two people she loved most. Where were they? She blinked, trying to focus.

She knew Cassie had set out as normal that morning. Anna had kissed her goodbye and watched her head off down River-side Road. So, what had happened to prevent her arriving safely at school?

It came to her in a single stroke. Her hand reached for the counter and she steadied herself, forced herself to take deep breaths.

Of course. It makes perfect sense.

31

Anna knew the route backwards. She turned out of the street into the main road which led out of Otley centre and soon rose steeply as it climbed the Chevin.

Gradually, as she pulled away from the town, the houses became larger and grander, the shops more sparse. The densely packed streets gave way to fields, dotted with horses, and heavy wooden gates which led down rutted tracks to converted barns and farmhouses.

She and Mike used to walk it, hand in hand, when they would trek back to his parents' house on days when his mother needed her car. They would talk so much, so intently, that the distance would always shrink. Now she gripped the steering wheel, heart pounding, hearing the pump of blood in her ears.

It was the perfect place to hide a child, of course it was. Somewhere out of the way. Cassie would be all too willing. Anna imagined Mike pulling up beside her in his car and inviting her to hop in. Maybe he'd called it an adventure, just the two of them. Maybe he'd lied and pretended he'd spoken to Anna and she'd agreed. What child wouldn't be excited by an unexpected day off school with the man she thinks is her long-lost father?

A light drizzle pattered on the windscreen. Up on the hillside, the pale autumn sunlight slanted through patches of cloud, long fingers touching the dry-stone walls, the grazing sheep, horses and cows. She reached their gate, permanently propped open, just as she'd remembered it, and turned down the grassy, rutted track to the farmhouse.

She had to bang on the door for some time. Finally, shuffling footsteps sounded inside and locks scraped.

'Hello?' Mike's father's voice was quavering. He held the edge of the door firmly in both hands as if he were steadying himself against it as he peered out, blinking. He'd aged. His shoulders were stooped and his white hair stretched thinly over his scalp. He gazed at her with a puzzled frown, as if he were trying to place her. It had been a long time.

'I need to see Mike.' She spoke loudly, giving herself confidence. 'It's urgent.'

He seemed distracted, anxious. 'I'm afraid he's not here.'

From somewhere inside, behind him, a high, querulous voice called, 'Who is it now?'

Anna fixed him with a glare. 'Don't you remember me? Anna. Anna King.'

He hesitated. 'Anna?'

Something in his manner sparked a flare of anger. This was how they'd made her feel, all that time ago. Belittled, out of place, not good enough for their darling son. They'd hardly known her and yet they'd thought themselves so superior. And now they thought they had the right to interfere in her life, to have access to her child. They were wrong.

She stepped briskly forward, pushing her way past him into the hall. The smell reached for her. A stale scent of furniture polish and seasoned wood. It took her back in a heartbeat to being sixteen years old, sweaty-palmed and nervous, awkwardly perching on the edge of a chair in their uncluttered lounge, trying to eat a biscuit, sip tea and answer Mrs Adams's coolly polite questions without embarrassing herself.

'Excuse me, young lady!' Mr Adams, flustered, was still in the doorway, clutching the open door, as if he couldn't understand how she'd passed him. 'What on earth are you—?'

Anna stepped into the lounge. It was over-heated and sickly with an air of neglect. The side tables, which she'd remembered as so pristine, dotted only with coasters, were piled with old newspapers and books, dirty teacups and glasses, a clutter of discarded pens and pencils. There, sitting by the mantelpiece on a cushioned recliner, sat Mrs Adams. A shock of white hair. A powdered, plump face, unnaturally rounded by steroids. A glinting eye which she fixed on Anna, her gaze malevolent.

'What are you doing here?'

Anna wasn't sure if the old lady recognised her.

'Who are you, anyway? Where's my son?'

Anna braced herself. 'I'm looking for my daughter,' she said. 'I think Mike's taken her.'

She blinked rheumy eyes. 'What're you talking about? Your daughter? There's no one here. Just my son and my husband.' She screwed up her eyes, suspicious. 'If it's about the cleaning job, you're too late. It's gone.'

Anna scanned the room. It was smaller than she remembered and shabbier now. There was nowhere here to hide a ten-year-old girl. She turned, crossing the hall in a few fast paces and checking the kitchen, the pantry, the messy study, thick with dust and mildew now, and the small downstairs toilet. They were all empty.

Behind her, Mr Adams loomed, following her, objecting but fearful. Anna felt empowered by her own youth and strength.

'I'm warning you,' he said. 'If you don't leave this instant, I'll call the police.'

'Go ahead.' She gave him a pitying look. 'I think they'd be interested to know why I'm here.'

It was a bluff but it worked, at least for now. He hesitated, reached a hand for the wall and supported himself against it, breathing noisily.

She turned on her heel and headed at a trot up the grand staircase. She took a particular pleasure in it. In the past, the upper part of the house had been out of bounds to her. Mike's mother had made it clear that it was inappropriate for her son to entertain a girlfriend in his bedroom, as if the mere sight of a bed would drive them to uncontrollable passion. As a result, her visits had always been stilted, unnecessarily formal affairs and Mike had come over to her home a hundred times more often than she'd come here.

From downstairs, Mr Adams's voice drifted towards her. 'That's it! You've had your warning! I'm calling the police right now!'

She didn't have long. She ran from one room to the next, checking inside wardrobes, crouching on rugs and carpet to lift trailing counterpanes and scan quickly under beds, peering in a cupboard which housed an old-fashioned water tank and peering into bath and shower rooms.

She called as she went: 'Cassie! Are you here? It's Mum. Cassie, come on out now. I'm not angry but you need to come out. You need to come home.'

There was no reply.

Mike's bedroom had hardly changed. Only the décor was different. The *Star Wars* and *Lord of the Rings* posters had been replaced by framed photographs of local scenes. The cobbled square on market day. A view of the Chevin. The medieval seven-humped bridge. His parents' choices, she was sure. The painted shelves held a different, more sophisticated collection of books. A suitcase lay open on the floor, spilling clothes, as if he were still only half-committed to being here.

Finally, she took the steep steps to the converted loft. She'd only seen it once, when Mike's parents had been out for the afternoon and they'd had the run of the place, but it had stayed with her, her favourite room from the moment she'd walked in. The ceilings were sloping, reflecting the architecture of the roof, so in places she had to duck to avoid catching her head. It was the nearest the family had to a dumping ground. An old sofa bed stood along one wall; a desk, piled with books, was against another; and Mike's old gym equipment – a rowing machine and sets of weights – dominated a far corner. Down one side was a row of walk-in cupboards, crammed with the sort of possessions all families store in their attics.

She ran down them, pulling open each door and peering inside, into the gloom. The interiors smelled of camphor and old parchment. She found herself lowering her voice: 'Cassie! Are you in here?'

No sight or sound. She stopped, sweating with exertion, trembling, her body suddenly exhausted. She'd been so sure. She'd really thought... She stood still in the quiet, forcing her brain to focus. *Somewhere else. Where else might he take her? A garage? An outhouse? What do they have here?*

She rushed to the loft window and peered down across the rambling garden.

From far below, a door slammed. Mr Adams's reedy voice, then the rumble of another, deeper one. The police, she thought, responding to his call, here already to arrest her for trespassing. Her legs trembled.

Footsteps sounded on the stairs, calling her name. She knew the voice now. Not the police but Mike.

She met him halfway down the stairs. At the sight of him, anger surged. She flew at him, knocking him backwards. He staggered, grabbed at the banister with one hand to steady himself and raised the other arm to fend off her blows.

'What're you doing?' He sounded more alarmed than angry. 'Anna!'

'You!' She was still slapping at him, hitting around the head, the shoulders. He didn't attempt to fight back, just did his best to defend himself. 'What have you done to her?'

'Me? Anna, no!'

'Where is she?' She snarled at him, her blows falling more feebly now, as her strength ebbed. 'If you've hurt her, if you've laid a finger on my baby, I'll kill you. God help me, I will.'

'How could you think I've—?' He must have sensed that she was flagging. He lifted his head cautiously to look at her, took a final smack across the face. 'Stop it. Please. I know you're upset. I know you're worried. But you're wrong. So wrong. How could I hurt my own daughter?'

'Stop saying that!' She stopped, exhausted.

He reached for her forearms and gently held them, anchoring her. His cheek burned red where she'd slapped him. They stood there, facing each other, both trembling. Her breath came in hard, short bursts.

He said again, more quietly now, 'How could you even think that?'

Something in her collapsed. Her muscles weakened and faltered and her knees buckled. He lurched forward, grabbing her as she fell.

His voice murmured in her ear, 'It's alright. I've got you. Easy now.'

She leaned in against him, felt him take her weight, manoeuvre her carefully down until they were sitting together on the stair, pressed close together in the narrow space, side by side, his arms around her, keeping her steady.

She sank into him. His body was firm with muscle and warm. She felt herself put down an impossible weight, a weight which she'd struggled to carry for such a long time, she could barely remember life without it.

His smell washed over her. A faint musk and his own fresh scent. The smell of their dates and of dancing, of holding each other close, of all those passionate clinches on the moors and in his mother's car. She'd almost forgotten.

Another thought jolted through her: *I don't know this man. Not now. How can I trust him?*

'Have you got her, Mike? Keep hold of her.' Mr Adams had reached the landing. His voice was breathy with the exertion, with shock. 'I'll call the police, shall I? They'll know what to do.' He sounded less certain now.

Mike raised his head. 'It's OK, Dad. We're fine. No need to call anyone. It was just a misunderstanding.'

'Your poor mother,' Mr Adams said. 'She's very upset.'

'I know.' Mike sounded soothing. 'She'll be OK though. Make her a cup of tea, could you? Tell her we're fine. I'll be down in a minute.'

A low moan sounded, so strange that Anna barely recognised it as her own. Mike was rocking her now, calming her, and, feeling the wetness where she pressed her face into his shoulder, she realised she was crying.

'We'll find her,' he whispered to her. 'She'll be OK. We'll find her.'

What if someone's hurt her? What if it's Mike? I want to trust him but – should I? Words tumbled through her head, fitting the same rhythm of the rocking. *What if I never see her again? What if she's dead? Then, God help me, how will I live?*

32

Tim

George rented a place on the far side of Otley. It wasn't the smartest part of town but clearly all he could afford on his wages. Tim drove slowly past the squat block of flats. He remembered Anna pointing it out when they'd driven that way once but he didn't know which one was George's.

Weak sunlight glinted off the windows, reflecting the hurrying clouds back to him. There was no sign of movement inside.

He did a U-turn at the end of the road and parked just beyond the block, then cut the engine and sat, hunched forward over the steering wheel, considering the building. It had a shabby exterior. A row of bins, some missing lids, stood by the main entrance. The woodwork round the windows and doors looked in need of repair, leaking scraps of dried paint.

To the side stood a set of six lock-ups for cars or storage. Numbers, presumably for each flat, were daubed in untidy letters on the front of each one. Tim hesitated. Would that be somewhere to keep a ten-year-old girl? It was possible, if she was bound and maybe drugged. He shivered.

He wondered whether to get out and investigate the lock-ups. He could bang on the doors and try the handles and press his ear to the cracks in the hope of catching any sound. It was risky. He'd certainly draw attention to himself. He was considering what to do when the door to the block opened and George stepped out. Tim's breathing quickened.

George hurried down the path, head down, dressed in an old baggy jacket. A canvas bag swung from one of his hands. Tim remembered what Mrs MacKay had described. He wondered what George had gone to such pains to retrieve from the house the previous night and if it was still there, in the canvas bag. Tools, maybe, he thought. Maybe he had food too, supplies for Cassie, if he'd imprisoned her somewhere.

George unlocked his battered old car, parked further down the road, climbed in and settled himself, ready to go. Tim clicked his seatbelt back on and put his hand to the ignition key, waiting for the right moment to slide out and quietly, steadily follow.

Tailing was harder than he'd expected. There was a lot of guesswork, a lot of thinking ahead. Once or twice, Tim thought he'd lost George. At one junction, they were separated when Tim was caught by a red light and he had to trust his instincts and guess which route George might have taken.

His hunch proved right. He caught sight of him again as George queued at roadworks, waiting to pick up Ilkley Road and head out towards the Dales. Tim kept carefully to the speed limit, thinking hard, letting George pull ahead.

It was a route they'd often taken together when they were teenagers, cycling before they were old enough to drive, heading off for picnics and hikes and even a swim in the Wharfe if the weather was hot enough. They'd both loved the countryside, the green, open spaces, criss-crossed by dry-stone walls, the sheep and cows, the gentle slopes. Tim loved the kindness of the landscape, vast and varied but rarely as desolate as the Pennines, with its curved, north-stretching spine.

He held his breath as George, past Ilkley now, approached the turn-off for Addingham and the moors beyond. Tim slowed, hanging back, as George's car nosed its way out of the forward stream of traffic and took the turn to the right.

Tim felt suddenly certain. He knew where his former friend was going. Of course. It was the perfect place to hide a child. They'd hidden away there themselves, when they were boys. It had been their secret refuge.

The traffic thinned as the roads onto the moorside twisted and turned. Tim, wary of being seen, parked in a layby and counted down five minutes, then ten. When he drove on, he found George's car parked ahead on the grass verge, abandoned, close to the gap in the dry-stone wall which they'd always used as an entry point when they were boys. He found a similar spot ahead, under a row of trees, parked his own car and crept back.

He scrambled through the gap in the wall, then stood, hands on hips, hearing the low wind whistle through the bracken and sweep across the wiry grass, chilling his cheeks and ears. Ahead, the slope of the hillside rose steeply, undulating, crossed by an occasional grey stone boundary, darkened here and there by scree.

He thought of all the times they'd come here, he and George, and wondered at the way their friendship, which had seemed at the time so deep, so permanent, had become so badly corrupted. He readied himself and started to climb, keeping close to whatever cover he could find – a wall, trees, rocks – in the hope that if George did pause in his climb and turn, Tim would stay hidden.

Finally, high on the hillside, the abandoned stone bothy loomed. Once used many years ago by sheep-farmers, it was more dilapidated than he remembered. One wall was crumbling, bifurcated by the trunk of a tree which had been little more than a sapling when they were teenagers.

As he paused to rest, his breath puffing mistily in the cool, a thin wisp of smoke rose from beside the bothy, straggling and gently dispersing in the breeze. He watched uncertainly. He remembered the stone circle, the cleared patch of charred earth where they'd once worked so hard to set fire to a mess of newspaper and twigs, thinking themselves outdoor adventurers. He set off again, quickening his pace.

His strategy worked even better than he'd hoped. As he climbed the final ridge and approached the bothy, moving as rapidly and quietly as he could, he found George with his back to him, crouched over the feeble fire, trying to shield it from the wind. Seizing his advantage, Tim crept forward.

After that, everything happened at speed. Tim jumped George, punching him hard in the head. George, tumbling heavily forward, a hand out to save him from falling into the fire, let out a gasp, part surprise, part pain. Tim's fist had struck him a glancing blow on the ear, knocking him to the side.

George twisted as he went down. Already, he was gathering his wits, struggling to free the arm pinned beneath his body, ready to fight back. He was a heavy-set man and strong. Once he steadied himself, he'd be a mean opponent.

Tim cursed. He brought his fist down hard again, this time catching the side of George's neck as he pulled away. His blow split the skin. A line of blood appeared at the surface, broke and trickled down into George's collar.

'Where is she?' Tim heard his own voice, visceral and wild. 'What've you done with her?'

George, turning now and seeing Tim for the first time, widened his eyes in surprise. 'What the—?'

Tim had his fists raised, threatening to strike a third time. 'Where... is... she?' he panted.

'What're you on about?' George shook his head, his eyes darting from Tim's face to his clenched hands.

Tim sensed him weighing up his options, figuring out a way of getting back on top. 'Last time.' Tim tensed his arms.

George jutted his chin towards the bothy. 'Go see for yourself.'

It was only a second but as Tim's eyes flicked to the stone hut, George seized his moment, bursting out from under him, hands grabbing for Tim's face. Grappling, arms flailing, hands grabbing at hair, eyes, chins, they found themselves rolling, grunting, down the slope. Tim, suddenly crushed by the bulk of George's body, felt the back of his head crack against stone. Sparks flew, multi-coloured, across the sky. He lay there, stunned, eyes struggling to focus on the moving clouds.

George, sensing the fight go out of his opponent, stopped too. He kept Tim pinned to the earth, his thighs straddling Tim's legs, hands on Tim's shoulders. Tim, slowly coming to, knew he was overpowered, trapped by a man who hated him.

33

It was an effort for Tim to breathe. His head ached.

'Was it to get back at me?' he said.

George glared down at him. Streaks of blood down his neck and chin congealed as they dried.

'Was that it?' Tim managed to say. 'Because of your mum?'

'What?' George looked confused.

Tim blinked away the spangles of light still cascading through his vision. 'Cassie.' He shuddered. 'If you've hurt her—'

'Me? Hurt Cassie?' George looked disgusted. 'I've known that kid since she was born. I'm like an uncle to her. More than I can say for you.'

Tim hesitated, unsure whether or not to believe him. 'Why are you up here, then?'

'None of your damn business.' His face darkened. 'You followed me?'

Tim thought about the bulging canvas bag, about the fire. 'You have got her, haven't you? You were trying to cook something for her. Why else are you out here? You should be at work.'

'Yeah, at least I've got a job.'

Tim made a gagging noise in the back of his throat and rolled his eyes. 'I'm going to throw up,' He twisted his head, choking. 'Get off. Now.'

George hesitated, watching closely as Tim start to cough. 'Just don't try anything. OK?'

Tim couldn't speak for coughing. George eased away, lifting off his weight. The cold air rushed in. Tim twisted onto his side, still coughing. He sensed George's movements. He was touching his cut neck with his fingertips, seeing how they came away, wet and sticky with fresh blood.

'Another inch and you could've killed me, you nutter.' George reached in his pocket and brought out a large, crumpled handkerchief.

As George dabbed at his neck, distracted, Tim surged up and pounded his fist against George's skull. This time he found his mark. George crashed sideways, his head striking a jagged rock. His mouth opened in a silent cry. His eyes rolled back in his head. Tim stood over him, panting, waiting for George to come back at him. Nothing. George just lay there, eyes closed, chest heaving.

Tim ran to the bothy. He saw at a glance that it was empty. There was no indication that the dust, the piles of desiccated leaves, had been disturbed.

He ran around the outside of the hut, scrambling through brambles and bracken and kicking his way through loose stones, looking for any sign that the undergrowth had been trampled. Nothing.

He arrived back at the front. George hadn't moved. Tim crossed to him, careful not to get too close. George's eyes were shut, his face pasty. His breaths were shallow and laboured.

Tim shuddered. The surge of anger that had overtaken him, driven him to attack his former friend, was draining now, leaving him exhausted. He'd fought blindly, lashing out in his desperation to save Cassie. But where was she?

He took a step towards George, confused. Maybe he should help him. He should check his wounds, heave him to his feet, and see if, with his support, George could somehow make it down the hillside to the car. He didn't see any other option. There was no phone signal up here. There was no other way of getting help.

As Tim approached, his body casting a low shadow over George's face, the closed eyes flicked open. Tim froze. George's expression, as he fixed on Tim, was venomous. Tim instinctively backed away again. He couldn't afford to get within reach. He sensed that whatever strength George could muster, he'd use it against Tim. This was no surrender.

He looked round the patch of open ground, still uncertain why George was here, what he'd been doing. The dismal attempt at a fire still smouldered nearby, emitting dissolving wisps of acrid smoke. He picked up a stout stick, thinking he'd scatter the embers so it could cool.

A piece of cloth jutted out from the lattice of half-burned twigs. It had been light blue. Now it was singed and patchy with soot. He hooked it out with the stick and held it up to the light to see. A small towel, for the gym or kitchen. It was densely spattered with dark red. Tacky. He peered closer.

His heart stopped. It was blood. He thought of the secrecy, of Mrs MacKay's account of George's clandestine visit to the house, of George's strange trek up to the bothy, his pilgrimage to the remote hideout they'd known as boys. He'd gone to a lot of trouble to try to destroy a blood-stained cloth.

He felt bile rise in his throat as he looked at it. His instinct had been right. George had hurt her. Was he too late? Was Cassie already dead? He couldn't bear to think about it. He took a deep, hard breath. Even if he was too late to save her, he could still make sure George paid for what he'd done. He swung round to George, suddenly sensing that he was being watched, but George's eyes had fallen closed again. He seemed barely conscious.

Tim looked back at the cloth. This was important. Whatever had happened, it was evidence. Tim stamped out the remains of the fire, turned and set off at a run down the slope. The towel, its corner pinched by Tim's fingers, flapped as it cooled.

When he reached the road, Tim clambered into his car, dropped the towel onto the passenger seat, and checked his phone. Still no signal. There might be something in another few miles, when the road lifted clear of the valley. He could pull onto the verge there and alert search and rescue, tell them where they'd find George; then, once he'd raised the alarm, he'd drive on to Leeds, to the police station, to give them what he'd found.

He went to start the car but his hands shook so hard, he couldn't turn the key in the ignition. He fumbled the door open again and sat there, dazed, gulping in the chill, dank moor air. He tried to steady his breathing but his body started to convulse, bending forward, his arms across his stomach, gripping his waist, as he started to sob.

Cassie. Images of her came into his mind. His lovely niece. Bursting into the house after school, dumping her bag in the hall, racing through to the kitchen for snacks, bringing a surge of energy and life into the house. Her sudden, unexpected laugh when something amused her. That tensing of her forehead when she was deep in thought. Ten years old, on the brink of independence, ready to take the world by storm. He'd just begun to get to know her. Now he wouldn't have the chance. And Anna, what about Anna? It would kill her.

It's all my fault, he thought as he wept. *George did this for revenge. Because he hates me so much. It's all because of the accident. It's all because I came back.*

34

Anna

Anna let out a scream.

'What do you mean? What did he do to her?'

She jumped to her feet, shaking with adrenalin, with fury. Mike, jumping up too, reached for her flailing hand, trying to calm her.

They'd been back at Anna's house for half an hour. Mike had found his way around the kitchen and made them both coffee, leaving Anna to pace restlessly round the downstairs rooms, a caged animal, teetering on the edge of hysteria, obsessively checking her mobile phone and texting people, anyone she could think of who knew Cassie, asking them if they'd seen her or heard from her, please, please could they keep a lookout.

Now Tim was back, his face drawn and tear-stained, with the news they'd been dreading.

'We don't know yet. Not for sure.' He said that but, when Anna scrutinised his expression, he seemed sure. The fight, the hope, seemed to have drained from him. 'The police said they'll get the blood on the towel analysed. That should tell—'

'How could he?' Anna was possessed with the urge to tear, to scratch, to claw at her face. 'George? He knows her so well. He's like family.'

Tim hung his head. Anna realised from his expression that he felt responsible. That he had already decided that whatever George had done to Cassie, it was because of him.

'No!' she said. She pulled a hand free and pointed an angry finger at her brother. 'No! I'm not having that. This is not about what happened to her. Don't even go there.'

Mike gently moved her backwards and pressed her to sit down on the sofa. She seemed to collapse into herself, rounding her back.

Mike turned to Tim and asked quietly, 'What about George? Where is he?'

'He was up on the moors. Remember the old bothy up near Kettlewell? I followed him there.'

Anna looked up sharply, shocked. 'The old bothy?' Her mind whirled. 'Why? Is that where she...?'

She couldn't finish the sentence. The words were unutterable.

'She wasn't there. Not that I could see.' Tim couldn't meet her eye.

Mike said again, 'And George?'

Tim hesitated. 'We had a fight. I—' He broke off, stumbled, then collected himself enough to carry on. 'I hurt him. I lost it. I don't know if...'

Anna frowned, trying to understand. 'If what?'

Tim squeezed his eyes closed. He seemed to disappear into himself. 'I don't know what state he's in. His head... I left him there.'

Mike said, 'But the police know where he is, right?'

Tim nodded. 'They're sending a rescue helicopter to get him down. I guess they'll take him straight to hospital. If...'

Anna's eyes widened. He didn't need to finish the sentence.

She sensed exactly what he meant. *If George was still alive by the time they reached him.*

For a second, she felt a surge of hate. She hoped George was dead. If he'd hurt Cassie, he deserved to die. The world didn't want him. Then she thought: *But what if she's hurt and still alive? What if he's the only one who knows where she is? We need to find out. If he dies, we may never find her.*

She stared at Tim, unable to speak. She read the anguish, the guilt in his face and thought: *And what about Tim? He escaped prison once, after Mrs Taylor's death. What if he's charged with murder this time? What if I lose him too?*

'Oh, Tim.' She had a catastrophic sense of the life she'd known, of the very ordinary existence she'd taken so much for granted, unravelling in front of her. She felt weighed down by grief and hopelessness. How could an entire life change so suddenly? How could that be right? She felt exhausted. If Cassie – she could barely even think the words – if she didn't have Cassie, she couldn't go on. She knew that with a deadening certainty. Her life too would be over.

Mike looked from brother to sister. 'The towel,' he said quietly, 'maybe it's not Cassie's blood. Maybe it's George's. Like, he cut himself and used it to bind the wound or something.' He hesitated, looking at their closed, disbelieving faces. 'Maybe it's not even human. An animal's blood. Could be.'

Tim said in a wooden voice, 'Then why would he bother to go all the way up there, to the middle of nowhere, and try to destroy it?'

Mike didn't answer.

Anna said, 'How long?'

'How long is what?' Mike looked puzzled.

'Until they find out about the blood. How long does it take?'

'The police said they'd try to fast-track it,' Tim explained. 'But apparently it still takes time.' He stared vacantly at his watch. He had the air of a man who'd lost all sense of what time meant. 'So,' he shrugged, 'they might have an answer by late tomorrow, I think. Or the next day.'

'We won't know until then,' she said dully.

Mike said, 'We'll have found her by then, alive and well. Don't give up hope, Anna. We don't know what's happened, not yet.' He stooped awkwardly over Anna and touched her shoulder, patted it. 'I should go. I need to check in on Mum and Dad.'

He straightened up and, as he crossed to the door to see himself out, stopped near Tim.

'You will tell me, won't you?' he said in a low voice. 'If you hear anything? Anything at all.' He turned and looked back at Anna, who sat with her head bowed. 'And if there's anything I can do.'

After he'd left, Anna started to sob. It wasn't sadness; it was angry, bitter crying that threatened to split her apart. She rocked herself back and forth on the sofa, tearing at her hair, her cheeks, with her hands.

'No!' she cried when she found breath. 'No! Not Cassie! Not my baby! My poor, poor girl.'

Tim crossed the room in a moment and pressed himself to her side, put his arms round her and held her tightly, swaddling her. 'Hush,' he murmured in her hair. 'Hush now.'

'It's my fault!' she wailed. 'I'm her mother. I should have looked after her. I'm supposed to keep her safe.'

He rocked with her, the two of them falling at last into a steady rhythm, trying to numb themselves to the pain.

They were starting to quieten, slumped with sheer exhaustion, when Anna's phone rang. She pushed Tim away from her and snatched at it.

'Lily? I've been trying to call you. Did you get my messages?'

Lily sounded dazed. 'George has been attacked. Had you

heard? The police told me. They're taking him to hospital. I'm going there now.'

Anna started to sob all over again. She could hardly force her mouth to form words. 'I know,' she said. 'And Cassie's missing. We think George took her.'

'George?' The shock in Lily's voice was clear. 'No! You know that's not true, right? He'd never... Who told you that? What, Anna? What's going on?'

Anna, unable to speak, looked wretchedly at Tim.

35

'I don't know if I can bear it.' Lily's voice was hoarse with crying.

Lily and Anna clutched each other's hands. They were sitting close together in a bland waiting area in a corner of the hospital's emergency unit. Gradually, as the hours had passed, they'd seen the unit and the corridors around them quieten, an air of desolation settling in.

Slowly, as they'd wept and waited, the hospital had been drained of the day-shift workers and afternoon visitors. The flower shop, the newsagents, the main café had swept up, washed down their counters and closed. Now it was dark, fast becoming evening.

Their eyes were red-rimmed. Both of them were struggling to comprehend everything that had happened that day.

'I know,' Anna whispered. 'He's going to be OK, Lily. They both are.'

Anna's head ached. All she wanted was to have Cassie safe by her side, to crawl into bed near her and fall asleep listening to her daughter's breathing.

Was that so much to ask? For the clock to be turned back

and for everything to go back to normal? She needed to wake up and start all over again, to find out this whole desperate horror was nothing more than a nightmare, one she could put behind her and forget.

Please. The thoughts kept running through her head, unbidden, drumming in her mind. *Just make Cassie safe. Make all this go away. I'll do anything you want after that. Anything.*

And then there was George. Earlier, a doctor had come out to talk with them. George had a closed skull fracture, he'd explained. He wasn't expected to need surgery. He was heavily sedated and under observation. They needed to assess him for internal swelling and monitor him carefully but the initial scans gave every reason for optimism. The doctor seemed young, barely older than them, despite his grave tone. His eyes were heavy with tiredness.

'We should try to see him,' Anna said. 'They said go back at seven. It's nearly seven now.'

Anna was numb. She felt as if someone else, another person, was going through the motions of being alive on her behalf, while another Anna, her real self, watched from outside her body. It was overwhelming.

She grieved for herself and for Lily, her closest friend. She understood her anguish. George was the only real family Lily had now. No mother, no father. The two of them, brother and sister, had always been so close, as close as she was to Tim.

But if George had taken Cassie from her, if he'd hurt her... Anna shook her head. Was it possible? He'd grown into a strange man, a bitter person, prone to rages. But was he capable of harming Cassie?

Lily didn't believe it. Tim did. Anna didn't know what to think anymore. She just wanted Cassie safe. She just longed, with a physical, visceral yearning so intense it was painful, to hold her daughter in her arms again. If she could, she'd never let her go.

And if George did know anything, if he did hold the key to what had become of her daughter, Anna needed to be near him. As soon as he became conscious, as soon as he could speak, she needed to be here, to hear what he had to say. Right now, the hospital was the only place she could bear to wait.

They left the sterile waiting area together, with its rhythmically popping fish tank and shabby chairs, and the archaic drinks machine that they'd fed, periodically, with coins, pulling out plastic cups of undrinkable tea or coffee, just to pass the time. Mostly, they'd simply huddled together, their arms round each other, crying quietly, wondering at this fresh fracturing of their lives. Their mobile phones had rested silently in their laps, screens dark, waiting for news which never came.

Their heads were dizzy with the acrid smell of disinfectant, overlaying the stink of human disease, human waste.

Tim, at home, had promised he'd call the moment he heard anything. And surely the police would call Anna's mobile if there was news to share. Good or bad. Anna both longed for a call and was afraid of one. At least while there was no news, she could hope.

Now, the two friends shuffled along the corridor, clutching each other's arms for support. They seemed to have reached an unspoken agreement, at least for now. They would survive this the same way they'd survived Mrs Taylor's death, which had posed a similar threat to their friendship.

In all the time they'd sat together, waiting, worrying, Lily had said nothing to Anna about the issues burning between them. About the fact it had been Tim who'd attacked George, that the same man who'd killed her mother had now put her brother's life in danger.

Anna, understanding, had said nothing more to Lily about George and her suspicion that he might have hurt Cassie. Both women seemed to sense intuitively that, as they each struggled to survive this crisis, these were matters too painful to be addressed. They needed each other too greatly. If they didn't face this together, what hope did either of them have of making it through?

They turned into the main corridor and hesitated at the closed door to a side ward. Lily twisted to Anna, eyes brimming. *Here we are, then*, the look seemed to say. *That's George's room, in there.*

A nurse hurried over to them, in a crisp, starched uniform, her flat, rubber-soled shoes squeaking on the polished floor.

'Can I help you?' Her voice was coldly officious.

'The doctor said I might be able to see him at seven.' Lily blinked hard, stopping herself from crying in front of the nurse. 'I'm his sister. Lily Taylor. Next of kin. Can I?'

The nurse frowned, considered. 'Wait a moment.'

She opened the door to the side ward and bustled inside. Lily and Anna craned to see in through the opening.

It was George but not George. He was a still figure, lying in a caged bed with raised metal sides. His cheeks were sunken, his eyes black with bruising, his skin unnaturally pallid. His head was swathed in bandages. A thin blanket was tucked firmly round him, showing the contours of his torso, his legs. His arms rested outside it, straight and lifeless.

Anna swallowed. His pose looked so artificial, almost as if he'd been laid out, as if he were already dead.

A cannula fed into the back of one hand, secured by tape. Anna followed it back to a drip on a stand by his side. A low whirr sounded and, beyond it, the calm, steady pulse of beeps emitted from a bank of machines.

The nurse checked the chart at the bottom of his bed, satisfied herself of something, then scurried back to them.

'You can go in, for a little while,' she told Lily briskly. 'Sit quietly. Hold his hand, if you like. Talk to him but stay calm. Don't excite him.'

Lily's eyes widened. 'Talk to him? I thought he was unconscious?'

'He's heavily sedated.' The nurse gave her a shrewd look. 'But it's still best to assume he can hear you.' She shrugged. 'You can never be sure what the brain's picking up. I've known patients coming out of comas and you'd be surprised what they heard, what they remember. You just never know.'

Lily gave Anna a wretched look, then took a step forward into the room. When Anna made to follow her, the nurse stuck out a hand and barred her way.

'Next of kin only.' She looked at Anna more closely. 'Are you family?'

'Practically,' Anna said. 'We're very—'

The nurse interrupted her, shaking her head. 'You can wait down there, if you like.' She pointed down the corridor to a plastic chair. 'She won't be in long.'

Anna hesitated, trying to read the nurse's tight expression. 'Will he' – she felt for the words – 'will he be OK?'

The nurse gave her a long look. 'I'm sure the doctors will keep you informed.' She turned on her heel and strutted smartly away.

Anna hunched over on the chair. Her head was so heavy, she could barely support it. She let it sag backwards against the wall, defeated by tiredness. Her thoughts were a jumble.

When she closed her eyes, all she could see were images of Cassie. The baby with the red, scrunched face and skin so thin she felt as if she could trace every vein on the back of her tiny, closed hands. The delight on Cassie's face when she emerged from nursery and caught sight of Anna waiting, crouched low, her arms out, waiting for Cassie to hurtle out of the door and bang into her. The smell of her hair, of her skin, as Anna enveloped her in the world's fiercest hug.

The first days at school in freshly polished shoes and stiff pinafores when Cassie ran in through the main entrance without looking back, Anna biting her lip not to cry. And now, as Cassie approached her final days at primary school, she was already so much more independent, making the short trip to and from the school gates on her own. *If only I hadn't let her*, Anna thought. *If only I'd carried on taking my daughter in.*

Anna started to cry again. She wiped off her eyes and nose and swallowed hard.

Please, God. She wasn't someone who went to church, she wasn't someone who prayed, but the words came just the same. *Please bring her back to me. Make her be safe and well.*

In her lap, her phone started to ring. It took her a moment to register what was happening, then, as she did, she snatched it up, fumbled to press the button and take the call. Tim, it said. Tim was on the line.

'What? Is there news?'

He said something but she couldn't make it out. His voice was muffled. Perhaps it was the poor reception, deep inside the hospital. Perhaps it was him, the fact he too had been crying.

She pressed the phone as tightly as she could to her ear.

'What? What is it?'

Tim was shouting, desperate to make himself understood. 'Anna?'

She could barely make out the words. The line spat static.

'Anna? Are you there?'

36

EARLIER THAT DAY

Cassie

Cassie hadn't been able to sleep last night.

She was frightened. Everything had fallen apart since Dr Taylor had been killed. She couldn't bear to think about it but when she closed her eyes, pictures came. Of blood and a monster with a knife, coming to get her mother, coming to get her. In the darkness, she'd knelt on the end of her bed and eased back the edge of the curtain, looking out at the shadowy street, keeping watch for him.

Twice in recent days, Cassie had been crossing the landing, on her way to her bedroom, when she'd heard her mum crying in her own room. Once, Cassie had put her eye to the crack and seen her, sitting on the edge of the bed, hunched over, her face in her hands. Her mum had tried to stifle the noise but it was obvious. Sometimes, when she came downstairs, her eyes looked red and sore.

When Uncle Tim had come back, it had been weird but mostly in a good way. Cassie was still getting her head around that. Not everyone in the street had been pleased to see him.

She understood why now. Lily had explained to her about the car accident which had killed Mrs Taylor. Cassie was sorry about it, but she tried not to care about the past. It was all history to her, as old as the Romans, and, besides, it had been an accident. Accidents happen. And she liked Uncle Tim.

And then there was Mike. Cassie didn't know what to make of that. She liked him too. She didn't really know him, not yet, but he seemed gentle and funny and kind. He seemed to care about her mum as well. He couldn't look Cassie in the face when he talked about her mum. He looked right past her as if he could see her mum standing there, watching.

Did Cassie look like him? She'd spent a lot of time thinking about that, examining in the bathroom mirror the length of her nose, the shape of her chin, the colour of her eyes. She still wasn't sure.

He seemed to think he was her father. And her mum hadn't denied it, not properly. The thought of it was messing with her mind, though. She wished Mike and her mum would just tell her and sort things out.

And then, the murder and the rock through the window and the shock at the funeral of seeing her mum arrested. She'd thought she'd never see her again. Even though her mum was back home now, that fear hadn't gone away.

Sometimes, when she was trying to get to sleep, she heard a car in the street and imagined it was the police, coming to take her mum away for good. She imagined it so hard she could almost hear their boots coming down the path, the pounding on the front door.

She didn't know how she'd live without her mum. She was innocent, of course. Cassie knew that with all her heart. Her mum would never hurt anyone, especially not old Dr Taylor.

But mistakes did happen. Innocent people did get sent to prison and were locked up for years and years. Cassie had heard about it on the news. What if that happened to her mum? The thought of it hurt so much it gave her a stomach ache.

That was why she had to do something.

So, Cassie had pulled out her warmest, blandest clothes – jeans, a long-sleeved top and an old hoodie – and stuffed them in her school bag along with some snacks, her water bottle and her phone. Beneath the clothes, she'd hidden a pair of her mum's old washing-up gloves, to make sure she didn't leave fingerprints. She'd made room by emptying out all her books and folders and stashing them in the bottom of the wardrobe. Her mum would never notice.

The next morning, her mum was in a strange mood and her face was pale and drawn. She must have had another poor night. When Cassie kissed her goodbye at the front door, she longed to whisper: *Don't worry, Mum. I've got a plan. I'm going to fix this.*

Instead, she just turned away, making sure her mum didn't see her face, and headed off down the street. When she turned to see, a few doors further down, her mother had already vanished, the front door closed.

She let out a heavy breath. She kept an eye out as she walked but no one seemed to be watching her. At the end of the street, instead of turning towards the bus stop and school, she headed in the opposite direction, towards the centre of Otley.

Her heart raced. She almost expected someone to call her out, to shout at her, ask her what the heck she was doing, going the wrong way. This wasn't like her. She'd never played truant in her life. She was one of the good girls, known for it.

But this was different. This wasn't being naughty. She was on a mission. It would take backbone but it was what she needed to do. They'd thank her in the end.

For half an hour, she wandered round the centre of Otley, pausing now and then to look in shop windows. No one seemed to notice her. No one seemed to wonder why a ten-year-old girl wasn't hurrying to school.

Finally, at nine o'clock, the library opened. She slipped up to the children's section and hid in a corner with a book. Once she was sure the coast was clear, she raced to the toilets and changed her clothes, folding up her uniform and swapping it for the jeans and hoodie. At once, she felt less conspicuous, the hood raised to shield her face from security cameras. Every now and then, she checked her watch.

At school, they'd be in science now. She wondered if they'd missed her yet, if anyone had raised the alarm.

She huddled in her corner and read the book. She couldn't settle. Time dragged. She'd decided to wait until ten o'clock but it was so long. She ate one of the snacks she'd packed. Finally, at five to ten, she hauled herself to her feet and shouldered her bag.

The cold was lying in wait for her as soon as she stepped out of the library. She crossed towards the centre of Otley, picking her way through the market square, busy now with shoppers, past the Victorian arcade, and weaving through the almost deserted back streets. Despite the snacks, she was hungry and she breathed in deeply the oily smells of baked pies, frying bacon and hand-cut chips which drifted out from the cafés.

At a local nursery, a gaggle of children in plastic aprons screamed and shrieked in a tiny playground, shooting down a plastic slide, throwing handfuls of sand and pedalling toy cars. A young woman there glanced across at Cassie as she passed. Cassie turned quickly away, flushing. She bowed her head and quickened her pace as she hurried away.

When Cassie reached Riverside Road again, she didn't turn into it but crept on a little further and entered the narrow alley which ran along the backs of the houses opposite theirs, including the Taylors'. It was a dingy cut-through, even at this time of day. High, unfriendly boundary walls ran along the backs of the plots, some set with cemented broken glass to deter intruders.

Ordinarily, Cassie didn't like to use it. It had a slight kink which meant that, once she'd entered, it was a long time before she could see the welcoming light of the far end. Until then, it felt like a trap, easily sealed at both ends. It smelled of rotting rubbish and dog dirt. Once, Cassie's friends had found dirty needles dropped by druggies. After that, they were banned from playing there. Cassie had secretly been glad.

But today was far from ordinary. Cassie pulled back her shoulders and stepped bravely into the mouth of the alley. The air was still and silent. No dog walkers, no shoppers cutting through to the main road, no one at all. Except her, the slight, short figure of a child.

Cassie counted to herself under her breath as she strode forward, trying to keep her spirits up. It was something her mum had taught her to do when she was an infant and dragging her feet on the way home, cold and tired of walking. The alley carried a dank scent of mould and festering undergrowth and, now and then, the musk of a wild animal, a fox perhaps. She shivered and hurried her steps.

The Taylors' back wall was low, topped with rickety fencing. Cassie scanned up and down the alley. Nothing and no one.

She examined the wall more closely, working chunks of loose cement free here and there between the bricks to force a toehold, then scrambling awkwardly up onto the top, scraping knees and skinning the pads of her palms. On the top of the wall, she pulled herself to standing and, panting with the exertion, pressed herself flat against the planks of the fence. They left such a narrow strip of wall free for her that the struts were in danger of pushing her straight back down to the ground again. She inched along, sideways, clinging to the splintery wood and tentatively testing each piece of fence for sturdiness.

This part proved easier than she'd expected. The wood was slack with age and rotten in places. It had clearly been many years since it had been replaced, perhaps even before the Taylors' day. Cassie, her scuffling shoes sending loose stones flying, stepped sideways with care. Her cheek against the wood, clinging to the struts for balance, she couldn't see her feet, and every trailing finger of ivy which had forced its way through from the garden side became as hazardous to her as a tripwire.

Finally, she reached two sections which had warped to such an extent that one bowed away from the other, leaving a clear gap. Cassie crouched low enough to put her shoulder to the space and press herself between them, squeezing. At times, she found herself held fast by the hard wooden struts and, trapped, had to tamp down rising panic, only to free a stuck hand or foot inches further a moment later and carry on through.

She lowered herself down on the far side, her bag banging on her back, and stood there, brushing off her dirty, sore hands and looking round. The house was silent. Uncle George wasn't here often and Auntie Lily would be teaching at school. Cassie kicked through the long grass to the back door. The toes of her shoes darkened as they became damp.

She tipped the plant pot and slid out the key hidden there, then opened the back door. In the kitchen, she stopped, suddenly cold with fear. The silence was oppressive, menacing. She hadn't been inside the house since Dr Taylor's murder. She sensed him here, pottering at those counters, making his strong, smelly coffee in that machine, turning to her with a wink. *Well, hello there! Look who it is!*

She blinked and steadied herself. No, it wasn't the same. She looked more closely. It was different. The counters were tidy and freshly scrubbed. The floor, usually sticky, was clean. *Auntie Lily*, she thought.

She gathered her courage and crept forward into the hall. Sunlight, striking the stained-glass panel high in the front door, fell in eerie red and yellow shafts. The old grandmother clock in the corner ticked down a soft, steady heartbeat. She reached her hand for the banister and crept upstairs.

She stood on the threshold of Dr Taylor's room and stared. The bed looked strange. It was just a bare mattress, stripped of its linen. She set down her bag, opened it and drew out her mum's washing-up gloves, blew into them, as her mum always did, to open up the fingers, then slipped them on. She knew the police had been here but, even so, they might have missed something. She'd seen it happen on TV.

She crept into the centre of the bedroom and stood there, still and quiet, looking round, battling to stay calm.

She had one reason for being here. She had to find the murder weapon, the knife. It was important. She'd heard women in Riverside Road gossiping at their gates about it. No one had found it. It was the key which might unlock the mystery of who the murderer really was. If she could find that and take it to the police, they'd know for sure that it wasn't her mum.

Hands sweating in the rubber gloves, she searched the room, checking for places where the knife might be hidden. Nothing.

When she'd exhausted the bedroom, she crept out onto the landing.

The nearest door was the one to the shabby bathroom, right there. She poked her head inside, heart thumping. She didn't want to feel behind the toilet and washbasin. They were too gungy. She wrinkled her nose. It was smelly in here. Dr Taylor hadn't cleaned very well. She looked round, assessing the hiding places. The only decent one in here was the big, old airing cupboard on the far wall. She'd hidden in there once or twice herself over the years when she was playing hide and seek.

She tugged open the door and breathed in the warm, dry air, heated by the hot water tank. The main shelf was piled high with spare sheets and towels. She frowned, thinking hard. The knife could be in there. It was possible. Maybe the police hadn't bothered to check. Maybe they weren't as thorough as she was. She smiled to herself, excited about the idea of finding it, of saving her mum by proving her innocence. Everyone would be so pleased with her.

She started to excavate the threadbare bath-towels, searching with her gloved hands through the worn folds of pillowcases and sheets, shaking out each one and probing it with her fingers, feeling for anything hard which might be the knife. She moved each pile as she checked it and climbed into the space it made, so she could reach further in.

As she climbed further into the interior, the air became stuffier but she didn't care, she was elated, intent on her task. She was right, she was sure of it. She'd find it. She'd astonish everyone – the police, Uncle Tim and Auntie Lily and her mum. And that missing knife would lead the police at once to the real murderer and he'd be sent to prison, instead of her mum.

She was almost at the end of her search, her fingertips touching the back wall of the cupboard, when her flailing foot caught the open cupboard door and knocked it hard against the surround. It bounced back and swung shut behind her with an ominous click. Darkness closed in, pungent with moth balls and worn wood.

Caught on all fours, she lifted her leg and planted her foot flat against the door's wooden surface. However hard she pressed, it didn't budge. She squirmed round, scraping her arms and knees against the biting roughness of unfinished wood, feeling cobwebs brush her hair.

She hammered against the door with her fists. Nothing. With no handle on the inside, she was trapped.

She clawed at the wood, tearing her fingernails. Overcome by a rising tide of panic, she began to scream.

37

Anna

Anna flung herself out of the car and tore down the path, her hands outstretched as if she could lessen the distance.

As she scraped open the front door, Cassie appeared in the hall. She seemed cowed, her shoulders rounded, her eyes struggling to meet her mother's.

Anna couldn't speak. She just grabbed hold of Cassie, pulled her close and pressed her to her own body as tightly as she could. She was real. She was safe. She'd needed to feel her with her own flesh and bones to believe it. Her smell, her softness.

'Mummy. I can't breathe.'

Anna pulled back, held Cassie by the shoulders and inspected her anxiously, searching for wounds, for signs of trauma. Her daughter looked tired and pale. Her face was scratched. Her hands were red and grazed. But she was here. 'You're OK?'

'Fine,' Cassie mumbled.

Anna shook her head. She held Cassie's hand gently in her

own, lifting it to bring her elbow tucked into Anna's side, to keep her close. 'So what – what happened?'

Cassie didn't answer.

'Who was it? Who shut you in there?' Anna still didn't understand.

Cassie turned and looked over her shoulder towards the open door to the lounge. 'I don't know. I'm not sure. Maybe it was just—'

'But why were you hiding in there?' Anna was struggling not to let her impatience show. 'Who told you to go there in the first place? Were you meeting someone?'

'It wasn't like that. I was just trying to...'

'What, Cassie?' Anna bent down to look her in the eye. 'Trying to what?'

Tim appeared in the doorway, hesitant. 'She says she went over there on her own. She got trapped in that old airing cupboard in the bathroom.'

'But why?' Anna blinked, still at a loss. 'What was she doing in there?'

'I wanted to find the knife.' Cassie's voice was a mumble. 'It must be somewhere. But I couldn't find it. And then—'

Anna frowned. 'What knife?' She read something in her daughter's face and flushed. 'Oh, Cassie. Who told you to do that? You should have been at school.'

'We've talked about that,' Tim said quietly.

'So you were at the Taylors' house?' Anna looked from Tim back to her daughter, who was hanging her head. 'All this time?'

Cassie looked close to tears. 'I couldn't get out.'

'We only just found her.' Tim looked stricken, as if he were the one at fault. 'A man heard her. He stopped by the gate, walking his dog, and, well, he heard Cassie screaming from upstairs. She'd been in there for hours.'

'Oh, Cassie.' Anna folded her arms around her daughter and held her close.

She thought of the pain, the fear which had almost broken her today. She thought about the way she'd stormed into Mike's home and terrorised his elderly parents, searching the rooms like a madwoman.

She thought about George, sedated in hospital, his future uncertain.

She thought about Cassie, terrified and alone, screaming for help.

'But why, Cassie?' Anna's legs gave way under her and she leaned sideways against the wall to steady herself. 'Why?'

Cassie's lip trembled. 'I just thought—'

Tim stepped forward. 'She wanted to find the murder weapon so the police could catch the man who really killed Dr Taylor and stop harassing you.'

'You did it for me?' Anna put her lips to her daughter's hair.

Cassie pressed her face harder into her mother's chest and started to sob. Anna stroked her hair.

'She's safe,' Tim said. 'That's what matters.'

Anna's mind was still churning. 'But George,' she said, 'what about George?'

'I know.' Tim bit down on his lower lip.

Anna thought about the still, pale figure in the hospital bed, his head wrapped round with bandages, a drip feeding his arm. Tim had done that. Tim had put him there. What would happen to him now?

'I was wrong about him,' Tim said quietly. 'He didn't take Cassie, didn't hurt her. I know that now.'

He lifted his eyes to find Anna's. 'But the thing I keep wondering,' Tim went on, 'is why was he up there? Why did he go all that way to burn that towel? That still makes no sense.' He paused, his eyes on her face. 'And if he didn't hurt Cassie, if it isn't Cassie's blood on that towel, then whose blood is it?'

38

That night, Anna couldn't sleep. She lay rigidly on her back, staring absently at the moving shadows on the ceiling, watching the ghostly reflections of the passing cars in the street below.

Cassie was curled asleep beside her. Anna had insisted that Cassie stay where she could see her, hear her. She was possessed by an overwhelming physical need to have her daughter close at hand. It was almost as if Cassie were a baby again, their flesh connected. For now, at least, she wasn't sure she could ever let her out of her sight again.

She listened to the swell and puff of Cassie's breathing. She tried to tell herself it was OK, that she could let go now, that she could release the tension keeping her body so stiff. It was over. Cassie was safe.

She thought of George lying in his hospital bed. Lily had texted to say that the doctors were pleased with his progress, he was doing better. She'd agreed to go home to her flat to shower and change and try to grab some sleep.

Anna, thinking of her friend, let out a long, slow breath. Her eyes brimmed and when she squeezed her eyelids together, the shadows on the ceiling distorted, shooting into lines. It was a wonder Lily was still speaking to her. It was Tim who'd done this, Tim who'd followed George and hurt him. The two women had been here before, of course. They knew how important it was to stay close to each other, to keep faith, whatever happened between their families. But this time, it hadn't been an accident.

At some point close to dawn, just as the outlines of the furniture in the room were starting to emerge from the darkness, she dozed off.

'Mum.' Cassie's voice in her ear.

Anna's head ached. She reached out a hand, felt the emptiness of the bed beside her, the crumpled sheets. 'What time is it?'

'Half past nine.' A muffled thud as Cassie set a mug on the bedside table. 'I've made you tea.'

'Nine thirty?' Anna couldn't remember when she'd last slept that late. She forced her eyes open. 'You OK?'

'Uncle Tim's here.'

Tim was hovering behind Cassie, hanging in the doorway, trying not to intrude.

'Lily just called.' His chin bristled with overnight stubble and his cheeks were sunken.

Something in his look shook her awake. She scrambled to sit up.

'What?' Her voice was hoarse. 'Has something happened?'

'She's at the hospital.' Tim couldn't look her in the eye. 'I think you ought to go, you know, ought to be with her.'

Anna found herself stumbling out of bed and onto her feet, still fogged by sleep, staggering against furniture. Cassie watched, wary and silent.

'What's happened?' She groped for her clothes. Why weren't they telling her? What could be so awful they'd be too frightened for her to know? Not— 'Is it George? Is he worse?' She took in the bleakness in their faces. 'He's not—'

'He's OK.' Tim's sombre expression didn't match what was surely good news. 'He's conscious. They think he'll be fine.'

'Thank God.' She blew out her cheeks, pulling on jeans and a clean T-shirt. Thank goodness he was OK. For his own sake and for Tim's, too. There'd been a point, last night, when she'd imagined her brother facing a murder charge. She ran a comb through her hair, reached for the cup of tea and sipped.

She was about to head downstairs when she stopped. She could feel them both still watching her. The quiet was ominous.

'What?' She didn't understand. She could just sense that they were keeping something from her. Something important.

Tim and Cassie exchanged furtive glances.

'Maybe you should sit down,' Tim said.

At almost the same time, Cassie blurted out, close to tears, 'Oh, Mum!'

Anna sank onto the edge of the bed. Her eyes darted from Cassie to Tim. 'Tell me.'

Tim swallowed hard, his eyes on Anna's face. 'Lily wants to tell you herself. But they've got the results back. From the blood. The towel. They've identified whose it is.'

39

Anna saw Lily as soon as she burst through the main door to the emergency unit. She was a forlorn figure, hunched forward, alone in the waiting area. She looked up as Anna ran to her. Her eyes were red, her face white.

She sat beside Lily and wrapped her arms round her, squeezed her as tightly as she could. For a while, Lily couldn't talk. She cried into Anna's shoulder, heaving sobs which shook her as she gave way to the tears she'd been trying to suppress. Anna held her close.

When the crying started to ease, Anna passed her a wad of tissues from her bag and stroked her back, as if she were a child again, while Lily blew her nose and wiped off her eyes and cheeks. Slowly, Lily's breathing became less ragged.

Anna took one of her friend's hot, damp hands and sandwiched it between her own.

'Tell me,' she said. 'What the hell's going on?'

Lily couldn't look her in the eye. She stared at the shiny hospital floor.

'The police called me. They've got the results through on the blood samples, fast-tracked, like they said.'

Anna frowned. 'And?'

Lily took a deep breath. 'It's Dad's.'

'Your dad?' Anna shook her head. 'Are they sure?'

Lily sniffed. 'A hundred per cent.'

Anna's mind was racing. 'It couldn't be George's, could it? I mean, father and son. It's bound to be—'

'Similar, obviously, but not the same,' Lily said. 'I asked that. No, they're sure it's Dad's.'

Anna frowned, remembering. 'So what was George doing with it?' She looked at Lily's stricken face. 'I mean, they can't accuse him of murder, can they? He's got an alibi. He was with us, at the party.'

'The police say that's not watertight.' Lily started to cry again, more softly this time.

Anna struggled to think. 'But lots of people can say they saw George there. I did!'

'I know. I saw him too. But I wasn't following him round all evening, was I? No one was. That's the point. We can't all be certain exactly what time we saw him and where, not to the minute. Half of the people at the party were drunk by then.'

Anna stared at her. The implications for George were starting to hit her. 'It wasn't him,' she said woodenly. 'It wasn't.'

Lily bit her lip. 'They say all he needed was a few minutes. Long enough for him to run across the road, stab Dad and get back again.'

'But that's nonsense!' Anna stared at her, wide-eyed. 'That's just conjecture. They can't convict him on that.'

'They don't have to.'

Anna blinked. 'What do you mean? The towel? There must be a reason for that. What's George said? He's recovering, isn't he? Can he remember? Surely he can explain now what was going on with the towel?'

'Oh, Anna.' Lily started to shake her head. 'You don't know, do you? It's not just that.'

'What then?' Anna wanted to take her by the shoulders and shake her. 'What?'

'The police interviewed him.'

Anna looked round. 'What, here? In hospital?'

Lily looked miserable. 'The doctors said he was well enough.'

'Did he have a lawyer?'

'They offered. He said no, he didn't need one.'

'But that's—'

Lily pulled her hand away, roughly. 'Just listen, can't you?'

Anna froze, waiting.

'It isn't only the towel.' Lily took a deep, shuddering breath, trying to collect herself. 'He's confessed. He's made a statement saying he did it. That he stabbed Dad to death.'

40

Anna, stunned, opened her mouth to speak.

Lily lifted her hand to stop her. 'Don't, Anna. Please. Just listen.' Lily collected herself and carried on. 'Apparently, he told the police he just snapped. He said it was because Dad was always belittling him, making him feel he was never good enough, never the son Dad really wanted. He couldn't take it anymore.'

'Oh, Lily.' Anna could hardly speak, her eyes locked on her friend's face.

Lily said bitterly, 'And that's true, isn't it? Plenty of people would confirm it. We all know what he and Dad were like.'

'But—'

'Listen!' Lily was shaking. 'George told them he ran over there to confront Dad, to have it out with him, but they argued and then, well, he lost it. He grabbed a knife and stabbed him.' Lily broke down again, sobbing. 'Oh, Anna. I can't believe it.'

Anna shook her head. 'Lily, he doesn't know what he's saying. Surely we can challenge his confession? He's concussed, for heaven's sake. The police must have put pressure on him. And he didn't even have a lawyer. All that counts in his favour.'

She tried to get Lily to face her and concentrate on what she was saying. 'What did he tell you? Have you talked to him since they took his statement?'

'I've tried,' Lily wailed. 'He won't see me.'

'He won't see you?' Anna frowned.

Lily shook her head. 'The police said he refuses.'

'Oh, no.'

'What am I going to do?' Lily's voice was little more than a whimper.

Anna reached her arms round Lily and tightened them. She rocked her friend as she wept.

She tried to sound more confident than she felt. 'We'll think of something,' she whispered. 'We will. We'll get him to see sense.' She was suddenly hit by the enormity of what George had done. 'Whatever happens,' she said at last, 'he can't go to prison for a murder he didn't commit. Can he?'

41

Anna's phone buzzed.

She jumped, her nerves frayed. Her first thought was of Cassie, that something else might have happened to her. She fumbled her phone with fat fingers, struggling to focus on the screen, and muttered to Lily, 'Back in a minute.'

Lily barely shrugged. She seemed calmer now, her body exhausted from the lack of sleep, from the crying. She sat on the hard hospital seat, her eyes bleary, hunched in on herself.

Anna ran through the main doors into the corridor to check her phone in private. A message, from Tim.

Mike's come round. Wants to see Cassie. OK?

Anna bit down on her lip. She stared at the screen. She knew what she wanted to type back: *No, it's not OK. Tell him to leave her alone.*

She ran a hand over her face, calming herself down. Why had he come back? He'd stirred up so much. Too many memories, too much hurt. It was better off buried.

She remembered the expression on Mike's face the previous

day when she'd sobbed in his arms, worried to distraction by the fact Cassie was missing. He'd looked so distraught.

She shook her head. It was too much, too soon. There'd been so much hurt, all these years. She couldn't switch those feelings off just because he'd walked back into their lives.

She forced herself to type something measured.

If she wants to. But pls keep it short and stay w them.

She waited, watching as her phone told her that the message had been delivered, then that it had been read. She imagined Tim and Mike together in the house. She could almost see Tim's quiet frown as he read the message and thought how to handle her instructions. He'd be loath to upset either of them. He'd always liked Mike, even when they were teenagers.

Cassie. Her gut twisted at the thought of her. She wanted to be with her, at home.

She thought about how terrified she'd been when she'd thought Cassie had been abducted. What if something really had happened to Cassie? What if she'd been assaulted, hurt in some way – how would Anna ever have forgiven herself?

She looked blankly out through the windows at the rows of vehicles in the car park. The dead leaves piled in corners and along the verge. She should have realised how worried Cassie had been about the fact she'd been arrested. She should listen to her more.

She took a shuddering breath. Maybe she had been wrong, lying to her about her father being dead. How could Cassie trust her, now she knew? She had sensed how much Cassie had longed for a father, for a second parent to fill the gap in their family. It wasn't as if Cassie hadn't tried to tell her. But how? How could she possibly tell her daughter the truth?

The doors to the emergency unit slid open and Lily

appeared in the corridor. She looked broken. She gazed vaguely round, lost, then spotted Anna and came across to her.

'The doctor just spoke to me,' she said. 'He's doing fine but they want him to stay one more night, just to keep an eye on him. They're hoping to move him to a side ward. They're trying to find one.'

'And then what?'

Lily couldn't look her in the eye. 'I don't know. The police won't talk to me. The detective has disappeared, back to the station, I suppose. They've left a constable outside George's room, but he won't say anything. I don't know if George has been formally charged or not.'

Anna didn't know what to say. She imagined George being handcuffed and taken straight from here to Armley jail, on remand. She didn't suppose a man who'd confessed to a violent murder would be allowed to go home.

She looked at Lily. 'What about you? Can you try to see him again?'

'He's still refusing to see me. I asked the doctor. Sounds as if he can't face me.' She shrugged. 'I don't know what to do.'

Anna took in the pale, drawn face. 'You need to go home,' she said. 'Eat something. Have a shower. You can't do anything right now.' She reached for her friend's arm and started to guide her towards the bank of lifts. 'Let's grab a taxi. It can drop you first, then take me home. OK?'

Lily, letting herself be led, didn't have the energy to reply.

As soon as the taxi drew up outside Anna's house, she saw Mike's car parked there.

Her body reacted first, with a sudden trembling in her hands and an awkwardness in her limbs as she stumbled her way out of the taxi. She imagined Mike watching her from the lounge. Her key rattled as she struggled to insert it in the lock.

Inside, the house was quiet. She shrugged off her coat, hung it up in the hall, took a deep breath and headed into the lounge. It seemed empty. Then a shadow shifted, and she realised Mike was there, sitting alone in the silence in an armchair in the corner. He rose to his feet and faced her.

'Where's Cassie?'

Mike nodded towards the ceiling. 'Upstairs. Tim's up there too. I think she's going to have a shower.' He hesitated and his eyes swung from her to the carpet and his neatly polished shoes. 'She still seems pretty, you know, done in.'

Anna gave a curt nod. It was too weird, coming home and seeing him here in the lounge, as if he'd never been away. It hurt. She wanted to shout, to tell him to leave. She took a deep breath.

'I'm not sure I thanked you properly.' It was hard to get the words out but she owed him that much, at least. 'I'm sorry I accused you. Upset your parents and everything. You were... you were very kind about it.'

His eyes stayed on his feet. They were like teenagers all over again, tense, unable to say what they needed to say. 'I'm not sure it was *kind*,' he said after a moment. 'That's such a weird word.'

She started, taken aback. 'Weird?'

'That's what you say to a stranger. *How kind.* It's the polite thing to say, just before you turn and walk away.'

Anna rolled her eyes. She dropped her bag on the floor and sank onto the sofa. 'I'm sorry you don't like my choice of vocabulary. It's been quite a tough couple of days, you know? How about I write you a thank you note, would that do?'

'No need to be sarcastic.' He sat down heavily in the armchair, across the room from her. 'I know you've been through hell. I can see that. But she's home now. She's safe. It's over.'

She gave a hard laugh. 'Not exactly.'

He looked across at her sharply. 'What's that supposed to mean?'

She was torn between wanting to shock him and wanting to withhold the news from him. It was none of his business, after all. He was already interfering far too much in their affairs. She hesitated but the words came out anyway.

'George is in trouble.'

Mike frowned. 'He's worse?'

She shook her head. 'Not his health. They're keeping him in for now but he's doing OK.' She searched Mike's face. 'Did Tim tell you about the towel?'

'The one George had up on the moors. What about it?'

'It had blood on it, remember?' Anna swallowed hard. 'It's Dr Taylor's blood.'

Mike looked confused. 'Dr Taylor's?'

Anna shrugged. 'We're still trying to figure it out. Anyway, the police went to the hospital to question George and, apparently, he's confessed.'

Mike hesitated. 'Confessed to what?'

'To murdering Dr Taylor. His dad.'

'No.' Mike slowly shook his head. 'That can't be right.'

Anna sank more deeply into the chair, bone-tired. She wanted Mike to leave, she wanted to go upstairs to see Cassie, to satisfy herself that she was OK. But just at the moment, she wasn't sure she could move.

'You should probably go,' she said.

'Not yet.' Mike stiffened. 'We need to talk, Anna. This stuff with Cassie—'

Anna shook her head, weary. 'We don't need to talk. There is no *stuff*.'

'Yes, actually, there is.' There was a sharpness in his voice which made her look up, startled.

He raked a hand through his hair. It stuck up in clumps, spiky and boyish. In a rush, a memory came to her of the feel of his hair, of running her own fingers through it, all that time ago. *I was besotted with you*, she thought. She thought of her teenage self, so heady with love, so naïve. She'd brimmed full of emotion, of ambition, of confidence in the future. The memory nearly broke her.

'Tim said something to me. Lily as well, when I met up with her after school. I couldn't understand why they both seemed so hostile towards me. After all, what had I done?' He frowned. 'Then it clicked. You told them that I was the one who broke things off, didn't you? You let them think you were the victim, so cruelly abandoned, and I was the heartless villain. Right?'

Anna couldn't answer at first. Finally, she got out, 'That was years ago. What does it matter now?'

Mike looked incredulous. 'Matter? Actually, it really

matters, Anna. All these years, you've apparently painted me as the sort of guy who'd dump his girlfriend as soon as he found out she was pregnant. That I was the one who didn't care, who walked away. Only that wasn't quite true, was it?'

Anna squirmed in her chair. Her eyes traced the pattern on the rug. She sensed that he was staring at her and she couldn't meet his gaze.

'You lied to our daughter. You told her I was dead. And you even lied to your own family and your best friend. No wonder you were so frightened when I suddenly reappeared. You knew they might find out the truth about what happened. That I didn't leave you.' His eyes filled. 'I never could have done that, Anna. I loved you. I adored you. I'd have married you in a heart-beat if you'd wanted me. Knowing you were pregnant with our child? I wouldn't have walked away. You know that. It would have been the icing on the cake.'

Anna just sat, her body rigid.

'Can't you at least tell me?' Mike said. 'Why did you break it off? You never gave me a chance. For years, I just didn't get it. I couldn't believe you'd stopped loving me. It wasn't that, what-ever you said.' He gulped. 'You don't know how near I came to packing it all in at uni, to coming home and trying to make you change your mind and have me back. I couldn't make sense of it. And then, just a month ago, I found out about Cassie. I couldn't believe it for a while but slowly I figured out the dates and realised she must be mine.'

His eyes were on her face, as if he were waiting for her to contradict him.

He carried on, 'And then it all started to fall into place. That was it, wasn't it? You found out you were pregnant and – and what? You wanted to punish me, was that it? Punish me because I'd escaped to university and you knew you'd never escape now, never have your chance. Was that it?'

He was speaking so quickly and so emphatically that he

made himself breathless. 'I'm sorry, Anna. Is that what you wanted to hear? *I'm sorry.* But what did you expect me to do? You were the one who left me, remember. It wasn't what I wanted. It almost finished me. And as for Cassie, what did you expect me to do about her when I didn't even know? Look at her. Anna, she's beautiful. She's clever and funny and such a wonderful person and I want to get to know her properly, to be a dad to her, whatever way you like. This isn't only about you. You don't have to see me, if you don't want to. That's water under the bridge for you, I get that. But don't stop me from getting to know her. If you do, I'll fight you. I'll go to court if I have to. It means that much to me.'

Anna stared out of the window. A stout middle-aged man was strolling past with a Labrador on a lead. The breeze lifted the man's hair around his temples and mussed it. High above, light clouds scudded past.

She felt oddly disengaged from the world. Tiredness, perhaps. Or sheer emotional overload. It was so strange, being here in the lounge with Mike again, just the two of them. It was like going back in time. And yet their lives were so different. They were so different.

'It's not what you think.' She turned and looked him full in the face, all pretence gone. 'She might not be yours. That's why I broke things off. Because I couldn't be sure.'

He flushed. 'I don't believe you. You're just saying that.'

She shrugged, calm. 'I'm sorry. I know it's hard to hear. But you said you wanted the truth. That's it. That's why I didn't tell you. You don't know for sure if she's your daughter. But here's the thing. I can't tell you. Because I don't know for certain if she's yours or not either.'

43

Mike seemed too stunned to speak. He just stared at her, wide-eyed.

'You're saying there was someone else?' he said at last. 'You were sleeping with someone else at the same time?' He shook his head. 'No. I know you, Anna. You wouldn't do that. You loved me.'

Anna said quietly, 'Yes, I did.' *So much*, she thought. *More than you will ever know.*

He blinked. 'So, it's another lie then, is it? It's not true she might be someone else's?'

'Mike, it is true.'

His body tensed. 'Well, go on, tell me the whole story. You owe me that much, at least.'

'I can't. Don't you get it? All I can say is that I couldn't tell you for sure if she was yours or not. Because I didn't know myself. That's why I had to let you go.'

Mike shook his head, as if he were shaking off buzzing flies. 'I don't believe you. You're just saying that because you want to get me off your back. Well, I'm not going anywhere. I've wasted enough time. I don't want to waste another minute. We'll do DNA tests, Cassie and I.'

'And what if you're not a match? What if she isn't yours? Have you thought how she'll feel if you get her hopes up and then walk away?'

He glared at her. 'I won't walk away, I never did. You're the one who did that. You wouldn't answer my letters, refused to talk to me when I tried to phone. Don't pin this on me.'

Anna pulled her eyes away. Yes, she did remember. She remembered how hard it had been, the hardest thing she'd ever done in her life. How desperately it had hurt.

'So, you agree?' Mike said. 'You won't try to stop her doing a DNA test, will you? Don't, Anna. At least that way we'll know for sure. She'll agree, I know she will.'

'Of course, I agree.' Cassie's voice caught them both by surprise.

They both spun round. Cassie was standing in the doorway, her face stricken.

Anna started. 'I thought you were in the shower.'

'I was.' Cassie was looking at her mum as if she barely recognised her. 'I heard you two arguing and came down to see what was going on. I didn't mean to listen but I'm glad I did.' She crossed to Mike. 'I want you to be my dad, I really do. More than anything.'

Anna shook her head. 'Cassie, my love, it's not that simple. It's not just—'

'But we can find out, can't we?' Cassie appealed to her mum. 'Like he said, we can do a test. That'll tell us the truth, won't it?'

Anna gazed at her daughter, concerned. 'I don't think that's a good idea, Cassie. I'm so sorry.'

Cassie frowned. 'But why?'

'I can't explain that to you. It's too complicated.' Anna

sighed. 'You just have to trust me on this. Sometimes, it's better not to know the truth.'

'Says the woman whose life is built on lies.' Mike jabbed the air with an angry finger. 'You're just frightened,' he went on. 'You're frightened that now we've started asking questions, we won't stop. And what if a test proves that I'm not her father? What then?'

His eyes were intense. 'Then you'd have to face another question, wouldn't you? If I'm not Cassie's dad, who is?'

44

Anna slumped in the chair in the lounge. Her whole body ached. She was too strained, too exhausted even to cry.

After his outburst, Mike had abruptly left. Cassie, tearful, had run upstairs and disappeared into her room, slamming the door behind her. Anna's attempts to go in and talk with her had only provoked cries of: *Go away! Leave me alone!*

Now, alone downstairs, Anna felt utterly wretched. She could see exactly what they thought about how it looked. She understood why Mike was so angry, so hurt. Cassie too. She wanted so desperately to explain but how could she? Maybe it was better that they blamed her, however much pain it caused her, than that they knew the truth.

She had to remember what was important. It wasn't her. It was Cassie. She was safe. That's what mattered. She was OK.

Outside, the street was quiet. After a while, a neighbour strolled past, walking his dog. Anna thought of the man who'd heard Cassie's screams and managed to rescue her. She should find out exactly who he was and thank him. *Thank you for saving my daughter.*

A car drew up. A door slammed. Footsteps sounded on the path.

She didn't move when the doorbell rang. She didn't have the energy. She didn't care. Eventually, Tim came running downstairs to open the front door. A murmur of male voices drifted through. Mike. Mike had come back.

Now what?

Anna felt beaten. Mike and Cassie sat opposite her on the sofa, shoulder to shoulder, a united front. Tim, in a chair to one side, looked grave.

On the table between them sat an over-the-counter paternity test. Mike, fresh from the pharmacy, was explaining what they needed to do, steadily and patiently, as if he were instructing a small child. Anna struggled to take it all in.

'I'll pay the lab fee,' he said, as if that was the obstacle. 'But I was thinking, we could just give your email address for the results, if you like? That way you still keep control. OK?'

The three of them scrutinised her. *OK? In what universe is this OK?* They meant well, she realised that. Mike really seemed to think he was doing what was best for Cassie, trying to untangle the knots Anna had tied all those years ago.

Her hands trembled in her lap. Mike was right. She was frightened. She didn't know what she'd do if the test proved that Mike was not Cassie's father after all. Cassie wouldn't stop at that. She'd keep pressing for answers, answers Anna couldn't bear to give. It was bad enough that her daughter had heard her admit that she wasn't sure, that there had been someone else.

She let out a long sigh. She didn't have the energy to keep fighting. She was too exhausted to resist them all. She gave a weary nod.

Tim, doing his best to arbitrate, helped all three of them, Cassie, Mike and Anna, swab inside their cheeks. Mike, satisfied, filled in the paperwork and packed up the kit for return. The fast-track service gave results the very next day, he said. He gave Anna a long, careful look before he and Cassie drifted together into the hall.

Anna, excluded, stayed in her chair.

She wrapped her arms round her body.

Cassie is safe, she told herself, trying to focus. *She's alive.*

But all the struggle, all the pain, all the care she'd taken for more than ten years to keep her secret close, what had it all been for?

The results would come through the next day.

The very thought of it made Anna sick.

Tim touched her on the shoulder as he passed her, following them out. 'You've done the right thing,' he said quietly.

Anna wanted to scream. Of course, she hadn't. They were all careering towards a cliff edge and there was no way of stopping it.

45

The next morning, Anna was making herself a coffee when the doorbell rang. She jumped, the milk jug slipping in her hand, spilling a splash onto the counter. She hurried to mop it up. She'd had another night without sleep, too worried about George and Lily, about the DNA results.

Cassie, sitting at the counter and spooning cereal into her mouth, didn't move. She was wearing jeans and an oversized hoodie that she loved. Anna's heart squeezed in her chest. She could see her daughter doing her best to brave this out, to be tough, but underneath, Cassie was scared to death of what the day – and the DNA results – might bring.

Anna opened the door to find Mrs MacKay on the step, her eyes bright.

'I'm not intruding, am I? Just wanted to pop round to see if you were alright.'

'Of course!' Anna forced a smile. 'Come on in. Coffee?'

'Tea, please, dear, if you don't mind.' Mrs MacKay followed her into the kitchen. 'Hello, Cassie! Goodness me, you caused us all quite a fright!'

Mrs MacKay unbuttoned her coat and settled herself down

beside Cassie, whose cheeks had flushed scarlet. 'Honestly. To think you were right there across the road and I never knew. I can't forgive myself. You're alright, though?'

Cassie nodded, her mouth filled with cereal, and scraped her bowl.

'Well, that's something.' Mrs MacKay beamed at her.

Anna searched out a decent china cup for her visitor and poured the tea, set it in front of her.

Mrs MacKay waited. Cassie finished eating, slipped down from her stool and left the room.

Mrs MacKay turned back to Anna and lowered her voice. 'You've heard about George? Extraordinary, isn't it? I just bumped into Lily.'

Anna settled across the table with her coffee. 'I know.'

Mrs MacKay carried on, 'The whole of Riverside Road's talking about it. They say it was him. He killed Dr Taylor. His own father! I can't believe it. Can you?'

'Actually, no, I can't.' Anna stared into her swirling coffee.

Mrs MacKay swept on, regardless. 'He was a perfectly normal little boy. Not as chatty as your brother, perhaps. Not as bright, either. If I met them in the street, he always let Lily do the talking for both of them, even though he was the oldest. And then there was that awful business with his mother. I'm not sure he ever got over that really. He was such a difficult age when it happened, wasn't he? And they were very close.'

Anna's eyes strayed to her phone screen. Mike had said he didn't know what time the DNA results would come in. She wasn't sure how she could stand the strain of waiting all day, refreshing her emails every other minute.

'Anyway, you must be relieved,' Mrs MacKay was saying, 'that Cassie's safe and sound. Tim went white as a sheet when he heard she wasn't at school.' Mrs MacKay leaned forward. 'Not like Cassie, is it? To bunk off. Is she alright?' Her eyes flicked pointedly to the door as she whispered, 'Shouldn't she be in school today?'

'She's not well,' Anna lied. 'I thought she needed another day at home.' She made a sweeping gesture with her hand. 'She's had a tough few weeks. She was very fond of Dr Taylor. We all were.'

'Of course!' Mrs MacKay tutted. 'Awful! And poor Lily. Imagine. First, losing her father in such a dreadful way and then finding out that her brother did it.' She reached over and patted Anna's hand on the tabletop. 'She's going to need a good friend, dear.'

A few moments later, Mrs MacKay heaved herself to her feet, thanking Anna for the half-finished tea and announcing that she had to run. Anna didn't answer. Whatever else Mrs MacKay had said, Anna had barely heard her. She was just too overwhelmed.

When Anna closed the door on her, she was engulfed by the sad quiet in the house. She wandered through the empty downstairs rooms.

She ought to go to work and see the staff, catch up on paperwork. Tim would look after Cassie.

She plumped a cushion and set it back on the sofa. She couldn't face work. Not yet. She just couldn't concentrate.

What had Mrs MacKay said about Lily? Anna remembered the older woman's sharp eyes as she spoke.

She's going to need a good friend.

Anna forced herself to sit very still, her eyes on the sky, on the clouds racing past.

Time streamed around her. She sensed the secrets, which she had tamped down and protected with such care for all these years, rapidly unravelling.

She needed to focus, to think. Her head ached.

She thought about George and his clumsy attempt to destroy the towel coated with his father's blood. He'd nearly got away with it. He'd only been caught because Cassie had disappeared and Tim was fuelled by a guilty belief that the feud between the two men, the bitterness which had erupted after Mrs Taylor's death, had never been resolved.

Her mind raced. She focused on the moving clouds and forced her breathing to slow.

Anna thought about Lily and the times they'd spent together, growing up side by side, as close as sisters. She thought about the dreams and childhood secrets they'd shared, the way they'd always trusted each other with their lives. Nothing had broken their friendship, nothing ever could. Not even the terrible accident which had caused Mrs Taylor's death.

She thought about Cassie, frantically searching in the old airing cupboard through piles of worn towels and sheets for the missing murder weapon, hoping to find the final piece of the puzzle, to reveal the real murderer and exonerate her mother.

The knife.

Anna's breath stuck in her throat. She sat bolt upright and opened her eyes wide.

46

Lily

I'm cast adrift. The world is in chaos, spinning, whirling. I need something solid to cling to. But what is there? Who is left?

My mother is gone. My father is gone. And now George. I have never felt so alone.

I hate this hospital with its drab corners and security doors and cheap, squeaking floors. I hate it but, for as long as George is here, I can't bear to be anywhere else for more than a few hours.

He refuses to see me. I know why. He's consumed by guilt. He wouldn't be able to look me in the eye.

We always stuck together, the two of us. We've always had each other's backs. I'm the only one who knows how bitterly, how long George sobbed after we lost our mum. He was broken into pieces. I'm the one who held him at night, stroked his hair, the way Mum used to do, and murmured to him. I'm the one who brought him through it. Only he knows what it cost me. It took every ounce of strength I possessed to keep myself strong, to find a way of forgiving Tim for what he did, for protecting my friendship with Anna from all that blame and hurt. No one in this world knows my brother the way I do.

I've begged the nurses, the doctors, the police to give me just five minutes with him. I need to talk to him. But even a murderer, it seems, has rights.

The doctor, the young one with the kind, tired face, is the most sympathetic.

'I'm sorry.' He uses his hands when he talks, spreading his fingers now to show sorry as if he were an emoji. 'I can't force him.' He looks at me with such sadness in his eyes. 'But he is doing well. He is getting better.'

He doesn't mention the detectives. None of the doctors and nurses do. They just give me suspicious sideways looks as they pass in twos, wearing their scrubs, their lanyards bouncing on their chests.

We must be the talk of the hospital. George, the murderer, and his poor sister, a sister he refuses to see.

All I can do is sit here, sipping insipid overpriced coffee from plastic cups, and try to will George to hear my thoughts.

You can't do this, George, I tell him in my mind. *Don't try to bear this alone. Let me help. We need to fight these people, not give in.*

Only he's not listening.

The detectives, a posse of three, sweep back onto the ward at around ten, all bustle and importance. The ward round has just ended. I sense the stand-off between the police officers and the doctors, the battle for dominance.

The detectives stride into George's room. The young doctor with the kind eyes emerges from further down the ward and stands near the nurses' station, considering the closed door. He frowns to himself. It's his territory, after all, his patient.

Later, when the detectives emerge again, one of them shoots me a sudden look as he marches past. His face is set hard and his eyes are cold. His anger frightens me. He would make a dangerous enemy.

The young doctor goes at once into George's room. He comes out again a moment later and beckons to me. He smiles.

'You can come in, if you like.'

I blink, confused. 'He'll see me?'

The doctor nods. 'Just for a few minutes,' he says as he makes to withdraw. 'He needs to stay quiet.'

I creep into the room, wary of the humming, pulsing machines by his bed, the still, silent figure lying inside it.

'George?' I'm not sure of him at first.

There's a chair by the bed and I pull it closer and sit. I'm shaking, looking into the face of a stranger, searching for George.

'It's me,' I say. 'Lily.'

Slowly, his eyes open. His lids are heavy and dark. He struggles to focus on me, then I see the corners of his dry lips twitch. The ghost of a smile.

His arms are lying by his sides, outside the sheets and blankets. I reach for his hand, cool and smooth-skinned, and take it in my own.

'Are you alright?'

He gives a slow nod. Tears swell in his eyes, then burst and trickle down his temples.

'I'm sorry.' His voice is barely more than a whisper. 'I messed up.'

I frown. 'I'll help. But you need to do as I say. Please, George. Listen to me. I'll get a lawyer. I know you confessed but they can challenge that, I'm sure. You're not well.'

The tears still flow. Under the tightly tucked bedding, his body shakes.

'I know you, George.' I lift his limp hand to my lips and kiss it, the way our mother used to kiss us better when we were hurt. 'I know you didn't do it.'

He sighs. 'The police know too.' His voice is so quiet, I have to lean in to catch the words. 'They've thrown out my confession. They say they know it was all lies.'

47

I feel tears bloom in my eyes. I can't speak. Something deep inside me settles and shifts. I feel the words in my head: *Thank God!* I give out a long, slow breath that I didn't even know I was holding.

I squeeze his hand in mine and manage to say, 'That's wonderful, George.'

He shakes his head, wretched. 'They're angry. They say they're going to charge me. But not with murder. With wasting police time.' He takes a shallow breath, gathering his strength. 'Perverting the course of justice.' He blinks up at me and I see the fear in his eyes. 'I could go to prison, Lily. For a long time. I should never have done it. I was only trying to—'

'Shush.' I cut him off at once and look round nervously. 'Don't say any more,' I whisper. 'We don't know who's listening.' I bend in closer. 'Listen. I'll get you a lawyer. A good one. We'll fight it. OK?'

George gazes back at me, uncertain.

My mind is racing, trying to understand. 'But why? What's changed?' I think of the detectives' tight expressions as they left the ward earlier, the hostile glance in my direction. 'What happened? What made them realise you were lying?'

'I couldn't answer their questions. They kept asking me to go over exactly what I did. How many times I stabbed him and where and whether he fought back and, if so, how. I didn't know. I sort of made it up.'

I tut. *Oh, George, my sweet, foolish brother.* He was always a bad liar.

'And the knife,' he goes on. 'They kept asking about the knife. Where I'd got it from and what sort of knife it was and what I did with it afterwards.' He shrugs. 'I had to make that up too.'

I pull away from him and sit down hard on the chair again. Of course. The missing knife. The central piece of evidence which the police have so far failed to find. That could prove crucial in confirming the killer's identity. And, of course, George couldn't lead them to it. He must be as clueless as the police about where it is now.

'Listen.' I keep his hand tight in mine. We have so little time. Any minute now, a nurse or doctor will interrupt us and tell me to leave, to let him rest. 'Just don't say anything, George. OK? To anyone. Whatever they ask. I'll sort out a lawyer. All you need to think about is getting better. Nothing else. Just get strong again. For me. Will you do that?'

His eyes flutter closed.

I touch my lips to his clammy forehead, saying goodbye, then hurry from the room and out of the hospital, buoyed by fresh hope.

The knife.

48

Anna

Anna opened the gate and hurried down the Taylors' path, skirting the front and heading to the back of the house. At the back door, out of sight of the road, she looked round, nervously. Her heart hammered. The garden plot, always kept so neat by Mrs Taylor when she was alive, looked forsaken and forlorn. The grass was wild, the patio paving choked with weeds.

The back door key turned easily in the lock and she eased open the door.

Since their father's death, George and Lily had been coming and going regularly. Lily in particular had started sleeping here some nights, keeping the house ticking over while they decided what to do with it.

But already, it seemed different. There was a musty smell in the kitchen as if the place needed airing. Anna imagined Cassie standing here just two days ago and thought how eerie it must have seemed to her. She made her way through to the hall and paused there, listening. The grandmother clock in the corner, by the front door, ticked loudly, the pendulum swinging.

The door ahead to the lounge was ajar. She crept forward and pushed it open, peered inside. It was all just as she remembered it and yet subtly altered. The life had been taken from the room. The sofa and armchairs, with their neatly arranged cushions, were too pristine. The coffee table was cleared. Dr Taylor's reclining chair, which usually sat in the middle of the room with a good view of the television, had been pushed aside to face the far wall.

She sighed to herself, saddened by the changes, by the weight of all the memories here, then turned back to the hall and headed stealthily up the stairs.

As she reached the top, a recent memory flared. She stopped, felt her breath quicken, her heart thump in her chest. The last time she'd been here, all alone then too, had been the night of the party. The night she'd crossed the road to check on Dr Taylor and found him murdered.

She closed her eyes and saw again the anguish on his face, the horror in his eyes. She snapped her eyes open, forced herself to look round, checking for movement. There was none. She shook herself and carried on.

She went first to the spare bedroom. The bed was rumpled, the duvet crooked as if Lily or George had recently slept there. She stood very still in the centre of the room, remembering. This had been George's room, when they were children. One of the hiding places had been in here, out of bounds to them when they'd been girls. Lily had sneaked her in here once to show her and they'd giggled together, hearts pounding, as they'd eased it open and found a set of *Lord of the Rings* character cards stashed away inside. At the time, they'd been George's most precious possessions.

Anna got onto her hands and knees and started to make her way round the skirting board, looking for tell-tale cracks that could suggest a false panel. The hidey-holes had been in the house since she could remember, since before the Taylors had moved in. A curiosity, shared by the previous owners. A useful place to squirrel away valuables if they went on holiday. Dr and Mrs Taylor had never bothered with them but, as children, they'd been fascinated. Lily had sworn her to secrecy then shown her the two she knew about. They'd made it their mission to find more but, despite many searches during idle afternoons, they never did.

Anna bent closer to the woodwork. There was a section, just before the wardrobe, which looked cleaner than the rest. She peered more closely. It could just be that less dust had settled here. Or it could be because this panel had been moved. Anna pulled open the wardrobe doors, found a wire coat-hanger and untwisted the end of the metal, then jabbed it into the nearest crack. It gave slightly. She kept working it, rocking the wood back and forth, prising it free. It came out in a sudden rush, the force setting her backwards onto her heels.

She sat, panting, and stared. A small rectangular hollow lay behind it, cleverly concealed. No wonder the police had missed it. It was more compact than she'd remembered, perhaps six inches long and two inches deep.

She pulled out her phone, switched the torch on and shone it into the space. It was filthy in there. It had been a long time since George had used it for hiding collectors' cards. She moved closer, picking up in the light a splatter of dark, dried flecks. She stared. Blood. Dried blood.

She shivered. She had no idea how old those flecks were, but forensics would know. She suspected they were recent. She considered. Her hunch might be right. Maybe this was where the towel, stained with Dr Taylor's blood, had been hidden. But the towel had gone, partly burned on the moors, then gathered as evidence. The hiding place was empty now. There was no sign of the knife.

A clatter from downstairs made her jump. She froze, listening. Footsteps, slapping lightly outside, faded as they headed away down the path. The clink of the gate, roughly closed. She eased herself to her feet and crept onto the landing. A pile of coloured advertisements had appeared on the front door mat. She inhaled deeply and tried to force her heart rate to settle again.

It didn't take a moment to replace the panel and head into the front bedroom, the one which had always belonged to Dr and Mrs Taylor. She hesitated in the doorway, her nerves jangling.

The bed was bare, stripped down to the mattress. Pillows and sheets and duvet were gone. The only reminder of the scene she'd witnessed here was the remains of the stubborn bloodstain there on the carpet, beside the bed. She reached out a hand to the door-frame and steadied herself.

I need to do this, she thought. *If the knife's here, I need to find it.*

She crossed to the window and, grunting with effort, pushed aside the wooden chest of drawers which stood against the wall. This was the most secret hiding place of all, the one she and Lily had used to stash away their sweets. She dug her fingernails into the hairline crack in the skirting board and slowly eased out the stubby piece of panelling along one edge until she could reach in her fingertips and lift it out. She hunkered down on the carpet to peer in as she reached inside.

Her fingers closed at once round a cold, hard object. She drew it out. It was a kitchen knife with a serrated edge. It wasn't a long blade – six inches perhaps, but clearly sharp. She turned it in her hand, inspecting the metal. The blade had been cleaned but roughly. In the glinting light from the window, she could make out dark smears. They were the colour of rust.

She couldn't move. It was the weapon she'd come here to find, that Cassie had looked for too, and yet, now it was in her hand, she felt sick. She sat, staring, feeling the weight, the solidity of it in her hand. This blade had been thrust into Dr

Taylor's body, not once but many times, slicing through skin and muscle, piercing veins and releasing his lifeblood. She couldn't breathe.

A creak. She started, coming abruptly back to the present. Her body tensed. She didn't move, just strained to listen. A second shiver of wood, as if someone were creeping across loose floorboards. Downstairs. Someone was downstairs.

She pressed the wood panel back into place, then stared, panicking now, at the chest of drawers. If she tried to drag it back into position, whoever was downstairs was bound to hear. Instead, she left it where it was and scrambled to her feet, looking wildly round the bedroom, still clasping the knife, conscious of every sound she was making. Her breath was shallow, her blood loud in her ears.

A soft footstep on the stairs. The sounds were so much closer. She put a hand to her mouth, stopping herself from crying out, and looked round desperately for somewhere to hide. She wanted to run but she forced herself to move stealthily to the old wardrobe, there against the wall. The door opened with a low groan.

She balled herself inside, engulfed at once by the touch of dusty tweed and cotton, the smell of mothballs and polished leather. Shoes, Dr Taylor's heavy lace-ups, formed awkward lumps under her feet. She put her fingers to the side of the door and eased it closed, the knife raised in her other hand.

Darkness rushed in. Panic flared through her. Her breathing was so shallow that her chest burned. She strained every fibre to catch the faintest sliver of sound. For seconds, absolute silence. Then the bedroom door shushed across the carpet as someone pushed it wider. A soft footstep sounded, close at hand. She held her breath.

She sensed how close the intruder was, almost upon her. The hairs on the back of her neck rose. She imagined them seeing the displaced chest of drawers, noting the four black indentations in the carpet made by its legs and now exposed. She wondered if this person, in the act of hunting her down, understood at once what she'd been doing here, what she knew.

A board creaked, so close at hand she quaked. Horror flared through her. She gripped the knife more tightly and brandished it, ready to strike.

She tried to shrink into herself, her eyes pinned on the narrow line of light down the edge of the door. It was impossible to hide. As soon as that door was flung open, she'd be discovered, a crouching target, wide-eyed and staring among the shoes and suits.

She watched, terrified. The line of light expanded as the door slowly opened.

She wanted to spring, to sink the knife into her attacker, to save herself. Instead, she found herself petrified, the raised knife useless in her hand.

A figure loomed dark against the light in the room. It leaned in, a pale hand reaching for her, ready to pluck her out from her hiding place.

Anna started to scream. A high-pitched, guttural shriek. She scrambled backwards in the mess of shoes, wielding the knife in her outstretched hand, desperate to defend herself.

49

'Anna!'

Anna peered out, blinking rapidly, blinded by the sudden flood of light. 'Lily?'

'For God's sake.' Lily's breaths came in short, sharp bursts. 'What the—?'

Anna, collapsing in relief, slipped sideways. Her cheek brushed cotton, then came to rest in the folds of a musty great-coat, up against the side of the wardrobe. She gulped in air. Her heart raced.

The knife, in her closed fist, dipped.

Lily, recovering herself, opened the door wider and dispelled more of the gloom. The glancing sunlight flashed on the blade in Anna's hand.

Lily's expression shifted. 'That's what you were looking for?' She pointed at the knife. Her mouth tightened into a stern line. 'So, you've found it. Clever you. And now what are you going to do?'

. . .

They sat side by side, the two of them, settled on the carpet, their backs against the end of the bed, their legs stretching out in front of them. It was the way they used to sit in here when they were girls, when their idea of pleasure was giggling and gossiping and chewing on sweets from their hidden stash.

The closeness was still there. Anna felt it in the way their bodies pressed naturally together, leaning in towards each other so unselfconsciously that they were barely aware of it. Not just friends, she thought. *Sisters.* It was what she'd always felt.

But the innocence had gone. They'd been so amused by the world as girls, so excited by their own cleverness, their own wit and brilliance, by the thrill of the future waiting to unfold in front of them. Now all of that was behind them.

Lily said softly, 'You saw me, didn't you?'

Lily didn't need to explain. Anna knew exactly what she meant.

'All that stuff about seeing a strange man in a hoodie running down the road.' Lily shook her head in disbelief. 'I couldn't believe you said that. I was sure they'd know you were lying.'

Anna thought of the detectives. 'Maybe they do. They just haven't figured out why.'

Lily stared at her. 'And the smashed kitchen window. Was that you too?'

'Yep.' Anna spread her hands. 'Sorry. I thought it needed to look like a break-in. More convincing, you know?'

'Blimey. Cost me nearly two hundred pounds to replace that.' Lily blew out her cheeks. She said, more softly, 'You could have gone to prison. You still could.'

Anna shrugged. 'I know.'

'And all that was to save my neck?' Lily looked incredulous.

'What do you think?' It was the only answer she needed to give.

They sat in silence for a while. Images flashed back into

Anna's mind. Dr Taylor, murdered, glassy-eyed with shock. The soft hurried footsteps of someone running across the landing and down the stairs, desperate not to be heard. Her fleeting glimpse, as she turned to look, of her oldest, closest friend, Lily, disappearing down the stairs and turning sharply towards the back door to make her escape.

There hadn't been time to think. Anna had acted on instinct, trying to cover her friend's tracks, trying to stage a break-in, convincing herself that her story of a male intruder was the truth.

She remembered the way Lily had trembled and cried out, back at the party, when Anna had come running in to raise the alarm, to break the news. Lily hadn't needed to act. She'd been almost hysterical. Only Anna knew the real reason. It wasn't the shock of her father's death. It was the shock of having killed him.

Now, sitting together in that same bedroom, Anna reached for her friend's hand and squeezed it. The knife lay on the carpet between them, winking with reflected light from the passing clouds.

Anna said, 'So I guess George knows too, doesn't he? How did he work it out?'

Lily paused before answering. 'I'm not sure. He hasn't said. I think he just sensed it. Something about the way I was behaving, I suppose. I'm not a very good actress.' She smiled wryly. 'You're better.' She hesitated. 'Maybe he just knows me too well.'

'He must have watched you, felt something was off.' Anna was thinking rapidly, figuring it all out. 'He was quicker than I was in figuring out where you would have stashed the evidence, somewhere the police couldn't find it when they searched the house. You knew he wouldn't find the knife if you hid it in here but there wasn't room for the towel as well, was there? So you had to take a risk and use the other hidey-hole, the one he knew about, to stash that. And, sure enough, he found it. I'm right, aren't I?'

Lily nodded. 'And then he decided to take it upon himself to get rid of it. It was his way of protecting me, I think. Then, when Tim cornered him, he did the noble thing and tried to take the blame himself.'

'Oh, Lily.'

Lily wiped her eyes with the back of her hand. 'I know. When I heard he'd confessed... I didn't know what to do. I came this close to confessing myself. This close.'

Anna gave her a narrow look. 'You can't. Ever. You do see that? If you confess, what do you think they'll do to me?'

Lily pursed her lips. 'Thank God I never told George about the second hidey-hole in here. Our special secret. He never did find our sweets, did he?'

Anna looked at the knife. George had never found that either.

'How are we going to get rid of it?'

Lily shrugged. 'I'm not sure we can. Not yet, anyway. It's too risky. We put it back, for now. If the police couldn't find it, no one else will.' She put her hand in her cardigan and picked it up through the wool. 'You might have worn gloves, you muppet.'

She crawled to the skirting board, removed the panel and pushed the knife back into the crevice there. Anna jumped up and together they pulled and pushed the chest of drawers back into position.

'We could actually go downstairs, you know, now that's done,' Lily said. 'We are allowed to be in the house together.'

Anna looked around the room, thinking. 'Was that you too?' Anna said.

'What?'

'The threatening notes. All that stuff about hurting Cassie. Was that your way of warning me off?'

Lily reached out a hand and patted Anna's leg. 'I just thought you needed something concrete to take to the police. A valid reason to stop helping them, to distance yourself from the investigation. You seemed to be getting in deeper and deeper. I know you're a pretty good liar. You always have been. You were always the one who didn't get caught, weren't you?' She allowed herself a slight smile. 'But even so. It was too dangerous for you.'

Anna hesitated, thinking fast. 'And the rock through Cassie's window? Was that you too? How could you be so stupid?'

'I know, I know. I'm sorry.' Lily put her hand to her mouth, shame-faced. 'I didn't mean to hurt her. Really. It wasn't even that hard a throw. I don't know why it—'

'Bloody hell, Lily.' Anna gave her a light punch in the side. 'You should've seen the blood.'

'I know.' Lily blew out her cheeks. 'I'm so sorry.'

Anna shook her head in despair.

After a while, Lily got to her feet and crossed to the wardrobe, rearranged the scattered shoes inside and closed the door.

Anna, watching her, said, 'You nearly gave me a heart attack, creeping in like that. You do realise that, don't you?'

Lily just smiled. 'I might have known it was you. Who else would hide in there?' She shook her head. 'All those games of hide and seek. It was our favourite spot, wasn't it?'

Anna pulled her thoughts back to the night of the murder. 'Did you know I'd seen you? Have you known, all this time?'

Lily looked down, embarrassed. 'I wasn't certain.' She hesitated. 'I kept thinking, if you had seen me, well, I didn't know what you'd do. I thought you'd tell the police. You'd have to. But then you didn't.' She went across to Anna and gave her a clumsy hug. 'Come on, let's go downstairs. I'll make you a cup of tea.'

Anna hesitated, looking round the room. At the bare

mattress. At the chest of drawers. At the wardrobe. 'It's weird being in here. After all that's happened.'

'I know.' Lily's eyes followed her gaze. 'I keep the bedroom door shut when I stay over. It spooks me out.'

Anna gave her a searching look. 'Do you regret it?'

Lily didn't answer at first. Finally, she said, 'He was my dad. Of course, I regret it. But it had to be done, didn't it?'

50

Lily turned and headed downstairs to the kitchen. Anna trailed after her, biting back questions. She watched as Lily put the kettle on.

'No milk, I'm afraid,' Lily said matter-of-factly. 'Is black coffee OK?'

'Fine.' Anna went through to sit in the lounge, watching the dust motes falling through the shafts of sunlight slanting across the front of the room. The room had acquired an old-fashioned air. In recent years, she saw now, it had faded and turned shabby. The beige three-piece suite was worn, the arms shiny.

She thought of all the times she'd sat in here, watching television with Lily and munching snacks. She could almost see Mrs Taylor in the far armchair, reading a magazine. Dr Taylor puzzling over the crossword, lifting his eyes now and then to wink at her.

Lily walked in with the mugs and sat beside her. She tucked her legs under her haunches, the way she always did, and sipped her coffee. There was a new calmness about Lily. A silence. As if she were waiting for Anna to be ready, to take the lead.

Anna steeled herself. She had the sense that a door between them, which had always been closed, was opening, just a fraction. If she didn't push on it now, it might never open to her again. She shivered. She wasn't sure she could form the words. Her saliva dried in her mouth.

'Did he do it to you too?' Anna asked abruptly. She heard the words but they seemed separate from her, as if someone else had spoken. 'Is that why?'

Lily looked down into her drink, her face softened by rising steam. 'No.'

Anna flushed. 'But you knew what he was like?'

Lily stiffened. She seemed unable to move. 'I think I did. I've thought a lot about it since. I sort of knew but at the same time I didn't. I didn't understand. How could I? I was too young. I just knew it was wrong.'

Anna flinched. 'For a long time, I blamed myself. My dad was always telling me how kind they were, your parents, how we should be grateful and behave ourselves when we were here. I think he was embarrassed that he wasn't always there for us. He had to work such long hours. It wasn't his fault. He knew this was like a second home for us. He knew we needed it.'

Lily swallowed hard. 'Did you ever try to tell your dad?'

Anna shook her head. 'I couldn't. I don't think he'd have believed me anyway. And your dad said I mustn't tell. That it was our secret.' She frowned. 'He was such a charmer, wasn't he? I suppose I was flattered, at first. He was such an important person – Dr Taylor – and he made me feel special. And I was always a bit frightened of him too. What he'd do to me if I blabbed.'

Outside, a small boy, hurried past by his mother, shouted in the street, 'No, Mummy! No!' His shrill, indignant voice and their footsteps slowly faded.

Lily said, 'I tried to talk to Mum about it once. I must have been about ten, about the same age Cassie is now. I said I was worried about you when you came over to the house to see me and I wasn't here, when you and Dad were on your own. There was something weird about it, something about the way you behaved afterwards. It didn't feel right.'

Anna's eyes widened. 'What did she say?'

'She was angry. Told me not to talk nonsense. I didn't mention it again. I've often wondered since then if she did know what was going on. Or whether she really didn't believe me, just thought I was jealous because you and my dad always got along so well. I guess I'll never know.'

Anna turned back to the window. The branches of the tree in the front garden were gently stirring in the breeze, dropping its final leaves. She felt an overwhelming sadness, thinking back, remembering.

She saw it differently now, as an adult. She understood the way Dr Taylor had groomed and flattered her, the way he'd imposed both his will and his body on her, even when she'd begged him to stop, to leave her alone. Her chest tightened. He'd been a doctor. She'd seen him as someone with authority. He'd been her father's friend. She'd trusted him.

She shuddered. She could almost feel again his hands on her skin and the sense of repulsion, of panic, paralysing her.

She got to her feet and paced up and down, overwhelmed by the surge of memories, of feelings she'd suppressed for all these years. For a few minutes, she just marched back and forth across the carpet. It helped. She eased it out, trying to steady her breathing.

She could feel Lily quietly watching her. Anna couldn't look her friend in the eye, not yet. Lily had known, then, all this time. Not for certain. But she'd sensed something.

Anna let out a long sigh. When she turned to face Lily, she saw the compassion there, along with the guilt.

'It wasn't your fault,' Anna managed to say at last. 'It wasn't mine, either. It was him.'

Lily looked close to tears. 'I know. I'm so sorry. Really. I should have—'

'Stop it.' Anna's voice was firm. 'We were children, both of us.'

She came to sit beside Lily again. So this was it. They both knew. A barrier that had grown up between them since they were teenagers finally weakened and gave way. Lily reached out and they clasped hands, fingers intertwined.

Anna tried to imagine how Lily must have felt, confused and uncertain, sensing something wrong without understanding it. She squeezed Lily's fingers. She needed to find words for the questions which had been tormenting her since the night of the murder. This might be the only chance she had to ask.

'Why now?' she asked. 'You've lived with it all these years. We both have. Why hurt him now, when he was becoming an old man?'

Lily set her mug down on the coffee table. 'I should have done something at the time. I should have talked to you about it.'

Anna shook her head. 'I would have denied it.'

Lily raised her eyes and gave her friend a beseeching look. 'I'm sorry. I really am. I didn't get it, not properly. Maybe I didn't want to.'

'I know. But you haven't answered my question,' Anna persisted. 'Why hurt him now, after all this time? It's too late to help me. I came to terms with it a long time ago. I had to. It was the only way I could be a proper mother to Cassie. Otherwise, how could I have loved her, when I never knew, seeing her grow, if it might be his blood in her veins?'

Anna closed her eyes, thinking back. 'When I found out I was pregnant, I came over and told him. Your father. He looked terrified. He knew it might be his. I told him I wouldn't get rid of it, I was having it, this baby. It was mine. And he knew, when I said that, that I wasn't frightened of him anymore. That if he tried anything ever again, I'd go straight to your mum, to my dad, to the police. It was weird but the power shifted. I felt it. We both knew he'd never touch me again.'

'I always wondered,' Lily said carefully. 'About Cassie. If it was possible...' She broke off and swallowed, then steadied herself and carried on. 'If it might be possible that she was my half-sister. I thought maybe, maybe that's why I feel so close to her. Always have. Why I love her so much.'

Anna managed to nod. She'd wondered the same thing over the years but she'd had no idea that Lily had silently borne the same pain. So many things they'd never spoken about, in all this time. She thought about Cassie and Mike and the DNA test. After all the years of uncertainty, they'd soon have answers. Her breathing quickened. She wasn't sure she wanted to know.

What if Mike wasn't Cassie's father? Then what would she tell Cassie about how she'd been conceived? Her daughter wouldn't stop pressing for the truth, she knew that. She had the right to know. But how could she tell Cassie that she was the product of sexual abuse, of rape by a monster, by a man she'd loved as a second grandfather?

Lily cut into her thoughts. 'You asked me why I did it now.' Her voice were shaking. 'Cassie.' Lily hesitated. 'I did it because of Cassie.'

Anna's eyes widened. She didn't understand. Then pain shot through her chest. 'Cassie? No! He didn't—'

Lily's expression was anguished. 'I don't know. I don't think so. But I came in one day and she was sitting close to him, there on the sofa. Too close. His hand was on her knee.'

Lily hesitated. Her body trembled. Anna, waiting, couldn't breathe.

'I couldn't be sure,' Lily stumbled on. 'But there was a look in his eye. It made me sick. He looked proud and, I don't know, sort of possessive. As if he owned her.' She paused. 'It was the same way he used to look at you.'

Anna's stomach roiled. *Cassie? Could he really think...?* She was still a child. She blinked hard. No, not to him. She was ten. And she, Anna, had only been eleven when he'd started with her.

'So that's why?' Anna looked her friend full in the face, understanding at last. 'That's why you did it?'

Lily's eyes filled with tears. 'I didn't keep you safe, Anna. I failed you. But I couldn't let it happen again. Not to Cassie.'

Anna pulled herself to her feet. Her eyes fixed on the worn sofa as if she could see the scene replaying there, in front of her eyes. A sudden hot anger coursed through her. Her hands curled into fists at her sides. She wanted to punch something, someone. No, not someone, him. She wanted to smash his face. She imagined the knife in her hand, the sickening crunch as she plunged it into his bony chest, the suck as she wrenched it free, only to raise it and stab him again. If she'd known, if she'd seen him touch her daughter—

A noise jolted her back to the present. A jaunty, insistent chirping. Her mobile phone.

Dazed, she reached into her bag and pulled it out, then pressed answer. 'Hello?'

'It's Mike.' He sounded breathless. 'They say they've emailed you. Have you seen?'

'Who has?' She knew exactly what he meant. She was just stalling. They must have sent the results. They would reveal the truth. Once she read that email, once she shared it with them, their lives would be forever changed. There'd be no room for uncertainty ever again.

'The DNA company,' he said carefully. 'They've sent you the results. Could you look, please?'

She said brusquely, 'I'll call you back,' then ended the call.

Lily's eyes were on her face. 'Well?'

Anna steadied herself. 'We did a DNA test. Mike and Cassie and me. They insisted.' She let out a hard breath. 'Apparently, I've got the results.'

She didn't move. The two women sat, rigid, staring at each other, their eyes wide with fear.

Eventually, Lily asked softly, 'What are you going to do?'

51

SIX MONTHS LATER

Anna

'Come on, Cassie,' Anna hollered up the stairs, the bunch of flowers wilting in her hands. 'We need to go.'

She turned and shook her head at Tim in mock annoyance.

He gave her a sheepish grin. 'Always,' he said in a low voice.

She smiled back. He didn't need to say any more. It was something their father used to say years ago, when their mother was still alive. The three of them would be sitting in the car, waiting. The two children would be strapped in the back seat, patient, and their father drumming the steering wheel, ready to leave.

It was their private joke, a fond, eye-rolling bond between the three of them, that it was always their mother who was running late, rushing round the house, putting a last-minute comb through her hair and reaching for her coat, checking that appliances were switched off, that the sandwiches had been picked up.

With hindsight, Anna saw it differently now. She realised

that her mother was only last all the time because she didn't just get herself ready. She cared for all four of them.

Now Cassie, just turned eleven, was always the last, and all she had to do was look after herself. Anna watched her daughter bolt down the stairs to join them. She swallowed back the comment which came to mind about Cassie's hint of lip gloss.

'You look great,' Anna said. She put the flowers into her daughter's hands. 'These are for Auntie Lily,' she said. 'You give them to her, will you? She'd like that.'

Cassie took them without a word. Anna watched her daughter surreptitiously check her appearance in the hall mirror as they passed, angling her face for a better look.

Tim watched too as his niece shimmied past and out of the front door. Anna managed not to catch Tim's eye as she locked up and the three of them headed together across the road to the Taylors' house.

The old house, which had played such a central part in all their lives, was finally getting the makeover it needed. They'd shared so many happy memories here over the years and were resolved to move on from the darker ones. After all, this was where they'd all grown up, had shared birthday parties and playdates, a place where they could remember being young together.

So when Lily and George had sat down to discuss what to do with the house they'd jointly inherited, they'd realised they wanted to keep it, at least for now. How could they leave this house, leave Riverside Road? It was the perfect location, after all, close to the town centre in one direction and to the river in the other and just across the road from their oldest friends.

Using their dad's savings, they were in the process of modernising the place, using the cash to pay for professional builders and decorators who could do the job properly and give them a new look for their shared home.

Downstairs, the shabby, ageing furnishings had been stripped out and sent, along with the worn, stained carpets, to the tip. The wooden floorboards underneath had been sanded and polished and scattered with colourful rugs. The musty old books on the shelves had been replaced by family photographs in silver frames and hand-blown glass bowls and vases, made by a local artist. The faded wallpaper had gone, and the walls were freshly painted in biscuit and cream.

'Cool!' Cassie stood in the sitting room and gazed round, impressed by the little extra touches Lily had added for this small, homely dinner. The cascade of fairy lights around the gilded mirror, reality and reflection peering at each other, Narcissus-like. The warm glow of candles on the shelves and mantelpiece.

George, tending bar, hurried to offer them drinks. He'd lost weight since his injury but there was a calmness about him now which Anna had never known before.

'He's finally free to be himself,' Lily had said simply the previous week when Anna had mentioned it.

That rang true. George seemed to have set down a burden which he'd been struggling to carry for most of his life. That was the only way Anna could think of it. He'd moved on. He even seemed to have forgiven Tim, both for the accident all those years ago and for his frenzied, unjustified attack. The old tensions, which had plagued their friendship since Mrs Taylor's death, seemed at last to have dissipated.

Lily had even hinted that there was a new woman in her brother's life. It wasn't serious enough yet for him to introduce her to family gatherings like this one. But the way things were going, Lily had whispered, it might not be long.

Anna was just taking a glass of Prosecco from George's tray when the doorbell rang, and Lily winked knowingly at Anna before hurrying away to answer it.

Anna stood quietly, listening as Cassie and Tim chatted

easily with George. Both men knew how lucky they'd been to escape prosecution – Tim for his attack on George and George for lying to the police. They both recognised that they'd been given a second chance.

Tim was telling them about the new financial project he'd been asked to manage at work. He'd been at the Leeds investment company for four months now and was settling in well. Anna watched him, pleased and proud. He was relishing the challenge, she could tell.

She was happy for him. Maybe, in time, he'd be ready to buy his own place and enjoy more independence but, for now at least, she was grateful to him for keeping them company at home.

The lounge door opened, and Anna felt her eyes drawn to the man standing there, a light smile on his lips. He quickly sought out the person he was looking for and crossed to Cassie's side.

'Hey, you.' Cassie reached for Mike's hand and gave it a squeeze.

'Hey, yourself.' Mike beamed down at her.

Anna watched them. There had been moments, alone, in the middle of the night, when Anna had cursed herself for deleting that all-important email without reading it, for deciding not to find out the truth, not yet, about the real identity of Cassie's father. For preserving her secret. But, as the days passed, she'd felt increasingly certain that she'd done the only thing she could.

The only person who'd really understood had been Lily.

'It's too big a risk, isn't it?' she'd said carefully, her grave eyes on Anna's. 'Better to let the two of them build a relationship together, choosing to believe they are father and daughter, than to risk—' She'd broken off. They both knew how much pain the alternative would bring.

Anna had scrutinised her friend's face, reading her. 'And

maybe it's best for you as well,' she'd said slowly. 'This way, it's still possible to think you may be half-sisters, you two. Even if she doesn't know it, you do. That's precious too.'

That mattered to Lily, Anna saw now. Lily didn't only want to be the kind friend across the street. She wanted a blood bond, to feel she was a close relative. She'd cherished Cassie since the moment she was born. She'd killed her own father to protect her. Anna couldn't take that hope away either.

Lily had looked away. 'It's only a short-term fix, you know,' she'd said. 'Once Cassie's an adult, she can do what she likes. She and Mike could take another test, if they wanted to.'

'I know.' Anna had nodded. 'I can't keep it a secret forever. But I can for now. And by then, they'll have built a relationship. It won't be such a shock if...' She hadn't let herself finish the sentence.

Now, Mike reached for a glass and his eyes flicked across to Anna's. He smiled. And there he was, in an instant, the same man she'd fallen in love with, all those years ago. He was stockier now, the first hint of grey already declaring itself at his temples, but he was still Mike, her Mike, back from London for good.

Lily tapped her spoon on the side of her glass. 'Just wanted to say thanks for coming to celebrate the end of phase one!' She raised a toast. 'Here's to having a decent kitchen at last.'

'Not just the kitchen,' Tim said, gesturing round. 'You've worked miracles down here. I hardly recognised the place.'

Lily grinned round at them. 'Bedrooms next,' she said. 'Wait till you see what we're planning up there. En suites and everything.'

Anna smiled to herself as the murmur of conversation started up again. Lily looked so happy, so relaxed. The redevelopment of the house wasn't just an ambitious building project. It was far more than that, she knew.

It was a chance to move on from the burdens of the past, the chance of a fresh start.

At the end of the evening, Anna, Tim and Cassie said their goodbyes to the others and headed home across the road. The night air was crisp and still. Anna's ears buzzed. She and Cassie held hands as they walked, swinging their arms back and forth in time with their steps, the way they used to when Cassie was a much younger child.

Anna felt a rush of wellbeing. Her senses were softened by Prosecco and good red wine, her stomach comfortably filled by Lily's home cooking.

It wasn't only that. Mike had been good company. She smiled to herself, remembering. She'd forgotten how much he made her laugh. He made her feel young again, almost innocent.

It was several months now since she'd sat Mike down and told him what Dr Taylor had done to her all those years ago. It was one of the hardest conversations she'd ever had. She'd never seen him so angry. If Dr Taylor had still been alive, she was sure Mike would have stormed right over there and confronted him.

But after the initial shock, he'd finally started to understand how desperate the situation had been for her, once she'd realised she was pregnant. He realised now that she hadn't been unfaithful to him. She hadn't betrayed him. She hadn't stopped loving him. She'd only severed contact with him because she'd felt so trapped by Dr Taylor's abuse and, at seventeen, she couldn't see another way out. Because she was frightened that the baby growing inside her might not be Mike's.

He even understood now, he'd said, why she hadn't been able to read the results of the DNA test. She thought Cassie was still too young to face the truth. By the end of their late-night conversation, Anna felt as if she'd finally set down a heavy weight, one which had almost crushed her all this time. Slowly, since then, it was becoming possible for the two of them to start to trust each other again.

He and Cassie were getting on so well too. He'd asked Cassie this evening if she'd help him with plans to modernise the property he'd just bought, a modest terrace down by the riverside park. She'd looked so pleased, so flattered to be asked.

Inside the house, the hall was cold and dark. Tim took off his coat, said goodnight over his shoulder and headed upstairs.

Anna kissed Cassie on the top of her head and sent her up to clean her teeth and go to bed.

It was late but Anna wasn't ready to sleep yet. Her mind was still busy, her nerves singing. She pottered through to the kitchen and warmed a mug of milk, then lowered the lights and sat at the kitchen table in the gloom, cradled the warm mug in her hands and looked out into the shadows of their garden.

She'd learned to walk in that garden. She'd pushed a wooden trolley, filled with plastic bricks, up and down the patio at speed, crashing into chair legs. Cassie had toddled there too.

A breeze stirred the trees and a memory came to her of her mother hanging out washing on a line across the same space. Wet sheets and towels flapping. Anna used to dance in and out of them. She remembered the soapy smell of the washing and the damp slap of the wet cotton against her face.

Her mother had used an old-fashioned peg bag, inherited from her grandma. Anna had liked to help when the washing had dried and her mother had gone outside to bring it in. Her mother would hand her the pegs as she snapped them off the line, one by one, and Anna would stow them carefully away, feeling the rattling bag grow heavy.

She sighed and dipped her lips to the milk. The memory made her immeasurably sad. She thought of her father in later years, prematurely aged, sitting in the garden with the crossword and a cup of tea. He liked to turn his head like a sunflower, angling his face and offering it, eyes closed, to the falling sun.

He'd be so happy, she thought, if he could see Tim home again. It had wounded him terribly when Tim had left in disgrace. Her father had never been a cruel man. He'd never passed judgement on Tim after the accident. But his disappointment in his son was implicit. She'd sensed it and she knew Tim had too. She suspected it had been the worst blow Tim had had to endure. Worse than George's hostility. Worse even than being forced away from here to start again on his own. She wiped her eyes. He'd borne it all so bravely. Never complained. He had no idea how much she loved him for it.

She went into Cassie's bedroom. Her daughter was already in bed, curled on her side, a mound of shoulder hunched under the covers. Anna bent down low.

'You awake?'

No answer. Too late to say goodnight. Anna kissed her lightly on her forehead and picked her way across the scattered debris on the carpet to the windows.

The street was silent and deserted. She remembered the times they'd seen Mike standing there, half-hidden by the tree, watching them, wondering about the little girl rumoured to be his daughter. He'd admitted, at last, that the mystery man had been him. He used to go out for long, late walks, he'd explained, when the atmosphere in his parents' house had become too stifling. He'd often found himself here, in Riverside Road, trying to understand, looking up at the house where they'd spent so much time together as besotted teenagers.

She closed the curtains and crossed to her own bedroom, started to undress.

She'd enjoyed this evening. It felt like a fresh beginning. After all this time, the leads in Dr Taylor's murder case seemed to have gone cold. None of them had heard from the police for months.

She and Lily never spoke of it, but she sensed that they were both allowing themselves to look forward and to imagine the future. They'd been through so much together. It was more than a friendship. They trusted each other like sisters. Finally, they were daring to hope.

Lily had described tonight's dinner, at one point, as being 'a family gathering'. To outsiders, that might have sounded a strange term to use for this bunch of people, brothers and sisters, friends and neighbours, who'd collected in the Taylors' home.

But she was right. As Anna had gazed round at Tim and Cassie, at Lily and George and at Mike, she'd felt that they were the best kind of family.

They weren't relatives in the traditional sense, perhaps. But they'd proved themselves ready to do anything to save each other from harm. To lie to the police, if they had to. To confess to a crime they hadn't committed, if that's what was needed. Even, if they sensed the threat of a monster like Dr Taylor, to kill to protect the people they loved.

From outside, clipping footsteps sounded, coming down the path. Anna stiffened, listening. A moment later, the front doorbell rang, shrill as it pierced the night air.

Anna reached for her dressing gown and hurried downstairs.

She opened the front door to find Lily on the step. She had a strange, twisted look on her face.

'What's the matter?' Anna's mind raced, thinking about George, about Mike, wondering what could have happened to bring Lily to the door so late. 'Everything OK?'

'OK?' Lily's voice was strangled. Her words were slow and heavy. 'No, Anna. Everything is not OK.'

52

Anna blinked, struggling to understand.

She stepped aside and ushered her oldest, closest friend into the lounge.

'What is it, Lily?' She lowered her voice to a whisper, suddenly frightened. 'What's going on?'

Lily perched on the edge of a sofa cushion, her arms wrapped round her body. Everything about her seemed rigid.

Anna stared. She wanted to sit beside Lily, to put an arm round her friend's shoulders and draw her close, comfort her. But the hostility in Lily's manner held her off.

The silence was broken only by Lily's laboured breathing.

Anna ventured again, 'What? What's happened?'

Lily lifted her face. The look she gave Anna was filled with anguish. Her hands clenched into fists. 'How could you?'

Anna shrank back as if she'd been scalded. 'What?' she stuttered. 'I haven't—'

Lily cut through. 'I trusted you. All these years. Sisters, isn't that what we said? Closer than sisters?'

Anna opened her mouth but no words came. She felt the heat in her cheeks.

'It's true, isn't it?' Lily went on. 'I can see it in your face.'

Anna shook her head with a jerk. 'I don't know what you mean.'

'Yes, you do. I *know*, Anna!' Her tone spat venom.

Anna stared, wide-eyed. 'What?'

Lily narrowed her eyes. 'It was something Tim said tonight. He was talking to Mike about how sick he was last week. Some dodgy prawns or something. So bad, he had to abandon the car and get a taxi home. He hadn't been that ill for years, he said, not since – then he broke off. He'd caught sight of me, realised I'd overheard. He went crimson.' Her eyes bored into Anna's. 'It was the look on his face. The guilt. The horror. He knew he'd said something terrible, something I should never have heard. A bit like the look on your face right now.' Lily shook her head. 'It was like a knife going into my gut and twisting. I couldn't understand it, not at first. But I knew it was important. I knew from looking at him.'

Anna backed against a chair. 'He just had food poisoning, that's all. Something he ate. Probably happened before, years ago, in London.'

'Oh, it was years ago, alright.' Lily's face was hard. 'But not in London. Was it?'

Anna's mouth juddered. 'I don't know what's got into you, Lily. This isn't like you.'

Lily let out a hard laugh. 'It's exactly like you, though, isn't it? Lying. That's what's been eating away at me since you left. It gnawed at me, all the time I was clearing up, stacking the dishwasher, putting the place to rights. Your whole life's been built on lies, hasn't it? I thought I knew you. My closest friend. My rock. The one I could always trust. The one who was there for me when my mother was killed. You held me. You comforted me, the same way I comforted George. I trusted you. I loved you for it.'

Anna managed to get out, 'I know. Me too. We've always—'

'But you lied to me. Didn't you? About that. The thing that mattered most to me. About my mum's death.' Lily's eyes filled with tears. She blinked hard, gathering her strength. 'I finally remembered. Tim didn't drink that night because he was throwing up. I saw him at the party. Something he'd eaten, he said. But that was never mentioned at the inquest. His statement omitted the fact that he was so ill, he couldn't drive. So, you took the wheel, didn't you? It was you. You were the one who killed her. You!'

Anna's eyes widened in horror. 'I don't know what you—'

'Stop it!' Lily's fist beat the arm of the sofa in frustration. 'Just tell me why. Why did you have to lie about it?'

Anna sat very still. Her eyes were fixed on the carpet between them. Her voice, when it came, was soft and low.

'It was Tim's idea, not mine.' Anna couldn't lift her eyes from the carpet. 'He said it made sense. If he hadn't felt so ill, he would have driven. He always did. He knew no one would doubt us. And they didn't, not even Dad.' She took a stuttering breath. 'I was only seventeen. I was pregnant. We didn't know what might happen. We couldn't risk me going to prison, not with a baby on the way.'

'You coward.' Lily craned forward. 'You let him take the blame. Poor Tim. You let your father and George and everyone else think he'd done it when all the time it was you. You were driving. You killed my mum.' She seemed dazed. 'And then you comforted me. Knowing it was all a lie.'

Anna wrapped her hands round her body and hugged herself. She couldn't speak.

Lily didn't answer. She seemed lost, remembering, recalibrating everything that had happened between them.

Finally, Anna said, 'What are you going to do?'

Lily shrugged. Her face was hard. 'I haven't decided yet.'

Anna said, 'Please don't go to the police.'

Lily looked up sharply. 'Why shouldn't I?'

'What good would it do?'

The two women locked eyes, one fierce, the other supplicating.

Anna carried on, 'I know you're angry. I don't blame you. You're right: I was a coward. I was frightened that, if I went to prison, they'd take my baby away. She was all I had to live for. And, no, I shouldn't have allowed Tim to take the rap, of course I shouldn't have. Don't think that hasn't haunted me.' She took a breath. 'But is it so different from George confessing to murder because he wanted to protect you?'

Lily shook her head, still angry. 'It's very different. Don't think you can worm your way out of this one. It goes too deep.'

'And I lied for you too, remember?' she said softly. 'About who killed your father.'

Lily didn't answer. She pulled herself stiffly to her feet and pushed past Anna, heading for the door.

Anna followed her into the hall. As she let Lily out, she whispered, 'We've all told lies. Terrible lies. I'm not saying that was right. But we had good reasons.' She put her hand on Lily's arm. 'We told them out of love for each other.'

Lily, shrugging her off, strode away into the darkness.

53

'Wake up!'

Someone was shaking her. Anna, bleary, struggled to the surface. Her daughter's face hung over her, blocking the light.

'What?'

'Come and see.' Cassie disappeared again and light flooded in.

Anna groaned and stretched out an arm to check the time. It was mid-morning. She hadn't meant to sleep so late. The uneasy feeling deep in her stomach slowly came into focus in her mind. *Lily.* It came back to her in a rush. She knew.

Anna shook her head, forced herself to take a deep breath. She mustn't let herself give way to panic.

It was just a shock, she told herself. Her heart hammered in her chest. *She won't go to the police. She wouldn't. She wouldn't do that to me.*

She heaved herself out of bed and sat on the edge, thinking rapidly. Lily was clearly furious. She had every right to be. She felt hurt and betrayed. But she just needed time. She'd forgive Anna eventually. *Won't she?*

She frowned, shook her head. Well, even if she didn't, Lily

had no real proof. It was Tim and Anna's word against hers. And it had happened eleven years ago. She couldn't believe the police would be interested in reopening an investigation into an accidental death, however hard Lily pressed them. The fact she'd been the one driving wouldn't change the verdict.

'Mum!' Cassie's voice, calling from her bedroom, was insistent. 'Come on!'

Anna, still sleepy, pulled on clothes and went to see. Cassie was standing at her bedroom window, peering out at the street. She was wearing an oversized nightshirt, her hair tousled.

'Look!' She pointed.

Anna went to her side, threaded a lazy arm round her daughter's shoulders. Her skin was warm underneath the cotton. 'What?'

She blinked, focused, stared. A builders' van was parked on the far side of the street, outside the Taylors' house. It had become a familiar sight in recent weeks, as Lily and George slowly pressed ahead with their renovations, room by room. But now, tucked in behind it, stood a police car.

'What's going on?'

Cassie shrugged. 'I don't know. I drew the curtains and there it was. One of the officers just came back out to get a case from the boot. He was all dressed up in plastic, you know, those funny suits they wear to gather evidence.'

Anna shook her head. 'But what are they doing?'

Cassie pointed further down. 'She'll know.'

Mrs MacKay was standing guard in her front garden, her hands resting lightly on her gate, her sharp eyes observing everything that was going on across the street.

Anna slipped on shoes and hurried downstairs, scurrying out of the front door and along to her elderly neighbour. 'Everything OK?'

Mrs MacKay turned to her. 'You alright, dear?' Her face twitched as she slowly took in the state of Anna's unbrushed hair, her face, still encrusted with sleep, the feet pushed into shoes without socks. She clearly decided not to comment and leaned in closer. 'It's to do with Dr Taylor, apparently.' Mrs MacKay's eyes were shining. 'Some sort of new lead.'

Anna felt something shift in her gut. 'Really? What?'

Mrs MacKay shrugged, wrapped the folds of her cardigan more closely round her body. 'They won't say. But they've been here a while. The builders came at eight. They're always punctual. And then, about an hour later, the police turned up.' Mrs MacKay gave a discreet nod towards the house. 'They're upstairs. I've seen them at the window. In the front bedroom where, well, you know...' She didn't need to finish her sentence.

Anna stuttered: 'But how do you know that it's to do with the murder?'

Mrs MacKay turned back to her with a slight smile and lowered her voice. 'One of the builders is Mrs Johnson's son. Eddie. Nice boy. He told her and she texted me.' She held out her mobile phone, showing a scroll of messages. 'She knows I take an interest.'

Anna stretched out a hand to Mrs MacKay's gatepost and steadied herself. Her mind was whirling.

Mrs MacKay straightened up. 'Look, there's Lily! Poor love. What she must be going through!'

Lily had emerged from the front door, the door they never normally used. She paused on the step, then lifted a hand and crossed the road towards them. Her eyes were red-rimmed from crying, a scrunched tissue in her hand.

Mrs MacKay, leaning forward over her gate, said eagerly, 'Lily, dear. Are you alright?'

Lily focused her attention on Mrs MacKay, as if Anna weren't even there.

'Did you hear?' Lily dabbed at her eyes. 'They found it. This morning.'

Mrs MacKay was practically salivating. 'Found what?'

'The knife. The one that—' Lily broke off, blinked hard, blew her nose.

'Oh no.' Mrs MacKay's hand rose to her mouth. 'After all this time! But where?'

Lily shuddered. 'I'd asked the builders to start work on, you know, on my dad's bedroom this morning. I couldn't put it off any longer.' Lily gave a dramatic pause. 'I asked them to strip away the old skirting board. And it was there. Hidden. He, she, whoever it was, must have prised it free somehow. Pushed it in there.'

'Well!' Mrs MacKay shook her head. 'Imagine.'

Anna leaned more heavily on the gatepost. A grasping hand seemed to reach into her chest and squeeze her heart. She couldn't breathe.

Lily's face blurred and, in that moment, Anna seemed to see two other figures in the street behind her, pressing forward, reaching for her, both of them fixing her with cold, dead eyes.

Mrs Taylor, shoulders hunched, forever waiting in the cold for a bus which would never take her home. And, beside her, Dr Taylor, his features twisted, frozen in horror, as his daughter, leaning over him, plunged a blade into his chest, again and again. As Anna gaped, petrified, his shape morphed, spinning through a series of hazy images: from victim to trusted family doctor to predatory monster.

'Apparently, it's the breakthrough they've been hoping for,' Lily was saying, her eyes glinting. 'There are fingerprints all over the handle. Good clear ones.'

'Thank God.' Mrs MacKay reached over and clasped Lily's hand. 'That's wonderful. Whoever did this, they'll catch them now, for sure. You'll see.'

'Yes, I really think so.' Lily nodded demurely.

Her eyes swung at last to Anna's. They were hard.

'That's the wonderful thing about science, isn't it?' Lily's face twisted into a strange smile. 'It just never lies.'

A LETTER FROM JILL

I want to say a huge thank you for choosing to read *The House Across the Street*. If you enjoyed it and want to keep up to date with all my latest releases, just sign up at the following link. Your email address will never be shared and you can unsubscribe at any time.

www.bookouture.com/jill-childs

Have you ever kept a secret from a close friend or relative? Maybe it was something in your past that you felt ashamed of having done – or perhaps you couldn't disclose the truth because of a sense of loyalty to someone else?

Or what if you weren't the one holding the secret? How would you feel if you suddenly found out that someone you'd trusted, someone who you'd always thought told you everything, actually hadn't been so open after all – but had kept a huge secret from you about their own life... or about yours?

I suspect that, for many of us, it would be hard not to feel hurt or even angry.

But can that sort of secrecy ever be justified? What if it were a secret so damaging that telling it might blow a family – or friendship – into pieces? A secret that wasn't even of your own making?

They're tough questions. As I pondered them, it set me thinking about what might happen to two intertwined families and how their lives might be shattered if their terrible, long-held secrets were forced out into the open.

I've set the story in the West Yorkshire town of Otley where I was born. It's a thriving town on the banks of the River Wharfe. The traditional market in the old square dates back to the thirteenth century and is still held several times a week. The town's roots are in farming and it's dominated by the dramatic scenery which surrounds it, the craggy moorland rising steeply from the town centre surrounded by fields, criss-crossed by Yorkshire dry-stone walls.

It's also a tightly woven community where many people have deep roots and a keen sense of belonging. Many friends and neighbours have known each other all their lives.

In reality, that closeness is a blessing. But in the novel, I've imagined that it might also be a curse – a constraint which puts loyalty before justice and makes it far easier to lie than to risk telling the truth.

It was out of these thoughts on family secrets and lies that this novel was born. I hope you loved *The House Across the Street*. If you did, I would be very grateful if you could write a review. I'd love to hear what you think, and it makes such a difference in helping new readers discover my books for the first time.

I love hearing from my readers. You can get in touch through my social media. Thank you!

All best wishes to you and yours,

Jill

facebook.com/jill.childs.71

x.com/author_jill

ACKNOWLEDGEMENTS

Thank you to my amazing editor, Maisie Lawrence, for all your creativity and enthusiasm. It's such a pleasure to work with you.

Thank you to the many other brilliant members of the Bookouture family for everything you do – from outstanding covers to tireless marketing and publicity. I'm grateful for the team's support for this book and all my previous ones.

Thank you to my wonderful agent, Judith Murdoch, the best in the business.

Thank you, as always, to all my family for your love and support, especially you, Nick.

PUBLISHING TEAM

Turning a manuscript into a book requires the efforts of many people. The publishing team at Bookouture would like to acknowledge everyone who contributed to this publication.

Audio
Alba Proko
Sinead O'Connor
Melissa Tran

Commercial
Lauren Morrissette
Hannah Richmond
Imogen Allport

Cover design
Lisa Horton

Data and analysis
Mark Alder
Mohamed Bussuri

Editorial
Maisie Lawrence
Ria Clare

Printed in Great Britain
by Amazon